Matching Scars

Book Two in the Boone Series

by Jim Hartsell

House Mountain Publishing

Cover design by:
www.nickcastledesign.com

ISBN 978-1-7327549-1-1

Chapter One

So I'm sitting in the room where I first laid eyes on Gamaliel, not counting seeing just a little bit of him peeking through the front door those first times we talked. It's not my favorite room in the house, too dark and it feels old, like all those parlors you see on TV. Anyway, I'm sitting in the chair where he was sitting that day, and I'm holding the fiddle he was playing when I let myself in.

Today's phone call from Carrie was right on time, as usual. She and her asshole husband Jerry took Gamaliel to their house from the hospital after the stroke, not quite a year ago now. I liked Carrie almost from the start, still do. She keeps me up to date on how it's going with the old man. I'd like to talk to him more, but she says it wears him out, and I can tell it does. When she puts him on the phone it's like it used to be but just for a few minutes and then the silences get longer and pretty soon she's back on the phone herself. She never puts Jerry on, which is fine by me. I still hate that son of a bitch, and I'm pretty sure he feels the same way about me.

I'm turning the fiddle over in my hands; it's a good piece of woodworking, looks like the back is maple, maybe. Wonder how long he's had this thing. I can't see into the inside very well, it's too dark in this room. There's a label of some kind. I get up and take it into the back room where all the windows are. The light is better in this room than anywhere else in the house; I should be able to make something out.

As soon as I get to the window that has the most sun coming through, I hear a car pull in next to the house and the door open. It doesn't close, and I take the fiddle into the kitchen and set it on the counter. Just as I turn to head out the back door there's a knock at the front.

I go halfway down the hall and take a left into Gamaliel's bedroom. He's got those real heavy curtains to keep out all the light and they're pulled shut, just like when he left to go to the hospital. Even though I've been staying here for the last six or eight months, I haven't slept in his bed. Doesn't look all that comfortable, to be honest about it, plus it'd feel kinda weird. The back room, the one with all the windows, has a chair I usually fall asleep in.

The window is really dirty. When I pull the curtain back a little it's hard to make out, but it looks like Carrie's car. That doesn't make any sense, though. She hasn't had time to get down here. Just

6

then I hear the door open and close, and footsteps in the hall, and Frankie starts growling deep in her throat.

Jerry steps into the bedroom doorway and stands there with his arms folded across his chest.

"Where's the money?"

How does he know about that? I never told him, I don't think Carrie knows about it, and it's for damn sure that Gamaliel didn't tell him.

"What the hell are you talking about, Jerry?"

"That's Mr. Phillips to you, Boone's Farm — "

I take a step toward him and he stands his ground, but his eye twitches a little.

"Don't even think about it, Jerry," I say. "We talked about that, remember?"

He's trying to decide, I can see it in his face. I take a half step closer and this time he backs up a step. He puffs up a little and clears his throat.

"Where's the money, Boone?"

I decide to take a chance. "Gamaliel told me Carrie used to play with that box of silver dollars when she was a kid. I'll give it to her, but I'm not sure I want to give it to you."

Jerry's nodding and I think, he doesn't know about the box with all the rolls of bills in it. He's here for Carrie's silver dollars.

"Maybe," I say, "I'll give Carrie a call and see if it's okay to hand her silver over to you."

7

He steps all the way back into the hallway. "Go ahead. She'll tell you it's all right. I came down here to make sure you weren't wrecking the place, like you people usually do, and when I said I was coming down here Carrie told me to bring her the silver dollars."

Then it's like he remembers something, and he says, "You'll do whatever we tell you to do. This is our property, not yours. I could tell you to clean the place and you'd have to do it. Hell, I could tell you to wash my damn car and you'd have to do that, too." He's grinning now. "Maybe I'll do that. My car's awful dirty."

"You sure you want me near that piece of shit car?"

Jerry glares at me. "Just get that box of money, Boone. I'm going to look around outside, make sure you haven't sold all his tools."

"Go ahead, Jerry. I'll just give Carrie a call. Maybe I'll let Frankie out for a run while I talk to her."

"You keep that dog inside and away from me," he says, and he looks down at Frankie like he wouldn't mind putting his foot right into her side. She's standing right beside me, growling, and I reach down and grab her collar. He gets a little smirk on his stupid face.

"That's what I thought."

He heads out the back door and I follow him as far as the kitchen. I'm hoping he doesn't look around the shed too close; the coil from the still is in there.

I moved the still off the land I used to live on as soon as I saw people moving in. Even though it had been up there for a while I didn't want to have somebody snooping around the woods and finding it. I brought it back to Gamaliel's house in pieces. The grate and the vat and the straight tubing looked like they could be used for anything, but the coil looked too much like all those old pictures of stills to be taken for anything besides what it was.

Jerry opens the door to the shed, looks in, and turns around. He catches me looking at him from the house and gives me a look, then heads off around the side of the house. I'm lucky the stupid old fart couldn't find his own ass with both hands. Turning away from the window, I pick up the phone and call Carrie.

"Hello?"

"Hello, Carrie, this is Boone. I know we just talked, but Jerry's down here saying he wants the money. Gamaliel had told me about the silver dollars, so I figure that's what he's come here for, and I just wanted to — "

"Is that where he is?" she interrupts me. "He just got in the car and took off, didn't tell me anything. You put him on the phone and then I want to talk to you after that. Don't let him hang up."

9

I tell her okay and hold on, and go out into the side yard. Jerry is leaned up against his car and I hand him the phone. "Carrie wants to talk to you."

I can't hear but one side of the conversation, of course. Jerry listens for a minute and I can see him tighten his grip on the phone. Finally he breaks in.

"I don't see why I should have to tell you every time I do — "

He's looking at me like he wants to take a swing. I bite my lip to keep from saying, "C'mon, asshole. I'm right here."

"You used to tell me about playing with those silver — "

He waves his hand at me like he wants me to go away. I grin at him and wave back.

"I just wanted to surprise you. What's wrong with that?"

He relaxes just a little, and then he smiles into the phone. He looks like an idiot, which he is. Then he hands me the phone.

"She wants to talk to you."

I take the phone and walk a few steps away.

"Hey, Carrie."

"Boone, I want you to do something for me, and don't you dare let Jerry know about it."

"Okay." I'm wondering what the hell is going on here.

"You tell Jerry that I want to talk to him again and hand him the phone. I'll ask him to check on something in the front yard and while he's doing that, you go in and count those silver dollars before you give them to him."

"Okay."

"After he leaves, call me and tell me how many there were when you gave him the box."

"Okay."

"I hate asking you this, but — "

"Don't you worry about it at all," I say. "I'm handing him the phone now."

I hand the phone to Jerry and start back into the house. I hear him say, "What? What does Pop care about that old hickory for? Okay, okay, I'm going."

His last words are pretty faint because I'm already almost in the house. I go into the front room, the dark one, and get the box of silver. It's hard to see in there, so I carry it out to the back room and count quick. I can hear him coming up to the front door.

"Got that money, Boone?"

"Right here, Jerry. Say hi to Gamaliel for me."

He doesn't even answer, just grabs the box, tosses me the phone, and heads right back out.

Chapter Two

I wait until he's almost out of sight, just topping the hill, and call Carrie back.

"Hey, Carrie, it's me."

"Boone, I hate to put you in the middle like this."

I have no idea what she's talking about, but I don't feel like I'm in the middle of anything.

"Listen, Carrie, as far as I'm concerned, it was Gamaliel and you that wanted me to watch this place, and I'm glad to do it. Either of you need something, all you got to do is ask."

"Okay," she says, and then she's quiet for a minute. Then she clears her throat. "How many silver dollars were in the box?"

"Thirty-one. That's how many was in there the first time I looked, back when Gamaliel still lived here but he was in the hospital and I was checking on the place. One of them was an 1885. Anyway, they're all still there."

She's quiet again for a full minute.

"Sometimes I feel like there's money missing from my purse."

I don't know what to say to that, so I don't say anything.

"Did Jerry look okay to you?"

Now I really don't know what to say. I didn't pay any more attention to him than I had to.

"I don't know, Carrie, I guess so."

More silence. This is really uncomfortable.

"Okay, well, thanks, Boone. Sorry I put you in that position. I should go now."

"Is Gamaliel around? Can I say hi?"

"Sorry, Boone, I looked in on him just before you called back. He's asleep in the recliner. I'll tell him you said hello. I need to go now." And she hangs up the phone.

I put the phone down and look at Frankie. "Want to go for a run, girl?"

She's bouncing around like a puppy.

"Okay, just a short one. It's pretty damn hot out there."

It's hot enough to make even Frankie want back inside. Gamaliel's place is small and there's no air conditioner, but there's a big fan in the hallway ceiling and screens on most of the windows. There's enough big trees around so that when I open the windows and turn that thing on the place is pretty comfortable.

Jerry didn't look around much when he was inside the house, and it's a good thing he didn't. There's still quite a bit of shine from last year, when Gamaliel and I were working together. I've stayed out of the triple-filtered good stuff; I'd like to sip some of that with the old man when he gets back here. I pour a little of the regular stuff into a glass and fill it up with Thunderstorm soda. S&S, shine and soda.

The sunroom in the back isn't too bad, even this time of year, with all the windows open and the fan going. In the winter, when the sun pours in from the south, it's pretty warm. I head in there, Frankie right behind me, and sit down in Gamaliel's chair.

It took me about three months to sit here, and sometimes it still seems like I ought to be in the other one, but this chair's really comfortable.

When I wake up it's close to dark, and the house has cooled off; I didn't turn off the fan when I sat down. When I shut it off the evening noises that the fan covered up are all around me, frogs and cicadas and an owl way off in the woods somewhere, and somebody whistling.

Too far away for me to make out the tune, and there's a little wind, which snatches away bits and pieces of it anyway. Frankie's got her ears up but hasn't moved from where she's lying. I think it's coming from down the hill, from the house I was living in last year. My glass still has some S&S in it, so I take another sip and sit back down.

When I first moved in here, back in the winter, I thought I'd miss not having a TV. Turns out it's not so bad, never was much worth watching anyway. Lots of times back at the other house I'd turn it on and go through all the channels two or three times and then end up watching something I'd seen already. Evenings I usually sit and talk to Frankie; she'll listen to just about anything I have to say.

I have to admit, though, sometimes it gets to me a little, not having anybody around to talk to. Not bad, not bad enough to do anything about it most of the time, but tonight's harder than usual. I'm worried about Gamaliel; I know he wants to be here instead of up there, but sure seems like he's settling in with Carrie. I'm kind of worried about her, too, since that thing today with Jerry and the silver dollars and her asking me all those questions.

Momma and Hannah, well, I don't think about them much. Hannah's eight, almost nine, I guess, and she's up there with Aunt Claire and better off than she would be here with me. Momma, who knows where she is.

I wonder what's going on with Jerry. Carrie seemed nervous on the phone and kind of secretive. I can sure see how things might not be going so good with Jerry; he's a real shithead.

I go round and round with all this and before I know it the sun's coming through the windows and

Frankie is nosing at me to let her out. I don't even remember falling asleep.

Chapter Three

After I get a bite to eat I take Frankie outside and let her run. She makes a quick circle around the house, sniffing for any changes since yesterday's night patrol. She's out of sight around on the side of the house up toward the Thompson's when I hear her growling low in her throat.

Then she starts barking, that loud, angry, don't fuck with me kind of bark, and I speed up and turn the corner.

She's standing, facing away from me. The hair on her back is bristled, and her nose is low to the ground. I follow her stare; there's a raccoon at the edge of the yard, just standing there staring back at Frankie.

I call her. "Frankie! Come here!"

One ear twitches but she doesn't move.

"Frankie! Here, girl! Here!"

She starts to take a step back and hesitates, then breaks off from the raccoon and comes over to me.

She whirls around and starts in again on the raccoon. I really need to get her better trained.

Then I take another look at the coon and start to get scared.

It looks like it can't get its balance, and I can see a long, thin thread of drool hanging off the side of its mouth. It shakes its head and the drool drops off, and the coon starts snapping at nothing I can see. It looks around, trying to find something to focus on, and takes a couple of shaky steps toward us.

It has to be rabies, I think to myself. Frankie's a big dog, lots bigger than the raccoon, and it didn't run or climb, didn't even act like any normal animal would, and then there's that staggering, drooling, snapping stuff. I've never seen an animal with rabies before, but I'm betting that's what it is. I grab Frankie's collar and it takes all my strength to get her started toward the house.

The coon is still there when I come back out with the shotgun, and it's an easy shot to drop it where it stands. I leave it in the yard and go back in the house. I'm shaking like a little kid.

I go over every inch of Frankie when I get back inside. No scratches or bite marks anywhere. I sit there on the floor with my arms around her and start crying into her fur.

"I'm a terrible owner, Frankie, terrible," I finally say. "You are going to the vet today for a rabies shot. I can't lose you, girl, I can't."

There's only one vet anywhere close, and I call them as soon as I can let Frankie go. "You are staying inside, girl, until we figure out what to do about that coon out there," I say.

"Binfield Clinic."

"Hello," I say, "I need to bring my dog in for a rabies shot. It's been a year or so since I got her, and she was a pup. I don't know that she's ever had one."

The man on the other end of the line says, "Definitely get your dog in here. We've had reports of rabid raccoons in the area."

"Well," I say slowly, "since you mention that, I just shot a raccoon that was acting really strange. It's laying in my side yard."

He gets a very serious tone in his voice and gives me a number, says I need to call TWRA right now.

"And don't let any animals or people anywhere near that coon," he says firmly. "Did it get to your dog?"

"No, I had just taken her outside for her morning run and she started barking like crazy and when I came around the house she was in the yard and the coon was out on the edge of the yard. I've already checked her out, no scratches or bites or anything."

"You keep her inside for two weeks," he says. "Don't let her out except on a leash. Don't let her go anywhere. If she's infected, it'll show up by then. If she's okay, bring her in after that and we'll give her a rabies shot. What's your dog's name?"

"Frankie."

"Well, you keep a close eye on Frankie, and call TWRA right now, as soon as you hang up. And go outside and don't let anything near that coon. It's still dangerous."

I make the call, and then tell Frankie to stay put and go outside. The coon is still laying right where I shot it, and there's a kid walking toward it with a stick in his hand. He's whistling that same tune I heard last night.

"Get the hell off this yard!" I shout at him. He stops where he is, but doesn't back up.

"Is that coon dead?"

"That coon is dead, and it had rabies. You get the hell away, you hear me? Somebody's coming to get rid of it. That thing'll make you sick, and then you'll die. You get off this yard and stay off!"

He throws down the stick. "You don't have to be so mean about it."

He goes back out to the road and starts down the hill, then turns back.

"What's your name?"

"You go on back home. Go on now."

Shrugging his shoulders, he turns, then turns back. "Mine's Trevor."

"Well, Trevor, you stay off this property. You got no business here."

He doesn't answer, just walks away.

The guy from TWRA comes and gets rid of the body, and tells me to keep my eyes open for any other coons or other animals acting funny.

"It's a bad year so far," he says.

When I go back inside Frankie is bouncing around, and I say, "You're on a leash for the next two weeks, girl. Sorry."

Then I realize I don't have a calendar.

It's been a while since I've needed to know what day of the week it was, and, since I don't have school or anything else like that to worry about, it hasn't been that big of a deal. Now I need to know when it's been two weeks, so I'll know Frankie's okay and I can call the vet, and then I'll need to know so I can keep the appointment.

Surely, I say to myself, Gamaliel's got some kind of calendar around here. I've never really explored that front room, if you don't count the drawer where I found the silver dollars. There's a desk in there, one of the old style, big, wooden, lots of drawers and stuff stacked on top of it. Compared to the rest of the house, it's kind of a mess, which by itself makes me curious. Gamaliel, as far as I can tell, isn't much interested in stuff, and what stuff he's got he keeps in pretty good order.

I decide to go through the desk tomorrow. The kitchen's getting a little empty, and I've got enough money from what Carrie gives me to afford a good-sized trip to the grocery store.

Daddy's old truck is still running, but lately when I start it up there's a cloud of blue smoke. It goes away pretty quick, soon as I drive it a quarter mile or so, but I'm thinking that I may be back on a bicycle before long. Sometimes I wish he had taught me something about cars, but I'm not sure he knew very much.

On the way down to the store I think about Daddy. I don't much like to, considering how things ended up, but once I start I sort of have to run through it. I try to remember something good about him being around and I have to think way, way back, before Hannah was born, when Frankie was still around, before Daddy messed up his hand. There were a few times he wasn't angry or drunk or both, usually both, but damned few even then. I shake my head to try to get back to today, jerking the wheel a little and scaring some old woman in a big four-door something or other. She almost goes into the ditch trying to miss me, and I grin a little. I wasn't even really out of my lane. I glance in the mirror; she's back on track and there's nobody else on the road, no police anywhere, and I settle in for the rest of the drive.

The store is almost empty, so it's a quick run through the aisles. I fill the cart with some Thunderstorm, frozen pizzas, cereal, milk, crunchy peanut butter, bread, a big hunk of cheese, a pound of ground beef, dog food, and half a dozen other things,

22

including a jar of spaghetti sauce and some spaghetti noodles. On the way back down that row I see some hot pepper sauce and grab that too. I'm heading for checkout when I hear, "Boone? Is that you?"

I duck back down the aisle I just came through and head for the back of the store, even though I was finished and ready to head home. There was a page from the newspaper that they had taped up in the store window; I had seen it when I came in, all about a sale, ground beef, corn on the cob, cabbage and slaw dressing, stuff like that, and it said, "Two weeks of savings! Don't forget to stock up for the Fourth of July!! Sale prices good right up to the big day!!" I asked the clerk when the sale had started and he said today was the first day. So now I know that when I hear fireworks down at the ball field, Frankie's two weeks will be up and I can take her in to the vet's. I need to find out how much that's going to cost.

I go back through the store, sticking to the inside aisles, hoping I won't run into whoever called my name. On the way I see a jar of that salsa that Hannah talked Momma into that time and pick it up, and put it right back down when I see how much it is.

It looks like the coast is clear, so I head for the checkout line and the cashier says, "You've only got four Thunderstorms and they're on sale if you buy six. You want to go get two more while I ring this up?"

I'm pretty sure I brought enough to pay for everything and Carrie's due day after tomorrow to check on me and bring me some more money, so I say, "Yeah, go ahead, I'll be right back."

She's done by the time I get back, so I put the sodas on the conveyor, she adds them to the total, and I pay. This leaves me with nine dollars, but nothing's due for a week or so and the truck's got a half a tank in it, so I'm good until I see Carrie. I grab the bags, wait for the automatic door to open, and head for the truck.

Mrs. Thompson is leaning against the fender. "Hi, Boone. Guess you didn't hear me inside."

"Hi, Mrs. Thompson. How's the family?"

She pushes herself off the truck and steps toward me. "Let me help you with those."

I shake my head. "I'm good, I'm just going to put them in the back of the truck. Headed straight back to Gamaliel's house."

She looks at me blankly for a second and then her face clears and she says, "You mean Mr. Everett? You're staying with him now? Where's your family? I remember your daddy ran off. Is everybody else gone too?"

I put the bags in the bed of the truck and turn back to her. She's driving one of the family trucks, I don't know how many they have up there. It's parked one space over from Daddy's old truck, and I look at it and then look at mine and inside I'm mad at Daddy all over again.

Mrs. Thompson is talking. "You know, I haven't seen Mr. Everett around for a while now. Is he okay?"

I'm already mad about this piece of shit truck I'm driving, and she's being really nosy, so I start to tell her to mind her own damn business and then stop myself. She lives right up the road, I tell myself, and she's not being mean about it, just asking. The last thing I need to do is piss her off.

"Actually, I'm not staying with him, I'm watching the place for him. He had, well, he had a stroke last year and he's up with his daughter and her husband. They asked me to keep the place up until he can come back here."

"Oh, Boone, I am so sorry, I didn't know." She looks down for a second and then looks up at me. "You call him Gamaliel? I didn't even know that was his name."

I grin a little. "It's kind of a funny name, right? We got to be friends last year and about the fourth or fifth time I went up to see him he told me to stop calling him Mr. Everett, said to call him Gamaliel. Carrie, his daughter, said his parents named him after a president."

She grins back at me. "Well, well. He must like you quite a bit. He always kept pretty much to himself." She starts back toward her truck. "You take care, Boone."

"Bye, Mrs. Thompson," I say and then follow her to her truck. She's already inside and rolls the window down and looks down at me. It's a big truck and I have to tilt my head a little. "Was there something else?"

"Yes, ma'am. Yesterday there was a raccoon in the yard, acting real strange, drooling and not steady on its feet and snapping at nothing. I shot it and called the vet. They said call TWRA and some guy came and picked up the body and said it was a bad year for rabies. I know you got a lot of animals up there at your place, thought you ought to know."

She nods. "I had heard that from somebody just the other day. Glad you shot that coon. Thanks for letting me know."

"Yes, ma'am."

I turn and start back to my piece of shit truck.

"Boone?"

I turn back.

"You let us know how Mr. Everett is getting along, okay?"

I nod. "I'll do that. You take care now."

She gives me a wave and backs out, turns, and heads out to the road.

When I get home I unload the groceries and put stuff away, then get out the leash. Frankie looks at me like, what the hell are you doing?

"Sorry, girl, vet's orders."

She jerks at me a few times when we head out into the yard and then settles down. I can tell she doesn't like it much, but I'm not going to take a chance. I think about that old movie I saw when I was a kid, Old Yeller I think it was, and pretty soon my eyes and cheeks are wet and I'm looking at Frankie and wondering if I could do it if I had to.

I wipe my eyes. No sense borrowing trouble, I say to myself, and then, "C'mon, Frankie, let's go back in."

I give her some fresh water, a cup of food, and then settle down with an S&S. "Busy day, girl," I say to Frankie. She comes over to get her head scratched and then lies down beside the chair.

The next day I go into the front room and open the curtains on the two windows that look out onto the front porch. It doesn't help much as far as lighting the room goes, but there's a floor lamp next to the desk. I turn on the light and pull back the chair that's pushed in under the center drawer.

"Nobody ever said I had to stay out of the desk," I say to Frankie, who has followed me into the room and is sniffing around. We don't spend any time in this part of the house, so she's curious. To tell the truth, so am I.

It's true nobody ever said that, but it still feels a little funny, snooping around like this. I don't really even need a calendar for Frankie now, since I know that right after Fourth of July is when I need to go to the vet. So there's no good reason for me to be going through Gamaliel's stuff.

Unless something happens to the old man. I know I'm glad I knew about the two money boxes when Jerry came by the other day. Gamaliel had warned me about Jerry, and told me the box with the rolls of bills in it was mine if anything happened to him; he didn't want Jerry getting his hands on it. Thinking about how Jerry was when he was here and how Carrie was on the phone makes me think I need to move that box somewhere safe, in case things get really bad with Jerry and Carrie. I'll do that after I spend a little time in here, I decide, and sit down and open the center drawer.

At first I think it's just a bunch of junk — rubber bands so old they're brittle, paperclips of all sizes, some kind of little wheel with a brush attached to it. I have no idea what that's for. There's some old letters that I leave alone; I figure that would really be snooping, reading his mail.

Toward the back, under some of the letters, I find a little envelope with Mountain Laurel Bank printed on it. Inside there's a key. I don't know what that is either, but I get the feeling I ought to hang onto it, so I put it in my pocket.

The top left drawer has, right on top, a book with "Fiddle Tunes" on the cover, and an old guy with a big smile on his face and a fiddle under his chin. I pick it up and wave it at Frankie. "Better cover your ears, girl. This might get ugly."

Underneath the book is one of those manila envelopes with a bunch of names and "Law Offices" up in the corner. In the middle of the front, in big block letters, it says, "Last Will and Testament". There's a little scrap of paper tucked under the flap, held there with a paperclip, that says, "Boone".

Chapter Four

I just sit there with the envelope in my hand for a long minute. I'm looking at it, and at Frankie, and wondering, was I supposed to find this? Is this really the old man's will? Am I supposed to take it somewhere? To somebody? To these lawyers listed on the front? I don't know anything about this kind of stuff. I need to talk to Gamaliel, face to face.

Gamaliel's not here, though, and I don't know when I'll see him again. I really don't want to do this kind of thing over the phone, any more than I would plan our next run of shine that way. I look over at Frankie.

"What do I do with this thing, girl?"

Frankie gets up, sniffs her way through the room, and goes out into the hallway.

This thing needs to be in a safe place, and all of a sudden I'm aware that I don't really have a place, safe or not. I'm living in somebody else's house, and when I have to leave I got nowhere to go except the piece of shit truck. I can't see putting this in the glove compartment or behind the seat. I need a safe, like in a bank. And then I realize what that key must be.

We never used banks when Daddy and Momma were around, never had enough money to bother with them. Daddy always got paid in cash, we paid bills with cash or money orders, and his truck came from one of those car lots where you just went by once a month with the cash, and they gave you the title when you had it paid off. Probably had to pay double for doing it that way, but it wasn't like we had a choice. Daddy never made enough to put any back, so no savings accounts, and we sure didn't ever have anything that would go into a safety deposit box, at least I think that's what they're called. Anyway, we never had one.

Looks like Gamaliel does, though. So I'm wondering, can I just go down to Mountain Laurel Bank and open it, or do I need a note from him, or what? That doesn't seem right, I bet there's more to it than that, but I just don't know.

For the moment I just shove the will back into the drawer and close it. I keep the key, though.

I take the music book into the sunroom; the fiddle is still sitting in the kitchen. Sitting down in Gamaliel's chair, I open the book and look at the first few pages. They're all about how to hold the fiddle and the bow and how to tune it. It's already talking about stuff I don't know anything about, and if I'm lost on the first three pages, well . . . .

The next few pages are even harder to understand, so I put the book on the floor next to the chair and look over at Frankie. "Guess your ears are safe for now, girl."

The next phone call from Carrie comes a few days later. She just says hi, real quick, and then hands the phone to Gamaliel.

"Boone?"

"Gamaliel, how in the hell are you?" I am really glad to hear his voice; didn't realize how much I missed having him around.

"I reckon I'm all right for an old man, Boone. Listen, I need you to do something for me."

"Sure, whatever you need. Hey, the other day, I shot a raccoon in your yard, the guy from TWRA said it was rabid, and — "

"Stop talking and listen, dammit!" His voice is weaker than I remember, but it's still got some fire in it.

"Okay, okay. So what's going on?"

"There's a desk in the front room, the room with all the pictures in it, and in one of the drawers, I forget which one, there's an envelope that has my will in it."

I don't say anything. I don't want him to know I've been snooping around already.

"You still there?"

"Yeah, Gamaliel, I'm here."

"Get that envelope and hide it somewhere. Don't let Jerry know where it is. You hear me? He'll — "

He starts coughing, can't seem to stop, and in a few seconds Carrie is on the phone.

"Let me call you back, Boone, I need to — Oh God, Pops! Pops? What's — "

And then she's gone.

I spend the next three hours walking around, thinking all kinds of shit. Frankie follows me from room to room for the first little while and then goes to her spot next to the chair and lies down. Her eyes are on me every time I look at her.

After three hours the phone still hasn't rung, and I'm thinking that when it does it's going to be really bad. I wonder if Carrie's been lying to me about how he's doing. She always says he's doing okay. Well, he sure as hell wasn't okay when I had him on the phone. I'm going crazy here; I can't leave the house, she might call. I can't just sit, and I've already walked every inch of this place a thousand times.

When the phone does ring I just stand there looking at it. I don't know whether I want to know what's at the other end of the line. Finally I pick it up.

"Hello." I can't find my voice, so it comes out all scratchy.

"Boone, it's Carrie."

There's a long moment of silence. There's some static on the line, hissing and popping. I hate this, I

33

hate this. Don't know what to say or do, and I'm about ready to throw the phone through the window.

"Carrie, you tell me what the fuck's going on up there!" I can't take it any longer and I'm shouting into the phone and then I take a breath and I can hear her crying.

"Oh, shit, Carrie, I'm sorry, c'mon, Carrie, tell me something, you gotta tell me something here." Frankie's right next to me, pressing against my leg, and I push her away and wipe my cheeks, hard, and they're still wet after I do that, and I think I know what she's going to tell me if she'll just stop that damn crying.

She takes a deep breath and says, "It was awful, awful. It took the ambulance forever to get to the house, and they told me his heart stopped twice during the ride and we're at the hospital now and they're talking about . . . . Oh, Boone, he looked so, oh, I don't know, I don't know what to do."

I start to ask about Jerry and then think, I don't even want to know where that shithead is.

"Is he going to be okay, Carrie?"

Stupid question, I know that, I don't know what to say, there's no way he's going to be okay.

She doesn't answer.

"Where is he?"

"He's had another stroke and — "

"I said where is he?" I'm shouting again and I'm gripping the phone and my other fist is clenched tight.

"Don't shout, please don't shout. You understand me? I can't do this right now, Boone."

I'm fighting as hard as I can to get back in control, but I'm breathing hard, I can feel my heart pounding, I just need to know where he is.

"I'm sorry, Carrie, I'm sorry, just please tell me where he is."

"He's in a hospital up here, but they're saying he needs to go into one of those rehab places, there's one in Knoxville. I don't know, there's no way we can afford that."

I think about the box of money.

"Don't you have some kind of insurance?" I say.

"Well, we do, and that'll take care of some of it, but Jerry says we can't dip into our savings, he says we'll need that ourselves."

That son of a bitch. This is why Gamaliel didn't want Jerry to know about the money he had here at the house. There's no way he's finding out about it from me, I say to myself.

"What did you say, Boone? I couldn't understand you."

Oh, shit. I thought I wasn't saying that out loud.

"Nothing, Carrie, nothing. I just can't believe this."

"I have to go, Boone, Jerry just came in. I'll call when we're moving him. We'll take him to that place, I can't think of what it's called. Even though we can't afford it."

"Listen, Carrie, I gotta talk to you, I gotta tell you about —"

But she's already gone.

I'm still breathing hard and all knotted up and Frankie pushes on my hand with her nose and I draw back my leg and almost let her have it right in the ribs. I know I need to get out of there and I slam the door hard on the way out. I don't look back, I know Frankie's at the door, but I'm already across the yard and into the trees.

Then I'm crashing through the woods, along the trail that Gamaliel used to get to the still, and I'm stumbling and running into branches and one time I trip and catch myself with a branch and I'm so mad I try to break the branch off the tree. I push it and it slips out of my hand and comes lashing towards me and I try to get my arm up in time and it catches me right across the face. I can taste the blood and I don't even care.

I break into the clearing where the still used to be and stop, panting, and I hear voices. There's somebody down at my pool, the only place I used to be able to go when Daddy was all crazy mad.

"What the hell are they doing at my pool?" I'm talking to myself and then I'm headed toward the pool and I'm ready to throw their asses out of there. I need that place, all to myself, and there's somebody where they got no business being. I know what to do about that.

Back down the path to Gamaliel's house, I'm still running but this time I don't trip on anything. I shove open the back door, catching Frankie on the hind leg. She yelps and runs into Gamaliel's bedroom.

Daddy's shotgun is in the bedroom, too, leaning behind the door, and the shells are in a box on the chest of drawers right across from Gamaliel's bed. I grab the box and I'm about to pick up the gun when I catch a glimpse of myself in the mirror hanging on the wall next to the closet.

My face is covered in blood, and my skin is splotchy from where I've been crying. Across my forehead, where the branch hit, there's a line running up from my eyebrow on one side up to my hair on the other. Only part of it has broken skin, but scalp wounds, you bleed like a stuck pig, and I'm just a mess.

I think about crashing through the woods covered in blood, waving a shotgun, and the more I think about it the more it sounds like a really bad movie, and I can't help it. I start laughing, and I throw the box of shells on the bed.

That lasts about a half a minute until I remember Carrie's phone call. I go into the kitchen and splash some water on my face, do it again, and grab a paper towel to dry off with.

Back to the mirror. I'm still bleeding, so I start looking around for a box of bandaids. What I find, in one of the kitchen drawers, is a roll of gauze and some white tape. I take the roll and tape into the bathroom; the mirror in here is smaller, but the light's a lot better. I cut off a long piece and fold it over three times and hold it up to my forehead. It's about the right size, so I tear off some strips of tape and tape it to my head.

I look ridiculous. "That's the worst job of first aid I've ever seen," I say to the mirror.

Frankie sticks her nose into the bathroom and looks up at me. I'll bet if a dog could laugh, she'd be rolling on the floor, but she just comes up and nuzzles my hand. Then she trots off toward the back of the house.

I follow her and then turn right, into the kitchen. There's a glass on the counter and I grab it and fill it half full of shine and don't bother with the Thunderstorm. Gamaliel always said to sip it straight, and right now I want to do it his way.

It's about two thirds gone when the phone rings again. I pick it up and don't even bother with saying hello.

"Is he okay?"

"Is who okay?"

It takes me a second; the shine's slowed me down some.

"Nancy?"

"Yeah, it's me, Boone. Who are you talking about? Is who okay?"

It's been — I try to remember — at least two months, probably more like four, since I've heard from her. Maybe more than that. I'd figured she'd gotten together with Randy or Roscoe or whoever, so I'm kind of surprised to hear from her now.

"I thought you were going to be somebody else."

I don't say anything else and after a little bit she says, "Boone?"

"Yeah."

"Are you going to be there for a while?"

"I don't know, I guess so."

"I was going to just come by later to say hi, but I thought I'd better call first, make sure its okay if I do that."

There's another silence and I realize she's waiting for me to say something.

"Sure, I'll be here. Come on over."

She hangs up and I turn to Frankie. "Never thought I'd hear from her again, girl. Wonder what she wants?"

Back last winter, Nancy and I were getting closer and closer and then it was like she was always busy when we talked on the phone and had to hang up so she could go do something. I had gotten tired of it and just stopped calling, plus I figured she didn't want anything to do with me anyway. She was smarter than me, her family had money, hell, she still had a family, and she was definitely too good-looking to be spending time with me.

"So what is this all about?" I ask Frankie, who just thumps her tail against the floor.

I'm done with the shine and thinking about another one when I hear a car pull up. I go to the front door just in time to see Nancy get out of the car. She's wearing shorts and one of those tops that ties up under her boobs; she's showing a lot of skin, almost as much as one of those two-piece bathing suits. Damn, she looks good.

She waves at me and says, "Where's Frankie?"

Frankie pushes past me and is out in the yard before I can grab her, jumping around Nancy and she's laughing and trying to rub Frankie's head and the dog is moving around so much she can't catch her. I'm smiling, watching all this, and then I remember the raccoon.

"Get back up here, Frankie!" I shout, and Frankie looks at me a second and I think she's going to take off, but then she comes slinking on up like she's done something wrong. Nancy is looking at me with a funny expression.

"What's the matter with you, Boone? She was just happy to see me."

I grab Frankie and push her back inside and close the door.

When I sit down on the top step, Nancy looks at me for a second like she's trying to decide whether or not to just get back in the car, and then comes over and stands in front of me.

"You didn't used to be so mean to her, Boone. Did you see how she came up the steps with her tail between her legs? It was like she was afraid of you."

"Sit down a second, Nancy."

She just stands there looking at me.

"Please sit down."

"Not til you tell me what's going on here. And what's that awful bandage on your head about?"

When I tell her about the raccoon and how I'm supposed to keep her in until after the fourth, I can feel myself getting all teary again and that pisses me off, but I can't seem to stop it. I can feel my eyes getting wet and look down at the steps.

I hear her moving closer and climbing the steps and then she's sitting beside me. She puts her hand on my arm.

"My daddy told me yesterday that he had heard the same thing at the convenience store a few days ago. He said it's a really bad year. Is Frankie okay?"

I have to clear my throat a couple of times before I can talk. "Yeah, I think so. I looked her over pretty good and didn't see anything, but the vet said to keep her in for a couple of weeks. Then I'm going to take her to get her shots, unless, well, unless, you know . . . ."

"I'm sure she'll be all right, Boone. You didn't find any cuts or bites or anything, right?"

"Right."

"Right. So are you going to ask me to come inside?"

Chapter Five

Nancy stands up and holds out her hand. I wipe my hand on my jeans and grab hold and she pulls me up and we're standing next to each other in front of the door.

"You going to tell me what that was all about on the phone? And how you got that cut on your head?"

I stand there for a minute, stupid, not knowing what I want to do. It's really good to see her again; I can feel myself getting kind of nervous, because I've never had anybody in here before. The only people that I've ever seen inside this house are Gamaliel, Carrie, and Jerry.

Then I think, what the hell, Boone, you were whining the other day about not having anybody to talk to, and here's somebody standing right here waiting for you to open your mouth and ask her in.

So I grab the door and open it and say, "Frankie, you stay right there, girl." I turn to Nancy and say, "You want to come in for a minute?" and hold my hand out like I'm a waiter or something.

She's got a little grin on her face and she steps on in, I follow her, close the door, and watch her walk slow down the hall, trying to look around without being nosy.

"Best room's toward the back of the house."

She looks back at me and then turns and heads on down the hall a little quicker.

When I get into the room she's standing, looking around, and she says, "This is where you and Gamaliel sat and talked about making moonshine?" She still has that little grin on her face.

I nod and point toward the chair where I usually sat, and sit down in Gamaliel's. As soon as I sit down I'm back up and I say, "I'll go turn on the fan, it's kind of hot in here."

"Okay," she says. "Come over here and talk to me, Frankie, tell me what you and Boone have been up to."

Frankie's in heaven, wagging her tail so hard her whole back half is going crazy. I'd forgotten how much she liked Nancy. I open a couple of windows and go down the hall to turn on the fan.

When I get back Frankie is at Nancy's feet, like she belongs to her, not me. I don't think I could pull her out of there with a winch, and tell Nancy so.

She laughs out loud. "Don't you dare try it, Boone. We're both pretty good right where we are."

Then her face gets serious. "Okay, Boone. What was that on the phone earlier?"

"You want an S&S?" I'm heading into the kitchen, thinking that maybe I'll make mine a small one. That last one, the one I fixed the way Gamaliel likes his, I didn't exactly sip it.

"I'll just have a little of yours."

I get the Thunderstorm out of the fridge and a clean glass. I pour a little shine into it, less than I usually pour, throw in a couple of ice cubes, and fill it with Thunderstorm. When I get back to where she and Frankie are, before I can sit down, she reaches out her hand.

"You didn't make this too strong, did you?"

I shake my head. "Pretty weak, actually."

"Good," she says, and takes a sip. "I think I've changed my mind. I might just keep this one."

"Guess it's a good thing I haven't sat down yet," I say, and head back into the kitchen.

When I come back, her glass is on the table and she's back to scratching Frankie.

"You're going to spoil that dog," I say as I sit down.

"Does he not give you any attention?" she says to Frankie, who looks up at Nancy like she's the queen of the world.

I'm sitting there remembering how good it feels being around Nancy when she sits back and says, "So who were you asking about on the phone, before you knew it was me? Is it Gamaliel?"

My face gets hot all of a sudden and I can feel my eyes getting wet. Damn, seems like all I've done since she got here is cry. Like a damn baby.

And just like that Daddy's voice is in my head, calling me a baby, a pussy, all that shit he used to call me is right back just like it was the other day instead of a year ago.

"Why did you call me, Nancy?" I manage to get that out and it helps a little, so I keep going. "I mean, I thought you were, you know, done with me and on to somebody else."

I glance over and she's sitting straight up now, not relaxed, and I feel like I should say I'm sorry or something.

Instead, I say, "I figured I wouldn't hear from you again, and I didn't want to keep bothering you, you know, calling and all that. I mean, you can call me anytime you want to, you know, or come on over, or whatever...."

My S&S is sitting right beside me and I pick it up and take a big drink, two swallows, then set it back down. I can't think of anything else to say, so I just sit there.

When the phone rings I'm glad I don't have the glass in my hand. Otherwise it'd have gone all over all three of us.

"Oh, shit," I say, more to myself than to Nancy. "Guess I need to get that."

I look over at Nancy after I get up and I swear she's got tears in her eyes. She looks like she's about ready to say something, but I head toward the phone and get it on the third ring.

"Hello?" I say. Nothing.

I say hello again, and there's nothing for a second, and then somebody says, "Is that you, Adam? It's me, Debbie."

"There's no Adam here, lady. You've got the wrong number," I say, almost shouting, and hang up before she can say anything else.

When I turn back, Nancy is right in front of me, and before I can say anything, she reaches out and wraps her arms around me.

I stand there for a second and then bring my arms up and hold her tight against me. After a minute she lets go and steps back, looking straight into my eyes.

"All this is about Gamaliel, isn't it?"

I nod.

"Is he sick?"

I nod again, and head back to the chair.

She pulls the other chair over and sits down, facing me, our knees almost touching. Frankie stays where she is, ears up, eyes on the two of us.

When I raise my head, she's leaning forward, just waiting for me to be ready to talk. Her shirt is a little loose, and any other time I'd be looking at her bra as often as I could get away with it, but today I'm so beat down I barely notice.

47

I finally take a deep breath and sit up a little. "Can we talk about something else right now?" All this shit, the will, the safety deposit box key, Carrie, Gamaliel, whatever the hell's going on with Jerry, is going round and round in my head and I can't seem to make it stop.

"Sure," she says, and lays her hand on my leg for a second before she sits back in the chair.

I try to think of something to say that's not too lame and then give up and say, "So what have you been up to this summer?" Then I laugh out loud and say, "That's about the lamest thing I've said all year."

Nancy starts laughing too, and it takes us a minute to settle back down. When she starts to scoot her chair back, I reach out and put my hand on her leg, just above her knee. Her skin is so soft. I let it rest there for a second longer and I'm too embarrassed to look up, but she doesn't push my hand off or jump back or anything.

Then I lean back and I hear her chair slide against the floor. I look up and she's standing, looking right at me again, and her cheeks are red. I don't know what to do next and so I just start jabbering away.

I tell her running through the woods and cutting my head on a branch, and then I tell her about the fiddle, and how I first heard Gamaliel play, and how terrible I am at it. I tell her about the raccoon and about Trevor and start to tell her about Jerry and the silver dollars and all of a sudden I get an idea.

"Listen, Nancy, if I give you something, something really important, can you keep it for me? It's kind of private, so you can't show it to anybody."

She looks at me, real serious, and says, "Boone, what are you talking about?"

"Just a minute," I say, and get up, go into the front room, and come back with the envelope.

I hand it to her and she looks at what's written on the outside, and sets it down on the table.

"Why are you asking me to keep this, Boone? It's Gamaliel's, right? I mean, shouldn't you just leave it here?"

"Gamaliel asked me to make sure that Jerry, his son-in-law, doesn't get ahold of it. He doesn't trust him, I guess, and neither do I. Jerry's a real asshole."

She starts to say something, and then doesn't.

"I can't get it to Carrie without Jerry seeing it, they always come down here together. If I could I'd just give it to her. Gamaliel didn't say to keep it away from her, just Jerry."

Nancy is shaking her head. "I can't promise nobody would find it, Boone, I don't have that kind of place at home. Why don't you get a safety deposit box down at the bank? Then you could just give the key to Gamaliel or Carrie."

"I don't know anything about how to do that."

"It's easy, you just go down to the bank and get one, tell them you have some valuable stuff to keep in a safe place. Then you sign your name and . . . ." Her voice kind of trails off.

"What?"

"It won't work to give them the key. They couldn't get into the box unless their signature was there with yours, you know, like you giving them permission to get into it. The bank won't just let anybody with a key open the box. They have to sign for it."

I think about that key in my pocket. No use keeping it, I realize, I might as well put it back in the drawer.

"You could still do it, though, if you wanted to make sure it was safe. You'd be the only one that could get into it."

"What if they ask for some kind of I.D. at the bank?"

"I've never gotten a safety deposit box, so I don't know about that. You could probably just show them your driver's license."

She can tell by the expression on my face what I'm about to say.

"Boone! You don't have a license?"

I shake my head.

"But, I see you out on the road . . . ."

"I don't go far, try not to hit anybody."

"Why don't you just go get a license?"

"You mean, drive up to the place and say I don't have a license yet, but I'd like to get one? Besides, isn't there a written test?"

Nancy's looking at me with a smile on her face, one of those that's just barely there. She pulls the chair back over to its place, sits down, and picks up her glass.

"You need a tutor, don't you?"

I sit back down in Gamaliel's chair and look at her. Her smile gets bigger.

"Yeah, I guess I do. Know anybody that could do that?"

"I've got a little time before my senior year starts. I guess I could maybe give it a try."

She raises her glass to me and I grab mine real quick and we click them together and I think I need to do that softer the next time. Don't want to break the glass.

She takes a sip, sets the glass on the table, and says, "So when do you want to start?"

"I got nothing but time," I say.

"How about first of next week? Monday, middle of the day?"

"Sounds good."

She finishes her glass. "Okay, I gotta run." She stands up and so do I. When we get out on the porch she puts her hand on my cheek and says, "It'll work out, Boone, really."

And then she's down the steps and halfway to her car.

"Nancy?"

She half turns.

"I just wanted to say you look good, I mean nice, I mean, good to see you."

She turns back towards her car, but there's that smile again.

Chapter Six

It's a couple more days before Nancy comes over to start teaching me what's in the book, and I feel like a wild animal in a cage. No word from Carrie about the old man, and I don't feel like I can leave in case she calls. Frankie's going crazy and getting harder to hold back when I take her out.

I take the box of money out to the truck and put it behind the seat and throw a bunch of old rags and empty boxes over it. I'm starting to think that I might not be living here much longer. Not if Jerry has anything to say about it, for sure. That son of a bitch would throw me out in a rainstorm and laugh about it.

The shine, I don't know what to do with all that. I've got gallons of the stuff left, since it's just been me drinking it. The triple-filtered stuff I haven't hardly touched; I'm waiting on Gamaliel to really get into that, but I tried it once and he was right — it's smooth going down, not much of a burn at all. If I get kicked out there's no way I'm leaving that here for

Jerry to enjoy, because if I get thrown out of here it'll be because Gamaliel's gone.

I could just put it in the back of the truck and drive off with it, I guess. I'd want the coil, too, just in case I wanted to make some more sometime. Then I think of what Deputy Anderson would do if I got caught speeding or something and he pulled me over. He'd shit and fall back in it.

That gets me laughing, thinking about Deputy Anderson and me with no license and gallons of shine and thousands of dollars in that old beat up truck. Then I think, really it's not all that funny, Boone, after that first minute, after getting to see the look on his face. Not a bit funny.

I've never been to jail, and as far as I know nobody I know has been either. Mr. Timmons, he might end up there if he doesn't cut some kind of deal, and I hope he can't. But Daddy, as far as I know, never spent the first night locked up, which is strange, since he was a mean drunk and was forever picking fights and shit like that. Maybe he did some jail time and I just don't know about it. Well, nobody around to ask about that.

I know if I start thinking about Momma and Hannah I'm going to start crying and I'm tired of that, crying and feeling bad. I pour an S&S and go out into the back yard and just walk around a little. It's summer and hot, but not August hot yet, and Gamaliel has plenty of trees, so it's not bad in the morning. I lean back against one of the big trees and slide down so I'm sitting on the ground and look up through the branches. It's real peaceful and I'm feeling pretty good until I hear the owl.

Momma always told me the stuff her gramma told her; she said it was her duty to pass it on, the old ways and such. Daddy used to just laugh at her, but Momma was always serious about it, and one of the things she told me was that if you hear an owl in the daytime, it means somebody's going to die.

Great, I think to myself, just fucking great. I can't get away from it. I guess that means the old man's about gone. And then I think, because I don't want to lose Gamaliel, that maybe it's somebody else. Maybe it's Momma, or Hannah, or Nancy, or Carrie, or Jerry, or somebody that moved into the house I used to live in. That's right down the hill, and maybe the owl's for them, not for me.

I look up at the sun; it's the middle of the day, almost, but I got no place I need to be, so I go back inside and pour another S&S. This one I make pretty strong, and it doesn't take long for me to nod off.

The phone ringing wakes me up. I look outside, and it's still light, but just barely. I grab the phone and say, "What?"

"Is this Gamaliel Everette's home?"

"What? What about Gamaliel?"

"Boone? Is that you? It's Mrs. Thompson, from up the road."

It takes me a second to finish waking up. Then I say, "Yeah, I mean, yes, ma'am, it's me, Boone. Sorry, I thought you were somebody else."

"I was pretty sure this was Mr. Everette's number. I haven't called him in years, you know, he liked to kind of keep to himself. I hadn't seen you to ask, but you told me about the stroke, and I was just checking on him."

"He's not doing so good right now; he's back in the hospital."

"Oh, Boone, I'm so sorry to hear that. You're down there by yourself, aren't you? I'm going to send my youngest down to keep you company for a bit."

"You don't have to do that, Mrs. Thompson," I say, but inside I'm thinking, it might not be bad to have somebody to talk to for a while.

"Of course I do," she says firmly. "You don't know any of mine, they're all older than you are, but Philip isn't that much older, and he's home right now. I'll send him right down."

"Really, Mrs. — "

She's already gone.

I hang up the phone and sit back down, finish the S&S that I had started before I fell asleep, and try to remember who Philip is. I probably met him years ago, before Daddy stopped letting us go up to the Thompson's place for those bonfires they used to have. That doesn't help much; I was pretty small then, and he was probably one of those guys sneaking off into the woods with the girls. I'm still trying to remember when Frankie gets up and trots toward the door, and a few seconds later somebody knocks.

When I open the door there's a guy standing there, and I have to look up to see him. He must be 6' 4" or more, and so big he barely fits through the door when I say, "Come on in." He's not fat, just big, like football player big. I say, "You're Philip, right?" and he says, "Everybody calls me Tiny," and just stands there in the hallway. Tiny. I guess I get that; the guy is huge.

"The best room's back here," I say, and start down the hall. He follows me, and I look down at Frankie. She's looking okay, not mad or scared or anything, which is good. She's a pretty good judge of people, a lot better than me sometimes, so if she's not worried, maybe I'm not either.

We come into the room and I look around and it looks like the only chair strong enough to hold him is Gamaliel's and that really pisses me off. I just point to it and go over to my old chair and sit down. Tiny lowers himself into the chair and looks around the room.

Neither one of us says anything for a minute or two and I'm starting to think, how can I get this over with, when he holds his hand out for Frankie to sniff and says to me, "Good looking dog. Had her long?"

He's leaning forward in the chair and Frankie gets up from where she's been, on the floor right next to me, gives his hand a sniff, and lets him scratch her behind the ears. Nothing like the way she acts around Nancy, but friendly enough.

"You want something to drink or anything?" I say.

"What you got?" he's still looking at Frankie, scratching her, rubbing her head.

I start to offer him an S&S and then think, how stupid is that, Boone? You've known this guy for about five minutes. "I got Thunderstorm, you want a glass? Or I got water. That's about it."

"Thunderstorm's good. About half a glass and a little ice."

Damn, this guy thinks he in a restaurant. I get his glass and take it in to him and go back and fill my glass from before.

When I come in and sit back down, he says, "Don't tell Mom, okay?" and pulls out a bottle from his back pocket and puts it on the table. "You like bourbon? Mom told me the old guy's not doing so well, and I thought you might want to have a sip."

"Hell, yes, I like bourbon," I say. I've never tasted anything but shine, but I can't say that.

"Good," he says, and points. "Drink some of that Thunderstorm, make a little room in your glass."

Half an hour later we're like we've known each other for years. Tiny knows about Mr. Timmons, and fills me in on what really went on at that lake house of his. It's a lot more than what Nancy told me about.

If half that shit gets out they'll put him under the jail.

"Damn," I say.

"He did that, had those parties, for ten years that I know of, before he got caught," Tiny says, and laughs. "Knew he'd get it in the ass sooner or later. Can't keep that kind of thing secret forever."

He's looking right at me and all of a sudden I think, he knows about Daddy. There's no way he knows that, but that's what comes into my head, and I can't get it out. I take another drink.

"You okay, man? You just went white as a ghost."

I nod. "Yeah, fine. So anybody besides Timmons going down for this?"

"Maybe, I don't know about that. Some kid named Curt spilled his guts, named everybody he could think of, trying to get some kind of deal. So I don't think Timmons is going to be in this by himself."

Curt. What an asshole. Now I'm glad I wasn't hanging around with him that last year I sort of went to school.

Tiny is still talking. "Course Timmons'll get it worse than anybody, it being his house and all."

I nod.

He picks up the bottle. There's a little left in it and he turns it up and then hands it toward me. "Might as well finish it off."

I tilt it up, drain the bottle, and hand it back. "Thanks, man."

He waves the empty at me. "Mom says you and the old man are pretty tight. Figured you might be in the mood for something a little stronger than Thunderstorm. She told me his name, can't exactly remember it, kind of a funny name."

"Gamaliel."

"Yeah, that's it. Like the president."

I just look at him. "How the hell did you know that?" I finally say.

He looks down at the floor. "I really suck at math and shit like that, but I, I don't know, I read stuff like history and it just stays in my head."

"You in college?"

He stands up. He's not real steady, but gets his balance and says, "Nah. No college. I gotta go."

"Okay, well, thanks for the drink."

He looks at Frankie. "You want to come home with me, girl?"

Frankie thumps her tail on the floor, and I look at her and then at Tiny. "I don't hardly think so."

He grins. "Yeah, that's what I figured. See ya."

"Yeah. Next time you come by, the door's open."

He heads off down the hall and I hear the door and then the screen door.

Chapter Seven

The first lesson with Nancy doesn't start out so well. I wake up around ten in the morning because somebody's banging on the front door, and can't even get awake enough to head that way before I see her coming around to the back.

"You're still in bed?" She looks like she's been up for hours, which she probably has.

"Late night."

She gives me a look. "You sure you want to start today?"

"I gotta take Frankie out for a minute. You coming in?"

I pull the door open and stand back, holding the leash. Frankie is starting to get used to the idea; as soon as I got out of the chair and picked up the leash, she was right beside me. She's looking up at Nancy, waiting for her to step inside so she can go out.

Nancy backs up instead and says, "I'll stay out here with you two. Look at you, Frankie, ready to go out?"

Frankie pulls me through the door and into the back yard. I start toward the woods with her; she's straining at the leash, trying to catch up on all the smells from the night before. All of a sudden she stops and starts growling, looking into the woods.

"Go get the shotgun," I tell Nancy.

"No," she says, and I look back over my shoulder.

"What the hell do you mean, no? It might be another rabid coon. I need that gun."

"Let's just go back inside, okay?" she's close behind me now, and she reaches out and grabs my arm. I'm not expecting it, and I flinch, and Frankie almost pulls the leash off my wrist.

"Dammit, Nancy, don't sneak up on me like that!" I'm shouting now, scared for Frankie and mad at Nancy, and Frankie's big enough to be a real handful. She's still growling and trying to get closer to the woods.

"Boone, please, let's get her back inside," Nancy sounds like she's about to cry, and I can't turn around and look at her. I'm dug in, holding my dog from going into the woods after whatever the hell is in there.

Then Nancy is past me and heading toward Frankie. She comes up next to her and puts her hand on Frankie's back. Frankie snaps back over her shoulder, doesn't bite Nancy, but I've never seen Frankie do that to anybody, not even Jerry, and I'm thinking, oh shit, she's got rabies, what the hell am I going to do now?

I shout at Frankie, "Dammit, dog, get your ass back here!" and jerk the leash and Frankie chokes a little and steps back one step to get the pressure off her neck.

"Don't you talk to her like that!" Now Nancy is shouting at me and that really pisses me off and I'm thinking she can't talk to me like that, nobody can, not any more.

I almost let go of the leash and step up to tell her that, but before I can, I hear something up in the tree, moving fast, and Frankie is trying to track its movements, but she's not pulling quite as hard now.

Then she's calming down some, and I can get her to move, and I haul her back into the house and almost slam the door on Nancy's hand. She's right behind me and catches the door, pushes it back open, steps inside, and closes it.

I'm breathing hard and I just stand there for a second and then I undo the leash from Frankie's collar and she trots over to the window. I can tell she still hears something, but she seems okay.

Frankie won't take her eyes off the back yard; I watch her for another half a minute and then look over at Nancy. She's looking at Frankie, too.

She shakes her head and looks at me, then, and says, "What were you going to do with a gun, Boone? Did you think I was going to be able to hold her while you shot at something you couldn't even see? You could barely keep her out of the woods yourself, and what if it was somebody out there, and not a rabid anything?"

She's right, I know she is, but I'm still mad and I know I'd better not say anything or it'll be the wrong thing for sure. It's all I can do to keep quiet, but I just nod and turn and sit down in Gamaliel's chair.

Nancy stands there for a minute and then sits down in the other chair. "I know you have a lot of stuff going on right now, Boone. You're worried about Frankie and you're waiting to hear something about Gamaliel. You know you can't just go shooting into the woods, though."

She leans back in the chair and we're both quiet for a while. Frankie gives up on whatever she was tracking out in the woods and goes over to Nancy. She's sitting forward now, with her elbows on her legs and her hands dangling in front of her. Frankie sticks her nose up under Nancy's hands and pushes, asking for a head scratch or a rub. Nancy smiles a little and gives her a two-handed scratch, getting both ears at the same time. It looks like Frankie is planning to stay there for the rest of the day, but Nancy pushes her aside after a few more scratches and stands up. She comes over to me and stands right in front of the chair, holding her hand out to me.

"Let's go for a drive," she says.

I shake my head. "I don't think I'd be much good behind the wheel right now."

"We'll take my car. Let's get you out of the house for a while."

I got to admit it's kind of nice, sitting in the passenger's seat up front with all this room. One time Daddy had this old four door something, I can't even remember what kind it was, but me and my brother Frankie and then Hannah later on were always in the back, and when it was just the truck we were either in the bed or jammed together up front. Back in the bed was better, unless Daddy was too drunk to keep it in the lane and we got thrown around.

This is nice, just sitting, watching the fields and stuff go on by and watching Nancy drive. She's got great legs and I think about putting my hand on the closest one and decide I should probably let her drive. It's not easy, because I remember how smooth her skin is.

She glances over and catches me looking at her legs and says, "What are you thinking about?" I look away real quick, a little embarrassed, but when I look back toward her she's grinning. She's not looking at me, got her eyes on the road, but she reaches over and messes up my hair. She leaves her hand on the back of my neck for just a second and then it's both hands on the wheel, and she says, "When you go for your test you need to have your hands like this."

I look at her hands, partway up on each side of the wheel, and say, "Okay. I usually drive kinda like that anyway."

"We'll try that study time that we were going to do today later this week," she says. "You busy on Wednesday?"

I laugh. "I think I'm pretty clear most of the week, Nancy."

"Good. Let's just take a short drive today, then, and work on Wednesday. Want me to wait until after lunch so you can get your sleep?"

I was looking at an old barn on my side of the road and when I turn around she's got that look on her face and I realize she's teasing me.

"Anytime you can come by is fine with me," I say.

We take a left at the crossroads where I usually go straight into town and I say, "Where are we going?"

She shrugs. "I don't know, no place really. Just driving."

I settle back and watch out the window, not really looking at anything in particular. We're in and out of woods and I say, "Whose land is this?"

"I think the state bought it a couple of years ago, something about a day park, I don't know if they're going to do anything anytime soon."

"Who lives in that old place?" I point at a house sitting back from the road, woods on two sides and a grown up field right up to the front door.

"It's been two or three years since I've seen anybody around there," she says. "I hardly ever come this way, though, so I don't know for sure." She hits a straight stretch and speeds up.

About ten minutes later we come to another crossroads and Nancy says, "That way," pointing to the right, "is the interstate, I think, but I've never gone that far. Straight ahead is the state line, another hour or so. The left I have no idea, never been that way."

"I think we ought to head back," I say. I don't want to, because this is the best I've felt in a long time. "I got Frankie to tend to and, well, Carrie might call, and . . . ."

"I know, Boone. You're right. We'll turn around up there and head on back."

When we get back I ask Nancy if she wants to come inside for a while. We're sitting in her car and she doesn't answer for a moment. Then she opens her door and gets out, turns and sticks her head in the car, and says, "You coming?"

I get out as quick as I can and we head toward the back door. Frankie is there at the door, looking at me and then at Nancy, jumping a little. Nancy laughs and says, "You'd think we had been gone for days."

"She's not left alone very much," I say, opening the door and grabbing Frankie's collar. "We spend all our time together unless I'm going to the store or something. I think after I take her to the vet I'm

67

going up to that state land we were driving through and let her have a good run."

The phone rings and I pick it up, all my worrying coming back in a rush. "Hello?"

"Hey, man, it's Tiny."

I realize I'm all tensed up and try to let go of some of that. I hold the phone away from my mouth and say to Nancy, "Tiny Thompson, from up the hill."

She just nods and sits down. Frankie trots over and sits right up against her and puts her muzzle on Nancy's legs. Nancy starts scratching her behind the ears.

I go back to the phone. "What's up?"

"Not a damn thing right now. Me and a couple of the guys are thinking about doing a little hunting day after tomorrow, and I thought you might want to show us what that dog of yours can do."

"Can't do it, not until after the fourth. Your mom tell you about the rabid coon I shot? The vet says I gotta keep Frankie in until after the fourth and then get her a rabies shot before I turn her loose to run."

"Well, I can't really blame you for that, Boone. She's a good dog. I'd keep her up too. Next time then."

"Definitely. What are you going after?"

"Squirrel, probably. Mainly just going out to fart around with the guys. I guess if one of us sees a squirrel we'll try to knock it out of the tree."

"Don't shoot each other, all right?"

He laughs, a short, hard laugh that kind of sounds like a cough. "Yeah, squirrels only. See you."

I hang up and turn back to Nancy. She looks so good, sitting there, leaned back in the chair. I walk over to her and lean down close. She raises her head up and turns toward me, closes her eyes, and I kiss her. She opens her mouth just a little and I put all my weight on my right hand and put my left on her cheek and then let it drop onto her breast. She puts her hand on mine and I think she's going to pull my hand off but she doesn't, she just lets her hand rest there.

I want to stay like this, just like this, but I realize how off balance I am and then I start feeling like I'm about to ruin the whole thing if I move the wrong way and then I feel Frankie bump against my legs and I have to catch myself to keep from falling. Nancy looks confused for a second and then she figures out what happened and starts laughing.

"I think your dog is jealous," she says and shakes her finger at Frankie. "How many girls have you pushed him off of, Frankie? Has it been a lot?"

"Nobody makes me feel as good as you do, Nancy," I say with a grin and then stop because I think I didn't say that right. "I don't think I said that right," I say. "Frankie hasn't pushed me off any other girls, I mean she hasn't needed to, I, I mean, there haven't been any other girls up here."

I'm looking at the floor while I'm saying all this, stumbling around like a damn fool, and I'm mad at myself and a little mad at Frankie and starting to get mad at Nancy because I can still hear her laughing.

I turn away from her and walk over to the window. Outside the wind is blowing the trees a little and the light is fading even though it's only the middle of the afternoon, and then there's a crack of thunder that's so close I jump back from the window.

The rain starts then and it's a real frog-strangler, coming down in sheets and bouncing off the ground. The last time it rained was a couple of days ago and it was one of those summer showers that just wet everything down, nice and gentle, and then gradually went away. Not this one. This one is coming in hard and the wind is picking up. I wonder if the creek on the old property is overflowing yet.

Nancy joins me at the window, coming up behind me. "Wow, it's really coming down. No way I'm driving in this mess. Okay if I stick around for a while?" and she's sliding her arms around my waist and pulling herself close, right against my back.

When I try to turn around Nancy tightens her grip, so I try to relax and just enjoy how this feels, but relaxed is not how I feel right now. I don't know what to do or say and I'm about to panic when Nancy rescues me.

"I bet Gamaliel would call this sipping weather, don't you think?"

I swallow hard a couple of times and clear my throat, trying to get my voice to work right, and say, "I think that's just what he'd say."

"Good," she says, and turns loose of me. "Need any help?"

"No, I think I got it. You want an S&S?"

Nancy's back in the chair now, looking out at the storm. It's not letting up at all, and I'm sure the creek's overflowing by now. She doesn't look at me, just says, "I don't know, Boone, how did you and Gamaliel drink yours?"

I laugh out loud. "He'd shoot me and leave me laying there if he knew I was mixing anything with shine in his kitchen. He always took it straight, not even ice. Just something to sip on."

"Well, don't you think that's what we ought to do? I mean, we're in his house, right?"

I turn to face her and now she's not looking out at the storm. She's looking right at me.

"Yeah, we're in his house."

"Then I think we ought to follow his wishes." She sounds pretty sure, and I smile, thinking that that's exactly what I did just before she called the first time, I guess that was last week sometime.

"Let's do that. You just want a sip or two, I guess."

"No more than that, Boone. If this rain ever lets up I'll have to drive back home."

"Well, then, I wish it would rain all night long."

71

Chapter Eight

I say that without thinking at all, it just comes out of my mouth, and I can feel my face getting red and I'm afraid to look at Nancy. I know she's sitting there biting her lip to keep from laughing out loud, so I start toward the kitchen.

She says it so low, I can barely make it out. "You know I can't do that." There's a pause, and then she whispers, "I think it'd be nice, though."

At least I think that's what she says, and I'm afraid to ask her to repeat it, so I say, "You want just a taste until you get used to it?"

No answer, and then she laughs and says, "I guess you can't see me nod from there, can you? Yeah, just a taste would be fine."

I pour her about a half inch into the glass and fill mine about a third full. When I carry them back to the table she looks at mine and says, "Really, Boone?"

"I don't have to drive anywhere," I say.

The lights flicker and go out. All of a sudden the only noise is the storm outside. When it slacks off for a second there is no refrigerator hum, no fan, nothing.

It's afternoon, but the storm makes it almost dark outside, so the room is dark and quiet except for the rain. It's turned into a steady shower now, the only thunder is a long ways off, and for a few minutes we sit and sip and don't say anything.

Nancy talks first.

"Do you miss being in school? I mean, do you like living up here, all by yourself like this?"

I look over at her. Half of her is in shadow, and the light coming in from outside is just enough for me to see her, kind of outlined against the dark cloth of the chair back. She's looking right at me and I can't remember when I've seen anything so beautiful. I've never wanted to say the right thing so much in my life, and I'll be damned if I know what that is.

"Well," I say, and it comes out a croak, like I'm a frog, or like I'm twelve and my voice is starting to change. I take a drink and clear my throat and try again.

"Well, part of it I like a lot. I mean, school, no, I don't miss that, and the part about not having no bosses is great, but I miss the old guy, and, and I miss seeing you." I'm looking at the floor now. "I'm sure glad you called me up, didn't expect it. Why did you? I mean, it's been a while. How come you called me?"

She looks away, toward the window. "I don't know, exactly, I just thought about you the other day, and thought I'd come by and say hi."

I start to answer and she stands up and walks over to the window. She's got her back to me now, and I'm glad she did that, because I figure anything I was about to say would have been stupid.

When I was in school I used to watch the guys in the hallway, leaning against the wall, talking to the girls, and it looked so easy for them, and the girls would laugh and punch them on the shoulder, and then they'd go off down the hall, bumping into each other on purpose.

No, I don't miss school. Not a bit.

Nancy's still standing there, and I take a sip, get up, and start toward her. My heart is thumping so hard I figure she can hear it, and I'm scared to death that this is the wrong thing to do, but it's like I can't help it, I'm walking real soft and I'm almost up to her, and she takes a big breath and says, "No, that's wrong, Boone, I didn't just want to say hi," and whirls around, flinging her hands up in the air, and hits me right in the nose.

I take a step back and I'm standing there, blood dripping from my nose, and Nancy has this horrified look on her face.

"Oh my God, Boone, I am so sorry! I didn't know you were there, does it hurt? Of course it hurts, and you're bleeding, you need a napkin or a paper towel

74

or a washcloth, I am so sorry," and she's looking around but she doesn't know where anything is.

Frankie is up on her feet, alert, probably wondering what the hell is going on here, and I'm wondering the same thing.

"It's okay, Nancy, really, it's nothing," I say and I'm thinking, dammit, Boone, if you hadn't been such a chickenshit you would have already been up there with your arms around her and none of this would have happened.

"I need paper towels, Boone, you're bleeding all over your shirt."

I take off my tee shirt and hand it to her. "Use this. It's already got blood on it."

Nancy looks at me, then at the shirt, and shrugs. "Sit down over there. Don't tilt your head back, I'm going to get some ice."

She heads for the kitchen. "Pinch your nose shut," she says over her shoulder.

She's back in just a second with my shirt, wet and wrung out, and ice in a washcloth.

"Found a washcloth in the sink. Hold this on your nose with your other hand and let me get you cleaned up."

I let go of my nose. "How long do I keep the ice on it?"

She puts my hand back where it was, "Keep pinching. I don't know, just a few minutes and we'll check it. Now hold still."

She didn't let the water run, so it's pretty cold. She uses my shirt to wipe the blood off my chest; there's not much of it, but it seems like she spends a lot of time on it. I'm wishing I had more chest hair. Last time I checked, there were only half a dozen or so. I know some of the guys at school started shaving in eighth grade and I'm just up to once a week or so and don't really need to do it that often, but I always thought those guys with a mustache with only a real hair every now and then looked pretty silly.

Nancy stops and leaves her hand on my chest for a second, at least it seems like she does, and then stands up and says, "I'm going to rinse this shirt in cold water and see if I can get the blood out of it, and then we'll check on you. I'm glad Gamaliel is on the city water."

I start to ask why and then realize that with the power off, if he was on a well we'd run out of water as soon as the tank was empty. I slide down in Gamaliel's chair and lean my head back.

"Don't do that," Nancy says. "Tilt your head forward."

"How do you know so much about this?"

"I've got a little brother with a smart mouth, in case you'd forgotten. He gets in fights every now and then."

Nancy finishes with the shirt and comes over to me. "Let's have a look."

When I take my hand and the washcloth away there's no bleeding.

I grin at Nancy. "Thanks, doc. Guess I'll go get another shirt."

I get up and two things happen at almost the same time.

The power comes back on and the phone rings.

I look at Nancy and then go to the phone.

"Hello?"

"Boone?" It's Carrie.

"Yeah, it's me. How is he?"

"We're back down in Knoxville. Pop is stable, and he's asking for you. Can you come down right away?"

"You're back in the hospital?"

"We haven't moved him into the rehab yet, I'll tell you all about it when you get here. It'd be better if you came now, Jerry's not here. He's back home, says he has an early day at work tomorrow, won't be back til tomorrow afternoon."

"Want me to wait until tomorrow morning?"

"No," she sounds worn out. "He's asking for you, I don't want to wait, in case . . . in case . . . . "

"I'll leave right now."

"Thanks, Boone. Be careful, the roads are wet."

I hang up and turn to Nancy. "He wants to see me."

"Okay."

This was turning into something really good, and then I blew it and walked right into her arm. I need

77

to see Gamaliel, just to make sure he's still alive, and if Jerry's not there I can take the will to Carrie. But I was really hoping something was going to happen tonight. I still don't even know why Nancy called me in the first place.

"Let me drive."

"What?"

"I said, let me drive," Nancy says again. "I've been wanting to meet Gamaliel, the weather is awful, and I've got an actual license."

For a second I'm angry, and I don't know why. Then I do know, and it makes me kind of ashamed. Gamaliel's not my personal property; I can't find a good reason not to introduce him to Nancy besides selfishness, and it might turn out that he'd like her. I sure do.

"Okay," I say. "I guess I need to get a shirt on."

"Too bad," Nancy says. "I was enjoying the view."

I stare at her, not believing what I just heard. Then I start laughing and turn around to go get a shirt. Just as quick I turn back, grab the glass, and have another drink before I put it on the kitchen counter.

Nancy puts hers beside mine. I look at it and I can't tell she had any of it at all. I get a shirt and pull it on, tell Frankie goodbye, and we head out the back door. After the door closes I remember and go back in to get the will.

"That's a great idea," Nancy says. "She's the one Gamaliel wanted you to give it to, right?"

The drive to the hospital is pretty easy, no rain to speak of, not much traffic, and it's on our side of the city. When we pull into the lot I say, "I don't know what kind of shape he's going to be in."

Nancy nods. "If it's not good for me to go in I'll stay in the waiting room. Don't worry about that, Boone, we're here for you to see him. I'm just tagging along."

I look over at her. "You're great, you know that?"

Nancy grins at me. "You just now figuring that out?"

I start to apologize for being so slow and then realize she's teasing me.

When I think about it, we didn't do much teasing in my family. Fact is, we didn't do any. Everything was so serious all the time, always tense around Daddy. I want to learn how to do this. For one thing, it looks like if I'm going to be around Nancy much I'm going to get it, so I might as well learn how to give it back to her. For another, it feels pretty good not to have to be worried all the time.

We get into the hospital and it goes easier at the desk than the last time I was here, and I wonder if Nancy being along has something to do with that. Probably.

Gamaliel's room is on the sixth floor, so we find the elevators and ride up. I look over at Nancy and she's glancing around real fast and it looks like she's sweating.

"You okay?"

"Not really. I hate these things."

I start to laugh and then have to bite the inside of my mouth to get it back together. She's really scared, I can see that. We're by ourselves in the elevator, so I step over to her and put my arm around her. She's trembling.

"Hey, look, it's almost there." I don't know what to say or do here, so I just point to the display.

"I'm taking the stairs back down."

"No problem. I'll walk with you."

It stops on four and she's out. "Maybe I'll just walk the rest of the way. See you on six."

I start to say something but the door closes and I'm going up.

When I get off I look around for the stairs and go over to get Nancy. She's not in the hallway so I open the door. I can hear voices, and one of them is hers.

"I need to get by, my boyfriend's waiting." I can hear the fear in her voice.

"I don't see anybody but us two." It's a guy's voice, and I'm down the stairs to the fifth floor in a heartbeat.

Halfway up the stairs between four and five I see Nancy, and a big guy blocking her way. I catch her eye and point left and she doesn't nod, just moves, and I hit him right in the back, both hands, as hard as I can.

He manages to catch himself before he slams into the wall and I turn to Nancy. "Go! Go now!" and she takes off. I back up to the landing and stand there.

The guy looks up at me like he wants to throw me over the railing. I'm too mad to be scared, so I just glare at him.

Then I hear Nancy's voice. "C'mon, sweetie, I'm at six. We need to get on to his room."

I walk backwards across the landing and then turn around, and now I am scared. He's a big guy and I'm guessing he's really pissed. I take the stairs two at a time and when I get out into the hallway on six Nancy throws her arms around me.

We just stand there, holding onto each other, and then she lets me go and says, "Thanks, Boone, that was scary."

"No problem." Boyfriend, she said boyfriend, but she was just trying to get away from that asshole in the stairwell.

Nancy says, "I hope you didn't mind that whole boyfriend, sweetie thing."

I wave it off. "I know, you just needed to get away from that guy. I get that."

She looks hurt, and I realize that I've blown it again. I try to make it better and say, "Not that it would bother me much if it was real."

I look up and she's smiling at me. "Let's go see Gamaliel."

"Right."

Chapter Nine

We're walking down the hall and Nancy turns to me.

"Oh, Boone, I am so sorry."

I don't answer her.

That was the worst fifteen minutes I've ever had. Worse than out in the barn with Daddy, or what was left of him. What just happened keeps playing over and over in my head.

I walk in and Carrie's standing by the bed and there's somebody in it but it doesn't look anything like Gamaliel. This old man has no life in him; he's like one of those old-timey dolls they used to make, all cornhusks and dried apples. Carrie motions me over and I just stand there with Nancy. I don't want to be anywhere near that bed.

The head turns and for a second there it's Gamaliel again, but it doesn't last and his face gets all saggy and his mouth is moving and I don't hear anything. Carrie motions again and I take a step or two. Nancy's right there, squeezing my hand over and over.

I take the envelope out of my back pocket and hold it up, show it to Gamaliel, and hand it to Carrie. She looks confused, but Gamaliel almost nods his head. I think he does, it's hard to tell. Then he closes his eyes and kind of sinks into the mattress.

It all blurs after that.

In the hall, Nancy is squeezing my hand so tight it's starting to hurt. We're halfway to the elevators and my head is full of hate and anger and fear. I hate hospitals, hate them for what happened to Frankie and now for what's happening to Gamaliel. I'm so mad at him for turning into this bad copy of himself. I turn my head toward her and start to look at her but I can't.

"I'm scared," I say, looking down.

"I know," she says.

"How the hell would you know!" I must be shouting, because a couple of old women at the end of the hallway turn and stare at me and I look at them and say, "Mind your own damn business!" and Nancy is pulling me over to the side of the hall to a door that says Family Room.

I jerk my arm away and go over to the window, one of those tall skinny things that won't open. There's nothing outside but a parking lot.

I feel a touch on my shoulder and Nancy whispers, "I'm going to sit down right over there, Boone, okay?"

and I nod and she sits down. I can see her out of the corner of my eye.

It's all so damned unfair, all of it. I'm going to lose Gamaliel and there's not a thing I can do to stop it or slow it down. The thought of it makes me tired all over, and I lean my head against the skinny window. It's still light outside but won't be much longer.

"Boone?"

"Boone?"

It's Carrie's voice and I straighten up and turn around. She's standing in the middle of the room.

"I thought you said he was asking for me. Don't look to me like he could ask anybody for anything," I can barely get the words out.

"Sometimes he can say a little, it's not real clear, but he did say your name earlier, and I know he was glad to see you." Carrie sniffs. "I'm glad, too," She looks over at Nancy. "I don't think we've met before. I'm Carrie, Gamaliel's daughter."

Nancy gets up and goes to her. "Boone's told me a lot about you. It's so nice to meet you, ma'am."

"You can call me Carrie," she replies. "Thanks so much for bringing Boone down here. Pop was so glad to see him."

I"m listening to this and thinking, how in the hell would she know that? He can barely move, and his face, his face is just there, there's no life to it at all.

I realize Carrie's talking to me.

". . . and you got out of there so quick I couldn't really talk. We need to . . ." she stops and looks at Nancy.

"She stays, Carrie. She's my, well, my, uh . . . ."

Nancy says, "It's okay, Boone, I'll wait in the hall."

"No you won't," I say and make myself look right at her. "I need you with me right now."

"Okay," she says. She has a very serious look on her face when she turns to Carrie. "So how is Gam- I mean Mr. Everett? I didn't know him before this."

Carrie smiles a little half smile. "You might as well call him Gamaliel. I think he'd want you to."

"I think so, too," I say. "I mean, he'd give me a hard time about having a girlfriend" I glance over at Nancy "you know, how'd you manage that, Boone, that kind of thing, but I bet he'll like getting to know you." I say this last bit to Nancy, not Carrie.

Carrie clears her throat. "That's one of the things we need to talk about, Boone." She's having trouble, I can tell. "Pop has a DNR and he's told us no machines to feed him or breathe for him, nothing like that."

"What the hell's a DNR?" I'm not shouting yet, but Nancy slides over and puts her hand on my arm. I shake it off. "Well?"

"It means do not resuscitate, Boone. It means don't try to bring him back if he, if he . . . ."

I know what all the other stuff she said means, the no food or breathing help, and all of it makes sense, I mean for Gamaliel, but it just makes me furious.

"You don't have to do that just because he says so!" I am shouting now.

"Do what, Boone?"

"All that stuff! You need to keep him around! He's the only — " The tears are all over my face and dripping off me and I don't even care who sees that. I turn away from them and walk back over to the stupid skinny window.

Nancy is beside me but she doesn't touch me. "Boone, look at Carrie."

I don't move.

"C'mon, Boone, please, just look at her."

I turn around and Carrie's standing in the middle of the room, staring at the floor. She looks so tired and small.

"You two need to be helping each other through this," Nancy is saying, but I'm only half listening. I'm thinking about Jerry and what kind of asshole would leave Carrie here like this and I want to track him down and pound him into the dirt.

Nancy leaves me and goes over to Carrie, leads her to a chair, and sits down next to her. She looks up at me and points to the chair on the other side of Carrie.

I don't move and she gets up and comes over to me.

"I know you're hurting, Boone, but so is Carrie. It's her father in there."

Nancy's right, and I'm embarrassed and a little ashamed that I didn't think about that.

"Give me a second and I'll be over there."

The chair next to Carrie squeaks a little bit when I sit down and Carrie glances over at me.

I think I should reach over and pat her on the arm or something, but I don't. Instead I just sit there, both of us leaned forward with our elbows on our knees, hands together, staring at the floor. Nancy gets up and says, "I need some coffee. You two want anything?"

Carrie looks up at her and starts to say something, stops, and then says, "That would be good, Nancy, thanks. Just black for me." Nancy looks over at me and I shake my head no.

"Okay, then, I'll be back in a minute," she says, and steps around Carrie, puts her hand on my cheek for just a second, and she's gone.

Carrie looks over at me. "She's a sweet girl, Boone. You two serious?"

I shrug. "She's great, Carrie, really great. I hadn't seen her for a few months and she called, we were going to work on getting me ready for my license and you called."

Carrie starts laughing, and I look at her. What's wrong with her, her dad in the room down the hall almost dead and she's laughing her damn head off?

She takes a couple of deep breaths and leans back in the chair. "So how long have you been driving around without a license, young man?"

I can feel my face getting red and I start to say something and she waves her hand at me.

"Never mind, I don't think I want to know. Oh, Boone, I'm not making fun, I just needed something to laugh at, I guess."

Nancy comes back in with two coffees and hands one to Carrie.

"Thanks, honey."

She takes a sip and nods. "I like it quite a bit stronger, but for hospital coffee, it's not bad."

Nancy comes over to sit beside me and offers me her coffee cup. I wave my hand and go back to staring at the floor.

Nancy says, "I called Mom and told her I was at the hospital with you and I'd be back as soon as I took you home. She was all freaked out until I told her neither of us was hurt, we were visiting Mr. Everett."

We all sit for a while, not talking, then Carrie says, "Boone, I need to talk to you about some stuff."

I don't want to, but I say, "Okay. What kind of stuff?"

"Well, about the house. You know Pop isn't going to be living there anymore, right? I mean, you saw him in there."

The idea crosses my mind to get Gamaliel up to the house and take care of him myself, and I almost say that, but then I think about what a stupid idea that is. I don't want to feed him, give him his medicine, wipe his ass, all that stuff for who knows how long. So I nod.

"He told me last week, before this last episode, that he wanted you to be able to live there as long as you wanted to, even after he's gone."

Nancy grabs my arm and squeezes it tight, and I turn my head to look right at Carrie.

She nods and says, "That's what he said. He made me call Jerry into the room so Jerry could hear him say it too."

I can't think of anything to say, so I just wait for Carrie to say something else.

"He likes you, Boone, likes you a lot. So you can keep taking care of the house until you decide to, well, you can stay there as long as you want to."

"Okay." I know that's a dumb thing to say, but I'm just realizing how worried I have been about the house. I don't really have anyplace else to go, so if I can stay there I sure will.

"The thing is," she goes on, and I think, here it comes. I knew it was too good to be true.

She takes a breath and starts again.

"The thing is, Jerry was really angry when Gamaliel said that to us. He doesn't like you much," I have to grin at that one, "and he had talked to me about selling the place and using the money to fix up our place, pay off some of Pop's bills, you know, stuff like that. So he doesn't want you in that house. Pop does, and it's his house, unless that will you gave me in there says something different. So I'm doing what he wants, but I'm telling you, Jerry is going to fight me on this."

She stops to give me a chance to say something. I don't, so she keeps going.

"If Pop leaves the house to me in his will, then Jerry will just have to be mad about it. But if he leaves it to me and Jerry, you know, husband and wife, then there's going to be a fight."

She puts her hand on my shoulder. "I know you need some time to let this all sink in, Boone. Pop wanted to see you and he got to do that, so he's happy for now. Why don't you go on home? I know you hate hospitals."

I start to say no, I'm staying right here, and then just as quick I think what I want to do more than anything else is get the hell out of there. I'm not even glad I got to see Gamaliel, not like that, like he's already halfway to the grave.

When I turn my head, Nancy is looking at Carrie, but she sees me and now she's looking into my eyes. "Let me give you a ride home," she says, real soft.

A ride home.

"Sounds good," I say, and give Carrie a hug, maybe the first time I've ever touched her, besides like shaking hands, and she hugs me back and we hang on to each other for a long time.

She pushes away from me and wipes her eyes. "I'm going to check on Pop. I'll call you tomorrow, sooner if something changes."

"Okay," I say, thinking that she must think that's the only word I know. Carrie goes out into the hall and Nancy and I follow her; she goes left and we go right, toward the stairwell.

Nancy grabs my arm. "If I can hold onto you I'd rather take the elevator," she says. "I don't want to run into that guy again."

Chapter Ten

I wake up the next day in the middle of the morning. Frankie is nosing me, asking to be taken outside, it's a half-cloudy day, and I feel pretty good until I finish waking up and remember yesterday.

While I'm outside being pulled around the yard by Frankie, I mostly think about Gamaliel, how I spent all that time living right next to him and never knew the guy, and that makes me think about Carrie and that leads to Jerry and now I'm just pissed off. I know that bastard's going to be trouble for me, whatever the will says.

We're so far away from the door, almost into the woods, that I can barely hear the phone ring. Frankie is not ready to come back in, not even close, so I'm having to drag her across the yard, and we just get to the door when the phone stops ringing.

"Dammit, dog, I bet that was Carrie," I say to Frankie, and she shies away from the anger in my voice. When I unhook the leash she goes over to

Gamaliel's chair and lies down next to it, looking over at me like she's scared.

I start to go over to her and tell her it's okay, and the phone starts up again.

Now I'm afraid to pick the damn thing up, but I do anyway, after a couple of rings.

"Hello."

"Hey, man, it's Tiny."

"You just call a second ago?"

"No, why?"

"I was outside and missed a call, that's all."

"Oh. Well, it wasn't me."

"Kill any squirrels?" I'm trying not to think about who that other call might have been.

'Leroy got one, nobody else even raised their gun. Left a couple of bottles empty out there in the woods, though. You should've come along, dog or no dog. Next time, right?"

"Yeah. Maybe."

There's a silence, then Tiny says, "What's going on, Boone? The old man die or something?"

Frankie jumps when I slam the phone down. I'm trembling and looking around for something to throw, somebody to hit, Frankie barks and I start toward her and the phone rings again.

I take another step toward Frankie and then spin around and grab the phone.

"What?"

There's a pause before she answers. "Boone, it's Carrie. I just talked to Jerry, he said he's going to stop by Pop's house this afternoon before he comes to the hospital. Thought you ought to know."

"Okay." I start to hang up the phone and then put it back to my ear. "How's Gamaliel?"

She takes a deep breath. "About like you saw him yesterday. He really perked up when he saw you, but now he's just there in the bed." Her voice breaks. "I don't know, Boone, I just don't know."

I stand there for a second and then say, "You want me to come down there?"

"No, I don't think so. Thanks anyway." She hangs up quick and after a second so do I.

It's early afternoon and I'm working on an S&S when there's a knock at the door. I go to it and open it just a little. It's Tiny.

"Mom says I need to come down here and check on you." He stands there a minute.

I'm about to say, well, you did, and close the door, but I change my mind. I don't know whether or not I can trust this guy, but right now I don't much care.

"You want to come in?"

He hesitates.

"C'mon, man, get your ass on in here. I need somebody to drink with."

Tiny looks at me and then steps into the hall. I close the door and start toward the back of the house.

When we get to the sun room I point to Gamaliel's chair and Tiny sits down. I take my drink into the kitchen and get another glass for him. I make two, nice and strong, and take them back over to the chairs.

I put my glass down on the table and stand in front of him with his.

"You can't tell anybody about this, okay? I don't want everybody and his stupid cousin knocking on my door."

Tiny looks at me for a second and then nods. I hand him the glass and sit down.

He takes a sip, then a drink.

"That's moonshine, right?"

"I call it S&S, you know, shine and soda. It's Thunderstorm and, yeah, shine."

Tiny grins at me. "Well, I'll be damned."

"You understand why you can't tell anybody, right?"

"This is real good stuff," he says. "Where'd this come from?"

"I don't have hardly any left," I lie. "Daddy had some in the barn, hid under some straw, he thought I didn't know about it. When he took off I got it, and then when I started watching Gamaliel's house I brought it up here."

He sips, and I sip, and we sit there for a minute or two.

"I hate getting this close to the last jar, but I needed a drink or three today."

Tiny takes a good long drink and sets the half empty glass down on the table.

"So how come you're sharing it? Not that I'm complaining," he says that last real quick.

"I went to see Gamaliel last night. He's about dead, Tiny. Hate to lose the old man, you know?"

He nods. "Lost a grandfather two years ago, he was a good guy."

He picks up his glass. "To the old guys," he says, and takes a big drink.

"To the old guys," I say, and do the same.

We both look at our glasses. There's a couple of half-melted ice cubes and a little S&S in the bottom of his; mine's not much better.

"Looks like I need to — " I don't finish because somebody's opening the front door.

"That'd be Jerry," I say to Tiny. "Ready to meet a real asshole?"

I hear steps coming down the hall, and Frankie starts growling.

"You put a leash on that damn mutt," I hear Jerry say, and then he's in the room with us. He looks from me to Tiny and back. He's swaying back and forth a little.

"Hi, Jerry," I say. "This is Tiny from up the hill."

Tiny just looks at Jerry. Jerry glances at him and then looks back over to me. He's got that stupid look on his face, the one that makes me want to punch him.

"You can't start bringing whoever you want in here," Jerry starts in on me. "You're supposed to be watching this place, not ent-ent-entertaining." He shifts over to Tiny. "And just who the hell are you?" He's already forgotten Tiny's name. I'm trying to decide whether to call Carrie or not when Tiny moves.

Tiny puts down his glass and stands up slow. Jerry kind of stumbles backward; Tiny is a head taller than Jerry and a whole bunch bigger.

"I'm a friend of Boone's," Tiny says. "And who the hell are you?"

"I own this place," Jerry says, but he's got a little shake in his voice. I'm loving this more all the time.

"Do you now?" says Tiny. He glances at me. "That right, Boone?"

"Not really," I say, and wink at Jerry. He gets all red in the face, but doesn't say anything. "This is Carrie's husband, Gamaliel's son-in-law. Gamaliel owns this place."

"Her name is Mrs. Phillips," Jerry is furious, but he's not making any kind of move. What the hell, I decide, and take a step toward him. Tiny slides sideways, out of my way.

"Well, she told me to call her Carrie, so that's what I'm doing," I say. "You look like you've had a few, Jerry. Want me to call you a cab?"

Tiny laughs out loud. "You know there's no cabs going to come all the way out to this part of the county, Boone."

I grin at him.

Jerry's fists are so tight the knuckles are white. I'm trying to decide whether or not to take another step when he takes one. Frankie is on her feet; she's growling low and the fur on her back is standing straight up. She's looking right at Jerry, showing her teeth. Jerry glances down and then back up at me. He gets a tight, angry smile on his face and draws his leg back, aiming a kick at Frankie's head.

I launch myself at Jerry, hitting him in the gut and knocking him on his ass on the floor. I can see Frankie out of the corner of my eye, getting ready to jump, and I say, "Tiny! Frankie!" and he snags her collar, bringing her up just short of Jerry's ankle.

Before Jerry can get back up I'm straddling his chest, fist back, my chest is heaving, and I'm thinking one right in the throat and I'll never have to hear his stupid voice again.

Then he's got one hand on the door frame and he's trying to pull himself out from under me. I can see the fear in his eyes; he's afraid I'm going to kill him, and I guess maybe he sees it in my face, that he's right.

"Boone!" Tiny is shouting at me. "He ain't worth it, man! Let him up!"

Jerry has mostly stopped struggling and he's just watching me. I look down at him and shrug, get to my feet, and step off of him. He uses the door frame to pull himself up and stands there, wiping his mouth with the back of his hand. Then he bends over, groans, and whirls around. A few seconds later he's throwing up in the bathroom. I go over to Tiny and take Frankie from him.

"Thanks for grabbing Frankie, man, she might've ripped his face off."

"Thought that's what you were going to do. You know he was faking it, right? He couldn't reach Frankie from where he was." Tiny looks at me. "A man might think you were kind of anxious to mix it up with him."

I don't look at him. "Maybe a little."

Tiny shakes his head. "Well, you took it right to him, I'll say that."

Now I do look at him. "What are you saying, man?"

Tiny smiles just a little. "I'm saying nice job, that's what I'm saying. Man goes after another man's dog, well, he deserves whatever he gets."

He reaches down and scratches Frankie behind the ears. "That's why I'm treating you so good, girl, you know that? Don't want to piss off your owner."

"Shit," I say, but inside I'm feeling pretty good right now. "I'd just be a greasy spot on the floor if I made a run at you, and we both know it."

Tiny grunts. "Yeah, probably. I think you'd get a few licks in, though."

"You two licking each other now?"

We look up and Jerry is standing in the hall, leaning against the door frame. He looks like shit.

Tiny straightens up from Frankie and says, real soft, "You want to say that again?"

Jerry looks around; I'm thinking he's realizing what a stupid thing he just said. He darts into the kitchen and picks up Gamaliel's fiddle. I hadn't done anything with it since that first try. He holds it by the neck and Tiny starts laughing.

"You going to play us a tune, Jerry?" He takes a step toward him.

Jerry swallows hard and edges back toward the hall. He sees me looking at the fiddle, catches my eye, grins, and drops the fiddle on the floor and brings his foot down on it, hard. I can hear the wood splintering and I see Jerry running for the front door. It slams behind him and he's out, on the porch and then out in the yard. A few seconds later I hear the car start, but I'm on the floor, trying to pick up what's left of Gamaliel's fiddle.

I hear Tiny behind me. "What an asshole," he says. "Want me to go after him?"

I shake my head.

"Want me to make you a drink, what did you call it, an S&S?"

He's moving toward the kitchen. "Yeah, that'd be good," I say.

I call Carrie while he's working in the kitchen and tell her what happened. When I tell her about the fiddle there's a long silence, and then she says, "Okay."

"He's been drinking," I say. "You be careful." She hangs up without saying goodbye and I realize I didn't even ask about Gamaliel, and feel like a jerk for forgetting the old guy.

I go sit down and take a sip from my refilled glass. I sit there for a minute, not moving, and then take another.

"You should be a bartender," I finally say.

Tiny takes another sip of his S&S. "You know you're right. I'm really good at this."

He looks down at Frankie. "When are you taking her in to the vet's?"

"End of the week," I say. "It'll be two weeks then since I killed that rabid coon."

"After she gets her rabies shot we'll take her out for a long run," he says.

"What do you think of that, Frankie?" I ask her. She's on her feet, tail wagging, looking at me and Tiny and then at the back door.

Tiny shakes his head. "She's past ready to get out of here." He finishes his drink and stands up. "I got to get back up the hill. Next time Jerry comes around, give me a call. I kind of enjoyed watching you kick his ass, wouldn't mind seeing another round of that."

"I'll do it," I say. "Listen, thanks for backing me up."

Tiny waves his hand. "Most fun I've had all week long."

"It's only Tuesday," I say.

"Oh. Right." He grins and heads out the door.

Chapter Eleven

It's too early to cook anything, so I'm eating cereal, and I start thinking about Tiny. I'm hoping I didn't make a mistake yesterday, trusting him. He and Nancy are the only two people who know about the moonshine, except Gamaliel, of course, and he's not talking to anybody.

Right away I'm mad at myself for thinking like that about Gamaliel, like he's just some guy.

I take Frankie out for a walk in the early morning. I'm not usually up this time of day, but Frankie loves it, and she's got her nose in the grass, pulling me all over the yard, and then she stops and stares at the road. When I follow her look I see that kid from where I used to live standing there, his hands on the handlebars of an old bicycle. I try to think of his name and it takes me a second.

"You need something, Devon?"

I've still got a tight hold on Frankie, but she doesn't seem mad or anything, just kind of curious.

"Name's Trevor."

"Oh. You need something, Trevor?"

He shrugs. "Nah, I'm just out riding. You get rid of that coon?"

"TWRA came and took it off. Listen, I'm busy, so you head on home now."

"Okay," he doesn't move for a second. "Is your dog all right?"

"She's good. We're going to the vet on Saturday. I'm going in now."

"What's her name?"

I can hear the phone inside.

"Look, Trevor, I got to go, the phone is ringing."

"Yeah, I can hear it. What's her name?"

"Frankie. I need to get the phone."

I start toward the door, look back, and Trevor's still in the same place. He's not on Gamaliel's property, so really there's nothing I can do, so I go on in. It bothers me, though. Kid has that stare, looks right through you. Like he knows stuff. If he starts poking around the field back behind his house and finds that marker . . . .

The phone stops ringing before I can get to it, but starts back up again about twenty minutes later. I pick it up.

"Hello."

"It's Nancy, Boone. Any word on Gamaliel?"

"I haven't called yet today. Yesterday about the same."

"Oh. You okay?"

"I guess. You coming over? I'll tell you all about Jerry coming by to make trouble."

"He's Carrie's husband, right?"

"Yeah, right, that's him. Hate that guy."

"Watch out for him, Boone," Nancy says. "He might cause you some real problems."

"He causes me problems every time I see him," I say. "He feels the same way about me I do about him. You remember last year when he came by the old place, where I use to live?"

"I don't think so."

"Well, it was pretty bad. Asshole just keeps coming back for more."

"You be careful now, Boone," She sounds worried. "I'm afraid one of these days you'll get into something you can't get out of."

It feels really good, having somebody worry about me. I guess Momma used to, but she's forgotten all about me since she took up with Jake whatever his name is, and Hannah's still too young to worry much. Besides, she's up with Aunt Claire, and Aunt Claire doesn't give a damn about me one way or the other.

I wonder who worries about Carrie. Not Jerry, that's for sure. Maybe that's why she's treating me so good, so she can have somebody around that doesn't treat her like shit. Wonder if they've got kids. I never thought to ask Gamaliel about grandchildren, and Carrie never mentions it. I sure as hell wouldn't want Jerry to be my dad.

"You there, Boone?"

I've been just standing here with the phone in my hand. "Yeah, I'm here. Just thinking about Gamaliel and stuff."

"Mom and Dad have me doing family stuff today. Okay if I just come by tomorrow?"

"You better call first in case I have to go, you know, check on Gamaliel or something. Make sure I'm here."

"You call me if something happens today. Otherwise, I'll call sometime in the morning, okay?"

"Sure."

When I go into the kitchen to make a sandwich, I realize that I'm almost out of food, so I head for the store. When I get there I see Mrs. Thompson's truck in the parking lot, so I'm not surprised when I hear her say, "Boone?"

I turn and she's pushing a half-full cart toward me.

"Afternoon, Mrs. Thompson."

She asks about Gamaliel and tells me how sorry she is that he's in such bad shape. I try to be polite, but I know that she and everybody else in the county had pretty much forgotten the old guy even existed until he got sick.

"You know Philip says you're taking good care of his house," she says, and I realize I've been kind of drifting. I hope she hasn't said anything I was supposed to respond to.

"Yes, ma'am."

"I just think that's wonderful, that you're being such a good friend to somebody like Mr. Everett."

I start to ask her what the hell she means by that when she sees somebody else she knows and she's off.

People sometimes just piss me off something awful, saying people like Gamaliel, like Daddy, like me. They think they're better than anybody else, with their fancy houses and big trucks and four-wheelers. Makes me wonder how Tiny turned out like he did. He never makes fun of me or Gamaliel.

At least not to my face.

I finish my grocery run in a really bad mood and go home, mix an S&S, and complain about people to Frankie until I nod off in the chair. When I wake up I'm starving and remember that the reason I went to the store in the first place was so I could make some lunch. It's close to dark now so I open a jar of sauce and boil some water for macaroni. I make too much and Frankie takes care of the leftovers in about three bites.

When it starts to get dark I hear a few fireworks and remember the fourth is only a couple of days away. I look down at Frankie; no sign of any problems at all. I tell myself I need to call the vet and make an appointment for Saturday morning, and I take Frankie out on the leash for an evening walk around the yard.

Chapter Twelve

Thursday starts out pretty bad. I'm caught right in the middle between Carrie and her shithead husband, and Gamaliel is so out of it he can't help. I'm thinking if he could talk worth a damn he'd tell them both to go fuck themselves, but he can't, and I don't think I could get away with it, even though I'm pretty sure that's exactly what he'd say. Maybe not to Carrie, but Jerry for sure.

I get a morning phone call from Carrie trying to tell me about Gamaliel and I can hear Jerry in the background running his mouth about me. Carrie's voice is low and tight, like she's really pissed off, and then she tells me she has to go and hangs up. I don't know much more about the old man than I did before the phone call, and I can't go down there because me and Jerry, well, we'd get into it for sure.

I spend the morning talking to Frankie and poking around the house, even though it still feels kind of wrong. I'm here, and there's not a lot of stuff, but there's some, and about halfway through the morning I realize what's going on.

I'm bored.

Part of it is this thing with Frankie, I know, and that'll go away after the weekend. Before that raccoon showed up Frankie and I could head off into the woods, up along the creek, and it was always good up there.

Except that I'm on somebody else's property now when I go up to the pool. I've never seen anybody up there, just heard voices that one time, but still, it doesn't feel the same, and anyway I can't do that like before with Frankie on a leash and all.

When Momma and Daddy were around I don't remember being bored hardly ever. I was still going to school then, but when I was at home I wasn't so much bored as scared. I guess if you're scared enough you don't have time to be bored. I remember always needing to know where Daddy was and what kind of mood he was in, so I'd know, or at least have some idea, of what to do or where to go next. Hannah, she had already learned the trick I used when I was her age; she could be so quiet and out of everybody's way that she was pretty much invisible. She was really good at it, like I used to be. Seemed like Frankie never used that trick, he'd always say or do something that would make Momma laugh and Daddy grin a little, and for a while then we'd all be okay. I never figured out how to do that, and sometimes I'd get mad at Frankie for being able to do it so easy. I feel a little ashamed now that I got mad at him for stupid shit like that.

I got too big to use the invisible trick before Hannah came along, and Daddy and I kind of moved around each other. Actually I think I moved around him; I don't remember him ever changing anything because of me, except to get mad and yell or beat my ass.

Now I'm thinking about Jerry again, and how he tries to be such a badass and how bad he is at it. That gives me a laugh, and for a minute I feel better, but then I'm back to being bored.

I can't try to play Gamaliel's fiddle because of stupid Jerry, and I don't know whether or not I would ever stay with it long enough to sound like anything. I look around the house again and then think about the shed and decide to go out there.

I'm halfway to the shed when I hear the owl again. It's been a while since I heard it, and I'd almost forgotten, but it's back and calling during the day. Gives me a shiver even though I mostly don't believe in omens and shit like that. I think about Gamaliel in that bed staring at the ceiling and it almost makes me cry, and I don't know whether I want him back up here, him being the way he is now, or I want him to go ahead and die and not have to live like that. I hate that choice, but there it is, I think that's what the choice is now.

Seems like when I'm not bored I'm feeling really bad about something. Except for Nancy. I'm not bored when she's around or when I'm thinking about her, and it's almost always good stuff I'm thinking. I think about how she looks with those summer clothes on and all that skin showing, and I realize I've never seen her in a bathing suit. I wonder what kind she has. I saw a picture of a model in that Sports Illustrated issue they put out every year and I had to look really hard to see the bikini, it was the same color as her tan, and it didn't cover up hardly anything.

Somebody up towards the Thompson place sets off some fireworks and I jump and look around, wondering why I'm out here just standing in the yard. Then I remember I was bored and was going to the shed.

When I open the door to the shed I turn on the light and look around. What this place needs is a good cleaning. I smile, thinking of what Momma would say if she heard me talking like that. Sounds like something she'd say about my room or the kitchen.

There's an old plastic bucket on the floor, one of the ones I stood on when I found the rifle, and I take it into the house and fill it about halfway with water. Gamaliel has a bunch of old dishcloths in a drawer next to the sink and I take two of them and the water out to the shed.

The rest of the day passes real fast and is ending up a lot better than how it started. By the time I decide to quit until tomorrow, two of the long shelves against the left wall are wiped down and the tools are pretty clean. Gamaliel only had one can of WD-40 and it was about half gone, so I used it up on the tools on those first two shelves. I'll need at least one more can and maybe two; I haven't gotten to the big stuff yet.

The chisels still need sharpening, but they're clean and oiled. So are the pliers and visegrips, the two hammers, and the three adjustable wrenches I find shoved back up against the wall. There's a small vise bolted to the wide shelf, the one about waist high that's built out past the rest, like a kind of workbench. That's the last thing I work on, and it still needs another shot of lubricant for it to really work smooth.

The dishcloths are more rags than anything else now and they're filthy, like the water in the bucket. I take them back to the house, throwing the dirty water into the yard on the way, and wring out the rags in the kitchen sink as best I can.

Last thing I think about before I nod off in the chair is to wonder how Nancy is going to spend the fourth. Maybe I'll give her a call tomorrow.

When I get up I try Nancy a couple of times and get no answer; the whole family's gone. She never said anything about plans for the holiday, but seems like we mostly talk about Gamaliel and all the other stuff going on with me.

She must think I'm a real jerk, I say to myself, always talking about me and my problems. I don't even know anything about her family, except she's got a little brother and I can't even think of his name. Simon, no, that's not it. Damn. I tell myself that the next time I'll be sure and ask about what's going on with her.

It's the Fourth of July for sure; not even noon yet and I can hear the fireworks from up at the Thompson place and down toward town, too. Frankie's a little skittish, but not too bad, like I've heard some dogs are. I had a friend, Gary, in eighth grade, told me his dog damn near tore their back door off the hinges every Fourth of July. Thunderstorms, too, according to Gary. Ended up being an inside dog, even though it was a full Lab and probably weighed seventy-five pounds or more.

I take Frankie outside on the leash. "Maybe tomorrow you can run, girl," I say, but I'm a little worried. She's been held back for so long she might take off into the woods and stay gone for a while. She does okay for me now, it's been a couple of weeks, and she doesn't fight me like she did. We go around the whole yard, front and back, and into the woods but not too far. I get tired of untangling us from the trees and roots and Frankie doesn't like it much either. After a few minutes we give it up and go back into the house, and I pour an S&S to celebrate the holiday and split a hamburger with Frankie.

Saturday morning I put Frankie in the truck and head out to the vet's. It's on the other side of town, heading toward Knoxville, and I leave a little early to make sure I can get there on time. The directions were pretty easy, but I'm still kind of nervous about being on a strange road and a couple of times I wish Nancy had been driving. I really need to get a license.

The parking lot is only about half full, so I put Frankie's leash on, get out, and head toward the door. A guy is coming out with some kind of huge dog, I have no idea what kind, lots bigger than Frankie, and when he sees us he goes crazy. I've got my leash with both hands and so does the other guy, and I'm thinking it's a good thing we're at a vet clinic. It looks like that other dog wants a big piece of Frankie, and she's not backing down at all.

The man and his monster dog finally get into his truck and he flips me off on the way out of the parking lot. All this puts me in a really shitty mood for my first visit to the vet.

Daddy never was much for pets; he said over and over that they just used up food money and didn't do a damn thing to earn their keep. The couple of times a dog followed me and Hannah home from school he'd grab it by the scruff of the neck as soon as he pulled in and saw it, throw it in the back of the truck, and that would be the last we'd see of it. I never knew whether he took them to the shelter, somebody he knew, or just tossed them out on the road somewhere. Anyway, we didn't have pets, so I never had reason to go to a vet's office.

The people at the desk, a guy not much older than me and a woman who looks like she's been working there for a long time, make a big fuss over Frankie, telling her and me what a beauty she is, and Frankie is eating this up. We go over to the waiting area, a big room with couches and chairs and dogs on leashes and cats in cages, and sit down to wait our turn.

The vet turns out to be an old black guy, hair going white, about the same size as me and strong for an old man. He picks Frankie up and puts her on the table and starts looking her over, asking me questions all the time. How old is she? When I say I got her as a pup last year he nods, then asks me if I got her from a pet store. I say no, a guy I know from school, his dog had a litter and Frankie was the runt, I got her before his dad tossed her out on the road or in the river. He gets real mad about that, the river part, and starts going off on how irresponsible people are with their pets. When he asks me about shots and I say this is the first time she's been to a vet he gives me a look but doesn't say anything, just turns back to Frankie and keeps working on her. I tell him about the raccoon and how I've kept her up and he nods at that like maybe I'm okay after all.

"You going to get her spayed?"

I get a little embarrassed by that, because I have to ask how much that costs. I don't want him to think I'm some kind of bum, but then I think about what I've got on and what kind of truck I drove in here, and I don't see how he can think anything else. When he tells me how much I shrug my shoulders and don't say anything.

"You know we can let you pay a little now and a little every month if that's what you need. You have a nice animal here, looks like you take good care of her, but she needs to see a vet every year. Also, getting her spayed is the right thing to do unless you're planning to breed her, and she's not a purebred, so you ought to give it some thought."

I tell him I'll think about it, and ask him about letting her run after this visit. He wants to know why I'm asking about that, and I remind him about keeping her up after me shooting the raccoon.

"Well, I wouldn't just let any animal run, not this year. This is a bad year for rabid animals. I'd only let her out if I was going to be out with her. You're not one of those people who chains their dog to a tree and leaves them outside all the time, are you?"

I tell him no, I'd never do that to Frankie, and he nods again. He does that a lot, nodding.

"Good," he says. "Now you take Frankie on home and keep on taking care of her. Think about getting her spayed; you don't want every male dog in your end of the county coming around every time she goes

117

into heat. Tell Jan at the front desk to give you the new customer discount, and call us when you make up your mind about spaying."

I start to tell him I don't need his damn charity and then stop myself. That's the kind of shit Daddy would say, all proud even though he always, always needed help. I say thanks instead and shake his hand, and he spends more time saying goodbye to Frankie than to me.

Chapter Thirteen

Frankie acts like she's still on the leash when we get home and I open the truck door and call her out into the yard. She gets out but stays right next to me. When I remember I have the leash in my hand I go over to the back door and hang it on the knob. I go back out into the middle of the yard and head towards the woods, Frankie right beside me. It takes her a second to realize she's not on the leash, and then I swear she jumps a foot off the ground. She starts running in circles around me as fast as she can go, and I'm laughing my head off. I don't hear the car pull in, right behind the truck.

Frankie skids to a stop, looking toward the truck. I turn and see Carrie walking toward me. She holds her hand out and Frankie trots over and gives her fingers a sniff, then a lick. She smiles, but it's a tired smile, you can barely see it on her face.

"Hello, Boone. Hi there, Frankie."

She sounds tired, too. Frankie is still hanging around her, and Carrie reaches out to give her a scratch behind the ears.

"How is he?"

I'm watching her with Frankie and she's not in any hurry, just scratching Frankie's head and really concentrating on that. After a minute she straightens up and says, "I wanted a dog when we first got married, but Jerry didn't. Said they were more trouble than they were worth. Are you more trouble than you're worth, girl?" and she's back with the dog and I'm getting really impatient.

"I said — "

"I know, Boone, I heard you. I came up to get you, actually, glad I found you at home."

I look at her.

"I want you to see something. You got a license yet?"

I shake my head.

"Too bad, I was going to let you drive. I'm worn out."

She tries the smile again, and it's still barely there.

"Can you leave Frankie inside the house? Will she be okay?"

"Sure, I don't do it much, but when I go to the store and stuff like that, she stays in. She'll be okay if I'm not gone long."

"Good." She gives Frankie a final scratch. and says, "Sorry, girl, I need to borrow Boone for a bit. He'll be right back."

She turns to me. "Ready?"

I put Frankie inside and make sure she's got water, close the back door, and get in Carrie's car. I've never ridden with her before, and, when I think about it, I've never ridden with much of anybody.

When Daddy was around he always drove and was usually off by himself somewhere. I never had many friends in school, so riding around on the weekend didn't happen. Besides, it's not like I had money for a movie or a hamburger or anything like that. Now I've been in the car with Nancy once, and I think I might end up going somewhere with Tiny and his friends sometime, but still, it's pretty rare for me to be riding with anybody.

I look over at Carrie and she's half watching the road, half watching me.

"What?"

I don't mean to sound mad or anything, but she jerks her head around to look at the road and says, "Nothing, Boone. Sorry, I didn't mean to stare at you."

Neither one of us says anything for a while, and then we make a turn onto a road I've never been on before. It's not the way to the hospital.

"Where are we going?"

Carrie doesn't look at me. "Almost there."

I don't like this. Are we going to a graveyard? Did Gamaliel die and she didn't tell me?

"Where's Jerry?"

"He's at work."

"What kind of job does he have? It's Saturday."

"He's a salesman, sells phone systems to businesses, and sometimes the weekend is the only time they can put the system in. He just goes in to make sure they get what he sold them, you know, that there weren't any mistakes along the way."

This sounds like bullshit to me, but I don't say anything. I'd bet anything Jerry's lying to her. That's just the kind of shit he'd do, tell her he's working so he can go out and get drunk or steal something from her, like those silver dollars. I never did find out how that ended and I'm about to ask, even though it's none of my business. She did kind of put me right in the middle, using me to see if he was telling her the truth. So I know something is bad between them. Just as I'm getting ready to open my mouth she says, "We're here."

I get out and look around the parking lot. There's a big entrance right in front of us, glass double doors and a roof that comes out over a place you can pull a car into and then drive on through back out into the parking lot. The main building is two stories high and only goes back a little ways before it splits into two sections going left and right. They're only one story tall, and there's lots of windows, looks like a dozen on each side. Carrie is walking away from the main entrance, along a sidewalk that curves around the left-hand section of the building. I can see two more buildings back a ways from where we are, a lot smaller than the one we're walking around. I have to speed up to keep up with Carrie; she's walking fast, like she's got someplace to be and can't be late.

"Where are we?" I finally catch up to her as we get to the edge of the main building and turn the corner. She doesn't answer me right away, but she slows down and then stops.

There, in front of us, is a yard with a bunch of bushes and a couple of trees that look like they don't belong there, like somebody dug them up and moved them out of the woods. The sidewalk winds in between them toward a circular pool, a little bigger than the one I used to sit beside, with one of those fountain things in the middle. It's not putting out much water, and I can see the sidewalk is cracked in a couple of places. The yard needs mowing.

She puts her hand on my arm and says, "Don't say anything about how the place looks, okay? The insurance company said we had to move him and this was the only place that had a bed that we could afford." She's pointing to the other side of the pool, toward an old man in a wheelchair.

It takes a few seconds before I realize who is sitting in that chair.

Chapter Fourteen

Carrie starts around the pool and then turns back. I'm not following her, I'm just standing there like a dumbass.

"The insurance company said we had to move him," she says, "and this place was all we could find that had an open bed and that we could afford." She's repeating herself and I don't tell her, I can't stop looking at Gamaliel.

The wheelchair is sitting so that it's angled toward us; I can see his face. There's no expression there. A blanket of some kind is tucked around his legs and the rest of it is piled up in his lap. He's got another cloth around his shoulders, and he looks just like the rest of the people I see when I glance around. They all look pathetic.

Seeing him like this makes me really mad, so mad I can't make myself go any closer or say anything to Carrie. I'm stuck, and I wish Nancy was here. Or Frankie.

"Hey, Carrie."

She's still looking at me, and after a second she says, "What is it, Boone?"

"Do they let dogs visit here?"

She frowns. "I don't think I've ever seen one here. Definitely not inside, never seen one inside. Are you thinking about Frankie?"

"Yeah, Gamaliel likes her a lot." I don't say anything else, because I can't think of anything else to say. I'm still mad at Carrie for dumping him here and mad at him for getting so old so fast. I don't like it here at all, and maybe Frankie would make me feel better. I don't know whether or not Gamaliel would even notice her.

I look up at Carrie and she's crying, that kind of quiet cry with just tears, no wailing or moaning or any of that stuff. Crying and smiling at the same time.

"I think that's a wonderful idea," she says. "Let's go find out."

The lady in the front office tells us to wait a minute while she gets the director and it takes almost no time at all, which I like. I hate this place, there's death all around me, and I think about the owl and wonder how often they hear one outside these rooms.

The director comes up, walking fast. She's older than Carrie, I think, and talks as fast as she walks.

"Not in the building, insurance regulations, you understand, and of course the animal would have to be approved by me or my assistant, and all the shots would have to be up to date."

She stops for breath and I say, "Just took her to the vet yesterday, I mean earlier today, and she's good, just got checked out."

She nods and goes on talking, something about organizing a schedule, and I'm already regretting I ever brought it up. All I wanted to do was bring Frankie with me the next time I came down to see Gamaliel.

" . . . and I just know the other residents would love to spend time with Francie!" She's getting all excited about this, and I'm just getting madder. I'm not sharing Frankie with anybody else. She knows Gamaliel, and he knows her. I just want to see if he can still recognize either one of us.

"Her name is Frankie, and, and, oh, hell, just forget the whole damn thing," I turn away from her and start toward the big double doors. I look back at Carrie. "I'll see you at the car."

Carrie comes out after about ten minutes and unlocks the car and gets in. I get in on the other side and we pull out onto the road, not talking to each other. After a mile or so I turn in the seat and say, "Sorry, Carrie, she just made me mad, is all."

"I don't understand, Boone, really I don't. She was just trying to cheer up the other residents, like you're trying to do for Pop."

She doesn't look at me when she says this, and I'm thinking she's mad at me now. I was about over it but now I'm getting mad all over again.

"Frankie's not some thing for her to parade around her, whatever that place is called, she's my dog and Gamaliel liked her and I just wanted to do something nice for the old guy." I take a deep breath. "And she just wouldn't stop, making all these plans and telling me what day to be there and how long to stay and she just wouldn't stop. And she got Frankie's name wrong."

Carrie laughs. "I heard that part. She's not really a Francie, is she?"

I can't help but laugh along with her. "No, she's not."

Now she looks over at me. "Tell you what. I'm going back there tomorrow. Let me talk to her, let her know that you want to take it slow, not promise anything you can't make good on. I'll see if she's okay with a couple of trial visits just to see how it goes. Okay?"

I look out the side window and then over at her. "Okay."

Three days later we pull into the lot and Carrie and Frankie and I get out of the car. Frankie looks around, trying to figure out where she is, sniffing the air and the pavement, and I clip the leash on her. She starts off and her head jerks back a little when the leash tightens. She looks back at me like, "What the hell is this about? I thought we were done with this." I give it a gentle pull and she trots back over to me, still a little suspicious.

"We're going to see Gamaliel, girl. Remember Gamaliel?"

Her ears are up and she's looking around, bouncing a little on her front legs. She remembers him all right.

Carrie is watching all this and it looks like she's about to cry again, so I say, "Lead the way, Carrie, let's see if he's out by the pool."

I'm following her down the sidewalk and I realize that I'm a little scared. What if Gamaliel doesn't remember Frankie? What if he doesn't remember me? What if this whole thing was a really bad idea? I'm thinking about going back to the car, but Frankie's pulling hard on the leash and I look up and there he is, in almost the same spot, and Frankie pulls me right over to Gamaliel's wheelchair.

Frankie sticks her nose under Gamaliel's hand and pushes her head into his lap. I've seen her do this dozens of times back at Gamaliel's house. He'd always pretend to push her away and then give in and rest his hand just behind her ears, scratching her now and then.

This time he doesn't do anything. His hand just lays there on her head, and neither one of them is moving.

I watch as long as I can stand it and then pull at Frankie's leash. She's not budging, and then I feel a hand on my arm.

"Let them be, just for another minute," Carrie says, her eyes locked on her dad's face.

So I stand there, looking everywhere but at the two of them, until Carrie says, "Okay, Boone, I think that's enough for today."

I finally get Frankie to come to me and I'm about to head back to the car when Carrie says, "Don't you want to say hi? He'd love to know you're here, Boone."

"No," I say, and walk back to the car as fast as I can get Frankie to move.

All the way back to the house Carrie is talking to me and Frankie.

"I think that was great, don't you? Frankie, he knew you, didn't he? I could see it, he knew you were there, he knew who you were. Boone, when can we go back? I think this was such a great idea you had. Pop needs this, he needs somebody around who cares about him. I could see it in his face, couldn't you?"

She goes on like this for a while and finally I can't stand it anymore.

"No, Carrie, I couldn't see it in his face, or his hand, or his big toe, or anywhere else. I don't know what it is you think you saw, but whatever it was, I missed it. It didn't even look like Gamaliel, not a bit." I can't look at her while I'm talking, I'm just watching the fields go by outside the car window.

She's silent for a couple of miles, and then she says, real quiet, "You're wrong, Boone, he knew, you just couldn't see it. I see him a lot more than you do, I saw how his face changed and his eyes, they were brighter."

I don't say anything.

"Don't give up on me, Boone, please? Pop needs this, I just know it."

I don't answer until we get to the house; when I get out and open the door for Frankie, I lean in and say, "Give me a couple of days, okay?"

She nods, puts the car in reverse, and, just before I close the door, she says, "Thank you, Boone. I'll call you in a couple of days, maybe Saturday?"

"Sure."

She pulls away and Frankie and I go into the house.

The next morning I call Nancy; I need to talk to somebody besides Frankie about this.

The phone rings four or five times and then somebody picks up.

"Hello?"

It's not Nancy's voice, but it sort of sounds like her.

"Is Nancy there?" I say, thinking, I bet this is her mom. I've never talked to her before, and all of a sudden I'm really nervous.

"Is this Boone?"

"Yes, ma'am." I don't like not knowing who it is I'm talking to. I wish she'd say who she was.

"This is Nancy's mother. I've heard a lot about you, young man."

I don't know what to say to that, so I just sit there with the phone in my hand like an idiot.

"Boone?"

"Yes, ma'am, sorry. I was just, I mean, is Nancy around?"

I sound like a damn fool.

"You know, we're going to need to have you over for supper sometime soon," she says. It doesn't seem like she's in any hurry to get Nancy, or even tell me if she's home.

"I'd like that, ma'am, thanks."

"Nancy told me all about the two of you," she says, and I almost hang up the phone right then. Does she know about the shine? The time I almost put a dent in her car I was so mad? The time Nancy was teasing me about staying all night?

"Well, I, uh, she's a real nice girl, ma'am. She helped me out an awful lot when I was, I mean when Gamaliel was . . . ."

"I know, she told me how pitiful he is now, how he's laid up in the hospital and all."

He's not pitiful, I start to say, but I can't. He is.

"He's not in the hospital now, ma'am, he's in like a home. The insurance — "

"Oh, I didn't know that. Is he doing any better?"

"No, not really." I don't want to talk about this, with this person I don't know, I want to talk to Nancy.

"I'm sorry to hear that, Boone."

There's a half a minute where neither one of us says anything.

I finally say, "Could you ask Nancy to call when she gets back?"

"I sure will, Boone, she's just out with some friends and, well, I could call her on her cell if it's urgent." She says it like she'd have to know what was so urgent before she'd make that call.

"No, nothing urgent, I just hadn't talked to her in a day or so."

"Okay, then, you take care. Remember, we need to have you over sometime soon."

"Yes, ma'am."

After I hang up I think, why do I not know Nancy's cell number? Why don't I know that she even has a cell phone?

I'm too sad about Gamaliel to get mad about it right now, so I go back to Gamaliel's chair and then get up as soon as I sit down and mix a strong S&S. The sky looks like it'll be raining soon, so I call Frankie and we go out into the back yard.

She doesn't call and I don't call her house, and I fall asleep early, just after dark, and wake up half a dozen times during the night thinking about Gamaliel sitting there in that chair and Carrie saying how good it was for Frankie to be there with him. Maybe I'll give it another try next week. It's just so hard to see him and then come back here and think about how he and I used to spend time here.

Friday afternoon I'm out in the shed, finishing the cleanup and thinking about what I'd like to do with the wood he's got out here. There's not much, but I don't think he'll be doing anything with it. Hell, I know he won't, and I hate to see it go to waste. There's some oak and cedar, and some other stuff I'm going to have to ask somebody about. I wonder if Tiny knows anything about wood. I'm thinking I'd like to try to make a little box, maybe give it to Nancy if it turns out okay.

There's the sound of a car pulling in, and then a car door opens and closes. Frankie's up on her feet, not leaving the shed, but alert. She's growling a little, I can barely hear it and I'm right beside her. Leaning over, I put my hand on her head and say, "Easy, girl. Let me have a look, okay?" I can hear somebody knocking on the back door.

Chapter Fifteen

It's a big guy, I don't recognize him, but he's driving an old Chevy and there's somebody in the passenger seat. He looks toward the car, shrugs, and goes over to the truck. He looks inside it and in the bed, takes out a tee shirt I had thrown into the floorboard, and throws it in the yard. When he turns to toss the shirt in the yard I see the pistol stuck in the waist of his jeans, right in the small of his back. He goes back to the car and reaches in, comes out with a yellow piece of paper, and leans over the truck's windshield. He looks at the paper and through the windshield, back and forth, and then nods to the person in the car, opens the truck door, and slides behind the wheel. I see him lean over and open the glove compartment. Then he bends down and I can't see him for a second.

I realize that the key is there, on the floorboard, lying there in plain sight. Sometimes I just drop it there, and I remember Daddy doing that same thing. I always thought it was stupid, like asking somebody to steal the truck, and now here I am, watching somebody steal the truck, me in the shed, and the shotgun in the house.

The guy starts the truck, it throws out that blue smoke, and whoever's in the Chevy slides over into the driver's seat and backs out to give him room. The car backs out and up the hill and I get a look at the driver.

It's Momma.

I start to run out and she's already gone, and the truck is right in front of her, and I'm standing there not believing what just happened to me.

When I get back up to the house there's an envelope stuck between the door and the frame. I grab it, go inside, make sure Frankie has some clean water, pour myself a straight shine, and sit down. I recognize the handwriting as soon as I take out the letter and unfold it.

I just sit there for a second and then take two big swallows before I start reading.

Dear Boone,

Jake's only giving me a minute to write this, so I've got to be quick. He was looking through the stuff I brought from the house and found the title to the truck. We're in Memphis now and he says we need a truck. The kid that lives in our house said there was a truck up here. I figure you're around here somewhere. Tell your Daddy it isn't your fault the truck's gone.

I'm sorry and I love you,

Momma

I sit back and stare at Frankie for a second and then I empty the glass in one huge swallow.

The rest of the day is kind of blurry.

The Saturday morning sun hurts my eyes when I take Frankie out for a run, and my head is really pounding. I cut the run short, and Frankie doesn't give me any shit about it. I might've taken it all out on her if she had.

The phone rings while I'm trying to get some cereal to stay down and I just let it ring. I'm thinking it might be Carrie, and I really don't want to talk to her about Gamaliel right now.

Fifteen minutes later the phone rings again and I ignore it again.

Half an hour later somebody is pounding on the front door and I try to ignore it but whoever it is won't go away, and I go down the hallway, Frankie right beside me.

It's Tiny; he's looking through the glass in the top half of the door and pointing at the knob. I open it

136

and say, "Before you come in here, you have to promise not to shout. I'm not in the mood for shouting."

He looks at me. "You drink everything you had left last night?"

"What?" I forget for a second that I had told Tiny earlier I only had a little left.

"No, there's a little left in the jar. I think."

He laughs and slaps me on the back and my head blows up to about twice its size.

"Man, you better watch getting into that stuff by yourself. Next time call me, we'll keep an eye on each other."

"What do you need, man?" I'm way past trying to be polite, I just want to go lie down.

"I was just wondering what your truck was doing on the side of the road on the other side of town. You leave it there and walk? That's a long ways to go on foot."

I'm staring at him, trying to follow what he's saying.

"I mean, if the thing up and died on you I can understand the temptation to come back here and tie one on, but it's just sitting there and sooner or later somebody's going to steal it. You want me to help you get it back up here?"

I start laughing, even though it hurts, and I'm barely able to stand up. Tiny gets this look on his face and says, "You okay, man?"

I nod, trying to get my breath.

Finally I say, "You can help me get it back here? Hell, yes, I want some help. When can you do it?"

"Anytime. I'm not doing anything this morning, and I've got the big truck," he points to the driveway.

"Let me get some shoes on, and I'll tell you about it on the way."

By the time I finish telling Tiny what happened, we're coming up on the truck. It's just sitting there, but there's a couple of guys looking in the side windows. Tiny pulls in and backs up so he's right in front of the front bumper and gets out. "Morning. You two want to help me get my friend's truck hitched up here so I can get him home?"

They're both shaking their heads, walking away from us; there's an old Honda parked just past the trucks and they get in and head down the road toward Knoxville.

Tiny takes a chain out of the bed of his truck and says, "You get under your piece of shit truck and hook this to the frame."

I'm grinning like a fool, under the truck, until I remember the box of money I had stashed behind the seat. I almost crack my head open getting out from under the truck. I go around to the passenger side and open the door, tilt the seat back forward, and reach under the pile of rags and papers I had thrown on top of the box.

The box is still there.

I put the seat back where it was and look around the inside of the cab. The key is down in the corner of the floorboard, like somebody threw it there, and I slide in and try the engine. It turns a couple of times, but there's a funny noise coming from under the hood and Tiny says, "Stop! Don't do that until we can get it back and take a look."

I sit back in the driver's seat and start laughing all over again. I wish I could have seen the look on Jake's face when he ended up on the side of the road.

After Tiny helps me get the truck into the back yard, he comes inside and we sit in the back room.

"S&S?" I say, heading to the kitchen.

"Sure thing," he says, leaning back in Gamaliel's chair and thumping Frankie on her side.

"So where's this note you were telling me about?" Tiny asks when I hand him his drink.

I point to the table beside him. "Right there."

He picks it up and gives it a quick look, then puts it back. "Damn, I'm sorry, man. Your Mom didn't even know you were watching? She doesn't know your Daddy took off?"

I shake my head. I'm standing at the window looking into the back yard.

"Think you could help me get that piece of shit running again?"

"Sure, but what are you going to do without the title? That Jake fellow has it, and that means he can come back and get it any time he wants to."

"Didn't I tell you?" I turn around to look at Tiny. "I was looking around while you were pulling me back here and I had nothing to do but steer."

I reach into my back pocket and pull out the title.

"It was in the glove compartment."

Tiny looks at me for a second and starts laughing. "Well, I'll be damned."

"How about that shit?" I say. "So, you know anything about trucks?"

"A little."

It isn't as good as making shine with Gamaliel, but working on that old piece of shit truck with Tiny is okay. We spend a few days going over the truck, mostly under the hood, but Tiny wants to look at the brakes and lights and wipers and all kinds of stuff. The engine takes the most work.

Turns out the damn thing's about to die for good, so maybe this thing with Jake wasn't such a bad thing after all. We drain the oil and it looks like sludge, black as tar and thick as molasses, and Tiny whistles when he sees it.

"When's the last time you changed the oil in this thing?"

I try to remember when Daddy did it last and can't. He used to get really mad at the truck but when I think about it, he never took much care of it. I try to think about how much I've driven it since last summer and finally say, "I don't remember Daddy ever changing the oil. I've been driving it for about a year and I doubt if I've put a hundred miles on it."

Tiny is looking at me like I'm some kind of criminal. "Just because your Daddy didn't take care of his machinery doesn't mean you can let it go, man. You can't just hop in and turn the key and never do anything to make sure everything's clean and lubed and . . . well, you can't treat a machine like that. It's not right."

I don't know what to say to him. He's right, I know that, but part of me is thinking he's got no right to talk to me like that. Nobody does.

I start to say something and Tiny sees the look on my face and says, "Don't do it, man. Don't say something you can't take back."

He takes a step toward me and I tense up, wondering how bad I'm about to get my ass kicked, and Frankie comes up and saves me. She's been outside with us the whole time, in the yard mostly, and she trots over and bumps my hand with her head. I look down and my knuckles are white I'm clenching so hard.

"Listen to your dog, man," Tiny says. "She knows."

I open my mouth and nothing comes out, and I close it and swallow and try again.

"So, how do I know when to do all this stuff you're talking about? I never saw a list anywhere."

Tiny drops the tailgate and sits down. "You got to either go by miles or time. Sounds like you don't put hardly any miles on this thing, so you ought to, like, change the oil every year whether you think you need to or not. It won't hurt anything. The rest of it, well, you just keep an eye on it. The oil's the big thing."

We work on the truck until we get to a good stopping place, and Tiny says, "Fresh oil, knocked some of the dust out of the air cleaner, cleaned the spark plugs, radiator's topped off. Why don't we try turning it over, see what happens?"

The idea scares me a little; we've not tried to start the thing since we got it back to Gamaliel's house. The last time we tried, or rather I tried, out on the side of the road, it made a godawful noise and didn't offer to start.

"You sure?"

Tiny laughs. "No, not even a little bit. Get in there and turn the key. Pump the gas a couple of times. I'll be under the hood. If you see my hand waving stop right then, okay?"

"Okay."

He pops the hood and leans over the fender, his head out of sight and his right hand resting on the fender next to the windshield. The driver side door is already open and I slide underneath the wheel and grab the key. I almost forget to take it out of gear, but I put it in neutral and say, "Ready?"

Tiny bangs on the fender with his right hand, and I pump the gas twice and turn the key. Nothing happens. I try again and nothing, then a real slow turn, then a couple of faster ones, and now it's spinning and there's no noise like before but it's not starting.

Tiny waves his hand and I let go of the key.

"How much gas did Jake leave you?" he asks, and I look at the gauge. Almost empty.

"Not much, but it looks like there's still some in there."

"Okay, then, time for a break."

"C'mon, man, the noise is gone, right? That's good, right?"

"Yeah, it is, but there's no reason to just keep on until we run the battery down. Let it be for a while, we'll come back to it later."

Chapter Sixteen

Later turns out to be the next day. "Listen, I've got some stuff to take care of," Tiny says. "Why don't I come by sometime tomorrow and we'll make another run at it?"

I wave my hand at the truck. "I'll be here."

He laughs that short coughing laugh of his and says, "I guess so. See you later."

"Thanks, man." I watch him head out the door.

Friday I get up midmorning because Frankie is wanting out. While we're outside I decide to do a little more in the shed. It's almost cleaned out now and I'm thinking I might spend a little time in there working after another hour or two of cleaning.

The back wall is about all that's left and I hit the light and start on the left, where the glass jar we filtered the shine with is sitting, on the floor next to a box with a pile of magazines on it. Last year I looked for the instructions Gamaliel told Carrie about and didn't find them, so that's the first thing I want to do.

"He told her next to the charcoal," I say, talking partly to Frankie and partly to myself. "The charcoal was right here, next to this box. But the box is empty, except for a bunch of old broken tools."

I move the magazines to the floor and lift the top off the box; it's a snug fit and I shake the box until it loosens from the lid and I can get it the rest of the way off. I toss it over to the side and look inside, expecting to see the pile of broken tools.

Lying on top of the rusty hacksaws and hammer heads and dirty rags is an envelope that I swear wasn't there before. I pick it up and turn it over and over in my hands; there's some clear tape sticking out from each side. I turn and look at the lid, upside down on the floor, and there's an envelope-sized outline right in the middle. I can see a couple of scraps of tape still sticking to the lid.

Gamaliel was really being careful with this envelope, I realize, taping it to the inside of the lid of this old box out in the shed. I forget all about the cleanup and head back to the house with Frankie right behind me.

She trots over to her food dish as soon as we get inside and I remember I haven't fed her yet this morning, so I take care of that first, even though I'm so curious about that envelope I can hardly stand it. I think I know what's in it, but with Gamaliel you never know. That makes me think I need to get that box of money out of the truck just in case Jake comes back. There's a place in the shed, high up on the shelves in the corner closest to the door, that stays kind of dark even when the light's on.

I leave Frankie to her food, go out to the truck, get the box and check to make sure the money's still there, and slide it onto the high shelf as far back into the corner as I can. Then I take a couple of old paint cans and some rags and cover it up. It looks like nobody's been up in that corner for years. Good enough.

Back in the house, I sit down in Gamaliel's chair and open the envelope. There's a couple of pieces of paper inside, and I set the envelope on the table and unfold them.

The top sheet is a list of stores, addresses and phone numbers. Most of them are out of state, and I have no idea why he would have written them down. I put the sheet with the numbers on the table and look at the other piece of paper.

The instructions are for making moonshine. I start smiling and in a few seconds I'm laughing out loud. All I need to do is find a place to set up and I'm good. I start reading the recipe.

Right away I realize I'm going to have to experiment with this, it's all, like, "a good handful" of this or that, and "until it looks right", and "until the smell changes". But the ingredients are there, and a kind of a rough guess about how long each step takes, and I still remember most of the fire-building and keeping it hidden stuff from when Gamaliel and I finished that batch last year.

Frankie starts growling and I jump up and fold the paper and stick it in my back pocket. When I turn around Jerry is standing in the doorway.

"What's that paper about, Boone's Farm Boy?" he asks, not getting any closer.

"Letter from my mother," I say. "You don't need to be sneaking around like that, Jerry, somebody might think you were a burglar and shoot your sorry ass."

Jerry pushes himself off the doorframe and stands there, looking around. "Mrs. Phillips wanted me to come by, make sure the house was still in one piece."

"That's bullshit, Jerry, and you know it. Carrie would have called me to let me know you're coming."

"I told you her name is Mrs. Phillips," he says, getting a little red in the face.

"And I told you my name is Boone," I say.

He starts to take a step toward me and I grab the other piece of paper and the envelope from the table and jam them into my pocket.

"You sure that's from your mother? I didn't figure she knew how to write," he says, grinning like a damn fool.

"Don't you remember the last time you stood right about there and ran your mouth?"

He puts his hand in his pocket and starts to open his stupid mouth again when we hear a car pull in and stop. A car door opens and then closes, and I say,

147

"I'm going to see who that is. I'll just leave Frankie here to keep an eye on you. Unless you want to go out there and check on it yourself."

Jerry's looking at Frankie and I can tell he's scared. He's trying not to show it, but there's a muscle in his neck that's twitching, and he keeps looking at Frankie, then past me at the back door, then Frankie again.

I'm about ready to say, "Well, what's it going to be, chickenshit?" when the door behind me opens and I hear Nancy's voice.

"Boone, Mom said you called but you never called back. Is everything — " she stops when she sees Jerry, and then says, "Sorry, I thought you were by yourself."

Nobody says anything for a few seconds. We're all just looking at each other, until finally I say, "Nancy, why don't you take Frankie outside for a minute?"

"That's what I thought," Jerry says, "You get that damn mutt out of here. It's a good thing I came by today. My wife will just love to hear about this, about you bringing all your little sluts in here to her daddy's house."

I can't remember ever being this mad before. I can barely focus my eyes, and Jerry's grin's getting bigger and bigger until that's about all I see. I feel Nancy's hand on my shoulder, but I don't turn away from Jerry.

"I said, get her out of here, Nancy. Right now," I say, my eyes hard on him. "You don't want to see what I'm about to do."

"Boone, please— "

"I said get Frankie out of here."

"You don't need to hurt him, Boone, I'll, we'll, tell Carrie all about what he's saying. You don't want his blood on your hands."

Jerry takes his hand out of his pocket and there's a click when the knife blade snaps open. He's still grinning, but it's a mean grin now and he's looking back and forth between me and Frankie. He's handling that knife like he knows what he's doing, and I want to jump him and break his head open on the hallway floor and I'm scared for Nancy and scared for Frankie and I can feel the anger growing and growing. I lean over and grab Frankie's collar and pull her toward me, past me, and I can feel Nancy's hand sliding past mine, gripping the collar, and she's pulling now and Frankie doesn't want to go, but Nancy's saying, "C'mon, girl, let's go outside," real soft, and Frankie starts moving.

The back door bangs, and bangs again, and a second later I feel her hand on my arm and she's pushing a cloth into my hand. I wrap it around my forearm.

"I'm calling 911," she whispers in my ear.

"No! They won't get here in time! Call Tiny," and I tell her the number. "He lives up the hill."

The door bangs again and it's just me and Jerry.

"That little slut looks awfully good without her shirt on," Jerry says, and laughs.

I look down at my arm and back up at Jerry.

"You ready, asshole?" I say. I'm holding his stare, trying to decide if he's got the balls for this.

Jerry tosses the knife in his hand, testing the weight. He plants his feet and goes into a crouch. He's definitely done this kind of thing before.

"I've been looking forward to this, Boone's Farm Boy."

I am scared out of my mind, but I can't back down. Not now.

He takes a step toward me and I tense, trying to figure out if I should watch his knife or his eyes.

I almost turn around when Nancy starts screaming at me. "He's coming! Boone! He's on his way! Get out of there!"

Jerry looks like he's getting ready to jump, and my eyes are darting around, looking for something, anything I can use. I've never been in a knife fight.

Jerry jabs the knife at me a couple of times; he's too far away to make contact, but every time he jabs, he inches toward me. Another step and he'll be on me and my back is almost against the door.

Now he's lunging at me, arm full out, and I jump sideways and he barely misses me. He stumbles a little and then he's back on the balls of his feet, and now I've got Gamaliel's chair between us. I take a deep breath.

"You're as bad at fighting as you are at everything else, Jerry," I say, and I know it's stupid, taunting him like that, but I can't help it. I hate this son of a bitch.

We're both breathing hard, and I'm still looking for something I can use, when we hear a voice from the hallway.

"I didn't know exactly where your gun was, Boone, so I brought my own. Hope you don't mind."

Jerry turns toward the front door and looks at Tiny. He's holding a shotgun pointed more or less at the floor.

"Why don't you put that little knife back in your pocket and get on out of here," Tiny says, and glances over at me. "You okay, Boone?"

I nod.

"That little slut must've called — " Jerry stops when Tiny raises the muzzle of the gun. It's not pointed directly at Jerry, but close enough to make his point.

"You know, Boone, I've never met your girlfriend. Soon as we get rid of this trash here I'd like to say hello."

He waves the muzzle at Jerry. "I parked in the road, so you've got room to get your car out."

Jerry starts to say something and Tiny says, "Don't say anything, and don't do anything stupid.

You close up that knife now." Jerry hesitates, and he waggles the gun again. "Right now."

Jerry closes the knife and slides it into his pocket.

"Smart move," Tiny says. "Get on out of here."

When we hear Jerry's car start I say, "I gotta see about Nancy and Frankie."

Tiny lays the gun on the kitchen counter. "You go right ahead. Want me to make a couple of S&S's for you and your friend?"

"Absolutely," I say, unwrapping the shirt from my arm. "Strong for me, just a drop or two for Nancy."

"They'll be ready when you get back," Tiny says. "Take your time." He points to my arm. "Get her to take a look at that while you're at it."

Chapter Seventeen

I guess Jerry didn't miss after all. I thought I had jumped quick enough, but there's blood running down my arm and, up close to my shoulder, a two or three inch gash.

First thing I think of is Nancy's shirt. I had the shirt wrapped around that same arm, but down on my forearm; things were happening awfully fast, though, and I'm not sure I didn't get blood on it. I look at the shirt and don't see any stains.

"Nancy?"

The back yard is empty.

"Frankie?"

Nothing.

"C'mon, Frankie, where are you, girl?"

The driver's side door of the truck opens and Nancy has her arms around me before I know what's happening. I look over her shoulder and Frankie is jumping down from the driver's seat.

"Oh, God, Boone, I was so scared! What is wrong with that awful man? I — "

She stops and pushes away from me. "Look at your arm!"

She's staring at my arm and I'm staring at her; she's got a green bra on and I can tell she's been out in the sun a lot this summer. I can't take my eyes off her. She raises her eyes to mine.

"Give me my shirt, Boone, before your eyes pop right out of your head," she says. "Go on back inside and I'll be in in a second. You need tending to."

I'm still staring, and she turns her back and starts fumbling with the shirt. "I said go on back inside. Is Tiny still here?"

"Yeah, he's waiting on us inside."

I've sort of got myself under control now, and I'm staring at her heels while I'm talking.

Her feet turn and now I'm staring at her toes. I don't look up; I'm afraid to.

"It's okay, Boone, I'm decent."

She's got her shirt back on and now I see the blood, just a little spot. I point it out to her.

"I need to get some cold water on that right away," she says. "I hope you've got an extra shirt I can wear for a bit."

I nod.

"Your arm first, though," she says. "Is it deep?"

She steps over to me and leans close to my arm. It hurts when she touches it, even though she's trying to be gentle.

"We'd better go inside," she says. "Frankie! Come here, girl."

Frankie trots up and stands between us, looking from one to the other. The three of us walk back to the house.

When we get close to the door Tiny opens it for us.

"Hi," Nancy says. "You must be Tiny. I talked to you on the phone."

Tiny puts out his hand. "Pleasure to meet you."

She takes it. "Thanks for taking care of Boone. I was afraid he was going to go after that stupid man, knife and all."

"Yeah, he's kind of crazy like that," Tiny says and grins at me.

I shrug my shoulders and wince a little.

"You need that cleaned up and bandaged," Nancy says. "Tiny, you know anything about this kind of thing? Have you looked at it?"

He shakes his head. "I just sent him out to you. I'll be glad to take a look if you want me to."

Nancy wets a dishcloth and wipes my arm; when the blood is mostly cleaned off they both look at the wound.

"You think it needs stitches?"

"I don't know. Doesn't look deep, but it's a good two inches long."

"No stitches," I say. "Just tape it up. I'll have matching scars, one on each arm."

I turn to Nancy. "There's a shirt on the bed in the room on the left, down the hall. You can change and get the blood out of your shirt."

"Is it clean?"

I look away from her, embarrassed. "Well, I've only worn it a few times."

Nancy rolls her eyes. "Great. I'll go do that after we get you taken care of. Where's the bandaids, gauze, or whatever Gamaliel keeps around here?"

I point to the kitchen with my good arm. "Top shelf, next to the sink."

While she's taping me up she says, "What did you mean, matching scars?"

"The scar from when Gamaliel shot me is on the other arm, about the same place."

They both look at me and Tiny says, "Exactly when did this happen?"

By the time I finish telling them about him shooting me and us trying to patch each other up, we're all laughing at the thought of the two of us trying to do first aid on each other.

"Okay, you should be good for now," Nancy says. "I'm going to change and do something about this little bit of blood on my shirt."

She gets her shirt soaking in cold water and comes back into the sunroom where Tiny and I are. My shirt is kind of tight on her; she looks really good.

"I think the ice is probably melted in your drinks," Tiny says. "Before he went out to find you I offered to make a couple of S&S's for you two. Boone said just a couple of drops of shine in yours, Nancy. Let me put some more ice in them and we can sit down."

"I think if there's room in the glass you might need to put another four or five drops in mine," she says with a little smile. "No more than that, though."

He nods and steps into the kitchen. Half a minute later he's back, his big hands wrapped around three glasses. He puts them on the table and hands ours to us. "Yours has the extra ice cube in it," he says to Nancy. "Mine and Boone's are a little stronger."

He raises his glass. "To matching scars," he says, looking right at me.

"To matching scars," Nancy and I reply.

We sit and sip for a few minutes, and finally Nancy says, "So, I'm guessing Tiny is because of how, you know, enormous you are?"

Tiny nods. "Eighth grade, I think it was, I just took off. Got so much bigger than the other kids that somebody called me Tiny and it just stuck."

After a little while Tiny drains his glass and says, "I need to get back up the hill. Mom's got some work out in the small barn and I'm supposed to move some lumber around for her."

"Let me grab some work gloves and I'll come help," I say. I know there's a pair out in the shed.

Tiny shakes his head and points to my arm. "Maybe next time, Boone. It looks like you've stopped bleeding and there's no sense in taking a chance. You just got that a while ago. Besides," he winks at Nancy, "I'm pretty sure Nancy here didn't come over just to patch you up."

I'm feeling bad about not helping Tiny; he might have saved my life, and definitely saved me from getting cut up. But I want some time with Nancy without anybody else around, so I don't try too hard to talk him out of leaving.

"No maybe about it, Tiny, next time for sure," I say, putting down my glass. "I owe you, man."

Tiny looks really uncomfortable all of a sudden and says, "Yeah, well, I gotta go. Anyway, I didn't do all that much. I saw you take him the last time, remember? I just hurried it along a little."

"Well, next time you get bored, drop on by. No telling what will be going on here," I say.

Tiny laughs and heads out the front door, waving to me and Nancy on the way.

"Guys are funny," Nancy says after the door closes.

I turn to her. "Funny like ha-ha? Funny like weird?" I don't like being called either one, not even by her.

She notices the look on my face. "I didn't mean anything by it, Boone, honest." Nancy looked a little scared for a second. I wonder what that's about, and then forget about it. She goes on, "Not funny, I guess. Different. You might have died, Jerry might have died, and the two of you are trying to pretend nothing happened. Girls aren't like that."

"I guess so," I say. "Me and Tiny, we just didn't want to go on about it, you know?"

She doesn't answer, and I don't say anything else, so we sit there for what seems like a long time. I look over at her and she's staring out the window, one hand on Frankie's head.

"Listen," I say, "thanks for your shirt, I mean, he might've cut it up pretty bad, and you, you know, just gave it up." I don't look at her while I'm talking. "I mean, I'm glad I didn't hurt it except for that spot of blood."

She starts laughing out loud and I look up. She's on her feet, heading toward the kitchen, and says over her shoulder, "Besides, you got to see me with my shirt off, right? I better get that shirt outside so it can finish drying."

She's back in a second with the shirt in her hands and takes it outside. There's a spot on the hood of the truck where the sun's been shining, and she puts her hand on it, nods, and spreads the shirt out in the sunlight.

"Shouldn't take long to dry," she says when she gets back inside. "So, what are you going to do about Jerry?"

I really don't want to talk about Jerry right now. I want to talk about me and Nancy. She didn't hesitate to give me her shirt even though that asshole could

159

see her. The thought of Jerry looking at Nancy half naked makes me furious. My heart is beating fast, and I can feel the tension in my arms; it makes the area right around the cut hurt a lot, and I guess it shows on my face.

"What is it, Boone? What's wrong?"

"I'm just thinking about Jerry, you know, seeing you, you know, like that, and — "

When I look up at Nancy her face is bright red, and I realize that I just made a stupid mistake bringing that up.

"Look, I did what I had to do, okay? Now can we please talk about something else? Please?"

I nod. "Right. So, I talked to your mom the other day."

This doesn't help, and I don't know why, but she's still worked up.

"Tell me about Gamaliel," she says. "Have you been to see him lately? How is he?"

Now I'm uncomfortable, but I figure I need to go ahead and follow her on this one. So I tell her about Gamaliel and Frankie, and how I told Carrie I needed some time.

"He was pitiful, Nancy, pitiful. I hate seeing him like that, and I don't know what to do," I say.

"I do," she says. "You need to go back and try again."

She's right, and I know she is, but it's damn hard seeing the old man like he is now.

"Well, Carrie said she would call on Saturday, and I guess I'll give it another try."

"Good for you, Boone. I bet you'll be glad when you do."

I'm not so sure about that.

Also, I'm thinking I need to start carrying a knife or a gun or something. Next time Tiny might not be around, might just be me and Jerry, and I don't want to get caught without something on me.

It'll be a knife, I guess. I can't carry around Daddy's gun, and I can't afford any kind of pistol.

Unless I get some money from that box.

No, I tell myself, I can't do that. Not now. Not yet. Gamaliel said after he's gone and he's not gone. I wonder if he has a knife around here anywhere.

"What in the world are you thinking about, Boone? You're a million miles away."

"Just thinking about Gamaliel," I say, and that's sort of true. He was the last person I was thinking about.

"What are you going to do? Carrie's going to call tomorrow, right?"

I stand up. "I'm going to call her right now, while I'm thinking about it. I guess you're right, I need to go back. I owe it to the old guy."

Chapter Eighteen

When I give Carrie a call the first thing she says is, "Oh, that's great, Boone, really, Pop will be so glad to see you and Frankie!"

Before I can say anything to that, the next thing she says is , "Have you seen Jerry? He's been gone all day, hasn't been answering his phone either."

I tell her about what happened and there's a long silence. Then she says, "No, no, no! I don't believe you! I know Jerry's got his problems, but he'd never do what you're saying."

"Well, I'll show you where he got me with his knife when you come by to get me and Frankie tomorrow."

She says, "That can't be — I have to go, that's his car in the driveway."

"What did she say?" Nancy is watching my face. I tell her and she says, "Oh, no, Boone, no telling what he'll do if she tells him about you calling her."

"I can't help that," I say. That asshole is making trouble for me and he's not even here. Now I'm pissed off and Carrie's worried, maybe in trouble, and

Nancy, well, it looks like our time alone isn't working out so well.

She sees me looking at her, how my shirt fits her real tight, and first she's looking kind of irritated, but then her face changes and she steps over to me and says, "I guess you're right, Boone, you can't help that. And, well, I didn't mean to get snippy with you earlier, you know, when you said that about Jerry. I guess I'd rather it just be you that sees me that way."

She stretches her hands way up above her head and says, "You think my shirt's dry yet?"

I start to say that I'll go out and check for her and she steps a little closer and I'm wondering why she's got her hands up so high and then I realize why and I take a step closer and we're almost touching and I reach down and grab the bottom of the shirt and pull it up.

It takes a little work to get it past her head but then it's off and I drop it on the floor. She lowers her arms and wraps me up and pulls me toward her and I put my arms around her and I can't believe how a day can go from so awful to so great in such a short time. Her arm brushes the tape over my wound and I flinch and she whispers, "Sorry," and then we're kissing and nothing else is happening anywhere else in the world.

She pulls her head back far enough to say, "You know, you're the bravest man I know, Boone Hammond," and I'm about to faint it feels so good. My hands are moving up and down her back, kind of stumbling over her bra strap, and I start to try to figure out how to unsnap it or unlock it or untie it or whatever the hell you do with it, and she lets go of me. I'm thinking she's going to push me away but she reaches around behind her back and then it's hanging loose and the skin on her back is smooth all the way up and down.

I step back and pull off my shirt and her bra falls to the floor and now we're skin to skin and this is like no feeling I've ever had before, it's like my skin is so sensitive it almost hurts when she touches it.

Nancy has to push me away and tell me the phone is ringing and I don't care, there's nobody I want to talk to right now, and I start to pull her to me. She backs up one more step and she's standing there, the most beautiful thing I've ever seen in my life, and the damn phone is still ringing and it finally stops. We're both breathing hard, like we've been running uphill, and she finally takes a deep, deep breath and says, "God, Boone, I mean, I can't, I mean we can't and it's driving me crazy, I got to get my clothes back on."

She bends down and picks up her bra and slips it on, comes over to me, and says, "This is how it hooks." She turns her back to me.

I'm staring at her fingers and she hooks it, turns around and says, "Next time you can undo it yourself, right?"

"There's going to be a next time?"

"Oh, Boone, you know there will be," she says, smiling up at me. "We both know that."

She picks up my shirt, the one she was wearing, and tosses it to me. "I'm going outside to get my shirt off the hood. Surely it's dry by now."

"Do you have to?"

She giggles. "I think I'd better."

"That damn phone," I say, and she shakes her head.

"I wish I could thank whoever was trying to call you," she says. "You're hard to resist."

I really don't know what to say to that. First of all, I don't think I believe it. Nobody's ever said anything that nice to me, maybe in my whole life. Second, until Nancy came along, no girl has ever paid me much attention at all. Third, pretty much every guy I know is bigger, or stronger, or hairier, or smarter, or richer than I am. So I don't know what to do with that, with what she said. So I say the only thing I can think of.

"I think you're the most beautiful thing I've ever seen, ever."

She's already halfway out the door and I don't think she heard me.

When she comes back in she's got her shirt on and the blood's gone. "It's been quite a day, Boone, you know that? I came here just to see you and tell you that Mom wants you to come over for Sunday dinner day after tomorrow, and then all this other stuff happened."

165

I think about going to somebody's house to eat, and what clothes I have that I can wear, and I'm ashamed, and mad, and I start to tell her no, that I've got something to do, even though I don't, and she holds up her hand.

"I told her I'd rather you come sometime when we're not just back from church. I hate to have to sit around all careful not to get anything on my dress, and everybody acting so churchy and all. I really want everybody to meet you, and I want to be comfortable, you know? I'll be nervous enough as it is."

So I don't have to say anything and I'm off the hook. I need to keep some clean clothes around, I guess. We never worried about that before, when Momma and Daddy and Hannah and I were living in the other house.

Trouble is, even when my clothes are clean they're old and ragged and I know they make me look like poor white trash, which I guess is what I am.

I spend the evening gathering up my clothes and laying them out. Most of them stink, or have holes in them, and I know there's some I should throw away, but I don't have but three or four shirts and a couple of pairs of jeans.

When Carrie gets to the house about ten in the morning, I watch her get out of the car. I'm trying to figure out whether she and Jerry got into it or not.

She looks okay and comes up to the front door and knocks once, then comes right in.

"Boone? Are you inside here somewhere?"

I stick my head out of Gamaliel's bedroom. "In here, Carrie. Can you come here a minute?"

I show her the pile of clothes on the bed and say, "Can we go by the laundry mat today, either on the way over or back? My clothes, well, they need washing."

She says on the way back would be better, and that there's a used clothing store, something called Amvets, close to the laundry mat, but she calls it laundromat, in case I need some more clothes. "Winter'll be here soon, you know," she says, "and you'll need something heavier than what you've got here."

"This Amvets place, it's not charity, is it?" I don't like the notion of taking charity. Daddy taught me that it's just a way for rich people to look down on poor folks.

She says no, it's just clothes that somebody outgrew, or somebody wanted the newest style, or something like that.

"Okay, then, let's go see the old man," I say.

It seems like a shorter drive this time, and we pull into the parking lot and watch the people coming out of one of the side doors.

167

"That's where the cafeteria is," Carrie points to the part of the building we're watching. "I guess lunch is just now over. Good timing, right?"

I nod, and start to get out, and Carrie puts her hand on my arm.

"You know we're going to have to talk about Jerry, you and me," she says quietly. She's got her hand on my arm still, and it's the one he cut, and she can see the edge of the bandage sticking out from the sleeve.

"I know," I say to her. "Can we do that later? If I don't go on in, now that we're here, I might chicken out."

"Okay, but, Boone, we can't pretend it didn't happen."

"I know."

She takes her hand off my arm and gets out. I get out and let Frankie out the back door and snap on the leash. She starts toward the same place we went the last time, pulling on me a little.

I turn to Carrie. "I think Frankie's anxious to see Gamaliel."

She's got a funny kind of smile on her face, like she's about to cry or something. I let Frankie lead me around the side of the building and, just like last time, she goes right up to Gamaliel and sits next to one of the wheels of his chair.

Nothing happens for a full minute, and then Frankie whines just a little; I can barely hear her and I'm only a few feet away.

Carrie pokes me in the arm, the one Jerry cut, and I don't even care, because Gamaliel is looking down at Frankie and then he puts his hand on her head just like he used to.

Chapter Nineteen

And that's it. That's all that happens; they stay like that for a few minutes, and then Gamaliel's hand slips off Frankie's head and his face changes. I don't think I even saw when it changed, but I can tell when it goes back to kind of slack and lifeless.

Frankie comes back over to me and stands for a second, looking around, and then heads toward an old man leaning back in a chair staring at the sky.

He looks down when he hears Frankie coming and reaches out a hand. "Hello, there," he says. His voice is raspy and I can barely hear him, but Frankie's tail is wagging and she noses up under his hand just like she did with Gamaliel that first time.

He looks around and sees me holding the end of the leash and motions me over with his other hand.

"What's her name?"

"Frankie."

So he starts talking to Frankie and she sits there and listens to every word and finally he pats her head and says, "I got to go inside, girl, it's time for my medication. You come back anytime, you hear me?"

He looks up at me. "Any time at all."

Frankie is visiting with her fourth person, an old woman this time, when I look up and see the woman I talked to before, the director, the one who wanted to organize the whole thing. She's got a big smile on her face, watching Frankie with the old folks.

I don't much like the way she's looking at me. Last time it felt like she was going to try to turn this thing with Frankie into some kind of job or something. I'm not interested in anything like that, having to be here at a certain time on a certain day of the week. Sounds like school, except no tests or anything like that, and I like being out from under all that stuff. She opens the door and heads toward me.

The old woman, the one Frankie is with right now, is talking to her and calling her Dusty and I start to say, "Her name is Frankie," and then I think why bother. She probably wouldn't remember that five minutes from now anyway.

"You go on now, Dusty, I've got work to do inside," the old woman says, and pushes Frankie away. She stands up and sways back and forth a little and I put my hand on her arm to steady her.

"Leave me be, Johnny, I can manage on my own," she says, and she sounds angry. She heads off into the building, not looking back at me or Frankie.

"That's Mrs. Sanderson," the director says.

171

I probably won't remember that five minutes from now.

Mrs. Sanderson disappears into the building and the director turns to me.

"I don't know whether you remember me or not, Boone," she says, "I'm Betty Franklin. I'm the director here."

Carrie comes up to join us.

Betty is saying, "Now if you'll come inside we can work on some kind of schedule, so the residents can count on you and Francie," and I'm about to tell her to shove it, this whole idea, when Carrie interrupts her.

"Betty, her name is Frankie, right, Boone?" I nod and she goes on. "I think this is just a wonderful thing, don't you, Betty? I'd like to see him here every day, but I don't think we can do that." She looks over at me.

"I noticed the truck was still in the back yard, Boone. Have you got it running yet?"

I'm starting to see what she's doing, and shake my head.

"Well, Betty, I think until he gets some reliable transportation he's going to have to depend on me to get here. You understand."

Betty's looking at Carrie now, not at me, so I keep my mouth shut, even though I feel like a little kid, with the grownups deciding what I'm going to do and when I'm going to do it. Carrie is still talking.

172

"Why don't I give you a call, say, a day ahead of time, and let you know about what time we'll be here? How would that be?"

Betty looks at me.

I'm trying to think of what to say, and finally say, "Tiny is helping me with the truck. I'll talk to him about how long it'll be."

Betty swivels back to Carrie, and they go back to talking between themselves. I give Frankie's leash a tug and we walk away as quiet as we can.

There's one old woman still outside; she's standing by that pool fountain thing that needs to be cleaned out and staring off into the distance.

Frankie and I stop kind of close to her and she glances over at me.

"Good afternoon, young man."

"Yes, ma'am." I'm not much in the mood to talk, still mad about Betty and Carrie talking about me like I'm some ten-year-old.

We stare off in the same direction for a bit; the Smokies are there, one range behind another, like they go on forever. Makes you feel kind of peaceful just to rest your eyes against them.

I look back at the old woman and she's looking right at me, examining me. I start to leave and she holds up her hand.

"You know, you favor my first cousin once removed, haven't seen her in years, not since she got married. Natalie was her name." She looks at me for another second or two. "Yes, you do look some like her. You have any kin by that name?"

I don't know what to say. My head is spinning and I feel like I'm about to faint dead away. She's got to be talking about Momma. Just before I start to say something I hear Carrie calling me, and I just about fall over Frankie's leash trying to get out of there and back to the car.

"What's the matter, Boone?" Carrie is already in the driver's seat.

I shake my head. "Nothing. Can we go to that Amvets place before we go to the laundry mat?"

They won't let me bring Frankie inside, which pisses me off a little, having to leave her in the car. It's not too hot, though, and there's a shady spot close to the store. We leave the windows open a crack and go inside.

This place is huge, and I see lots of stuff I want to look at, but I'm worried about Frankie and I guess Carrie can tell. She says, "Why don't I wait in the car with Frankie and let you look around?"

I nod and she goes out the door. There's a whole table full of jeans and I grab two pairs and head for the shirts. They've got all kinds and I get a long sleeved shirt and a sweatshirt and pick up a jacket on the way to the register.

It takes all but a couple of dollars of my money, and I'm worried that I won't have enough to wash my clothes, but Carrie says not to worry about that.

174

"You don't have much here to wash, and if you're a quarter short I can pitch in," she says. "You sure this is enough clothes for you?" and she points at the stuff I bought.

"It'll do for now," I say, thinking that this is the most new clothes I've got at one time, maybe in my life. I look at her and how she's dressed and think, I'll bet you've got a closet full at your house. Maybe two closets full.

She's right, it doesn't take long to wash what little I've got, and we're home with some light still left.

"I'll see you sometime soon," I say. "Thanks for taking me to the store and the laundry mat." I let Frankie out of the back seat and she goes around the yard, nose to the ground, checking on things.

Carrie looks at me from behind the steering wheel. "I can't stay, been gone too long already, but we need to talk about Jerry. Don't forget that."

I hold up my hand. "See you soon," I say.

Carrie shakes her head and puts the car in reverse. "Be careful, Boone. I'll call you in a couple of days. The people at the home really liked having Frankie there. You know, they'll probably like you, too, if you give them a chance." She turns to look over her shoulder and backs out into the road, and she's gone.

We go inside, I feed and water Frankie, and heat up some leftover pizza for myself. I start to mix an S&S and then put the Thunderstorm back in the refrigerator. Gamaliel wouldn't like me mixing it with anything, I know, so I pour a glass about a third full and take Frankie back out into the yard to watch the night come on.

Chapter Twenty

Monday morning I get a phone call from Nancy.

"You still want that driver's license?"

I'm about to say yes when there's a knock on the door. "Hold on a second," I say, and go down the hall.

Tiny is standing there with a box in his hand. It's got a dial and a switch on the top and a couple of cords running out of the side. He says, "I thought we ought to put this on the truck battery, keep it from running down."

I nod and open the door the rest of the way. "Tell Nancy I said hey," he says with a smile and a nod toward the phone.

I put my hand over the phone. "How do you know it's her? Could be anybody."

He laughs out loud and starts toward the back door. "Are you kidding? I saw the way you two were looking at each other. I'm not blind, man."

He goes out into the back yard and I get back on the phone. "Tiny says hey."

"Oh, do I need to let you go? Are you working on the truck or something?"

"No, he just wanted to hook something up to the battery. Why don't you come over in a little while?"

"Okay," she says. "You know school's starting up soon, so if we're going to get you a license we need to take care of it now."

When she gets here we spend about an hour going over the questions, about as long as I can stand to study anything, and Nancy closes the book, stands up and stretches, and says, "You could probably pass this right now, but I think we should go over it a couple more times and do a little driving just to be sure. You busy this week? Going back over to see Gamaliel? Maybe I could go along, say hi to him."

The thought of running into that old woman makes me kind of nervous, and I'm slow to answer, so Nancy says, "Something wrong, Boone?"

When I tell her about what the old woman said she says, "Wow. Do you think she's right? I mean, that your mother is related to her? What does that make you to each other?"

I shrug my shoulders. "I don't understand the whole once removed stuff."

Nancy sits back down and says, "I think it means that your mother's mother or father was her first cousin, so your mother is her first cousin once removed. So maybe you're a first cousin twice removed, or a second cousin. I'm not really sure. Mom

178

knows all about that stuff; she tried to teach me, but I'm not real clear on it." Nancy shakes her head. "So, anyway, are you going over there this week?"

"I don't know. I guess so."

"Can I come with you? I mean, the last time I saw him he was flat on his back in a hospital bed, and at least he's up and around now."

Before she leaves she has me talked into it, and to tell the truth, I don't mind too much. If the thing with Jerry comes up, she can tell Carrie what she saw and maybe that'll help Carrie believe me. I think Carrie knows I'm telling the truth, she just hates that I know stuff about Jerry that used to be her secret. I know Momma never wanted anybody to know how bad it was with Daddy. I figure Carrie's the same way.

Tiny's back the next morning and we try the truck again. It turns slow a couple of times, me in the driver's seat and Tiny under the hood just like last time, but he doesn't tell me to stop so I keep cranking and it pops a couple of times and then catches and runs for a few seconds and dies. Tiny stands up and I slide out and go around to where he's standing.

"I think we've got it," he says, staring at the engine.

"What are you looking at?" I say. I can't tell whether I'm looking at a problem or not.

He glances at me. "I just think better when I'm looking at what I'm thinking about," he says and

179

turns back to the engine. "At least with stuff like this."

He sniffs and then says, "Let's give it a few minutes and try again."

The next time it catches right away, starts running, stumbles around for half a minute, and then smooths out. I'm sitting behind the wheel and Tiny stands up and grins at me, then comes over to the window.

"Let it run for another two or three minutes, and we'll try again in a half hour or so," he says. "I don't hear anything that worries me, though."

The next time it starts right up and settles in smooth, and I back it out of the yard and leave it beside the house.

I offer Tiny a drink and he says, "Better not this early in the day. Last time Mom gave me a look when I got home, she might have smelled it on me. You go ahead."

I shake my head and say, "Maybe later on. Thanks, man. I was afraid I was going to have to just push it down the hill into the woods and leave it."

After he's gone I call Nancy.

"Truck's running."

"That's great, Boone! We need driving practice anyway, and it ought to be in your car, you know, the one you're going to test in."

"I'm not supposed to drive without a license."

She doesn't realize I'm teasing her. "Of course you'll need to be very careful until you pass everything, and you'll need a hardship license, for sure."

"I don't know what that is."

"Well, you're supposed to practice for half a year after you get your permit. You can tell them you're a hardship case, since both your parents are gone, and get them to let you apply early."

I don't like this hardship thing. It sounds like charity to me, and I tell her so.

"Oh, no, Boone, it's nothing you're getting that you didn't earn, you know, if you pass the test, it's the same test as everybody else. They're just recognizing that you're on your own, is all."

So we decide to meet twice more and then go for it, and I say, "I'm going to call Carrie and set something up for Thursday. You want to come along? I can call you and tell you what time."

"I'd like that, Boone. Listen, Mom's calling, got to go. Call me.

Thursday with Carrie and Nancy and Frankie and me in the car it's kind of crowded. I don't say much on the way over. Carrie and Nancy are talking away like they've known each other for a long time, and Frankie's looking from one of them to the other.

Four or five of the people hanging out around the pool wave to Frankie when we come around the corner of the building. I look around and don't see

Gamaliel and start to ask Carrie what's going on when Nancy says, "There he is, I think. Isn't he over there, under that tree?"

Frankie and I head that way and stop about ten feet away. It's Gamaliel all right, but he's not by himself. The guy crouched down beside the chair looks a lot like Jerry from the back, and I turn to ask Carrie what the hell's going on.

I can tell by the look on her face she didn't expect this. She motions me back and practically drags me around to the front of the building. Nancy is right behind us, and she looks pretty shaken up, too. Frankie's pulling at the leash; she wants to go see Gamaliel.

Carrie is standing in the middle of the sidewalk, breathing hard, and she looks scared and angry at the same time.

"I don't know what he's doing here, Boone, he's supposed to be in Kingsport, it's Thursday, he's supposed to be up in the Tri-Cities. What the hell is he doing here with Pop?"

Right then the front door opens and Jerry walks out. When he sees us he has this guilty look on his face for just a second, and then he smiles real big and I want to put my fist right into his stupid face. I start toward him and Nancy grabs me by the arm.

"Don't do it, Boone. Please, just don't, okay?"

He walks over to us and stops in front of Carrie. "Hi, Carrie. Didn't expect to see you here. What are you bringing him around for?" He doesn't even look at me, probably scared to. Frankie is right beside me, the hair on her back is standing up, and she's got that low growl, way down inside. I don't think Jerry can hear it, but I sure can, and so can Nancy. She's got her hand on Frankie's leash, right next to mine, and it's shaking a little.

"He comes down to see Pop, Jerry. Why aren't you up in the Tri-Cities?"

"I took the day off. I needed to take care of something," he says, and pulls a piece of paper out of his back pocket.

"I had a nice long talk with your dad, and told him how this piece of white trash was treating his house, and what a shame it was to see it go down like that. He was pretty worked up. I got him to sign this," and he waves the paper at me, "giving me the right to oversee his property, and make sure it's taken care of the way he wants." He turns to me. "I'll be expecting you to be gone by — "

Carrie snatches the paper out of his hand and rips it into half a dozen pieces. She throws them down at his feet and takes a step toward him. I see his hand draw back and start forward, and I'm in between them and I put both hands on his chest and shove as hard as I can.

He stumbles back a couple of steps and catches himself. When he straightens up he looks at me with as much hate as I've seen in anybody, ever.

Behind me Carrie is screaming at him, "You stay away from my father, you hear me? And stay away from his house, too. I saw what you did to Boone's arm, and you're just lucky he didn't press charges, you know that? With your record, you know — "

"You shut up, shut up right now!" He's looking like he's going to make another move and I step a little sideways so I'm right in front of him. Behind me Nancy says, real loud, "Boone, I'm not sure I can hold her back much longer."

Jerry glances over, and I take a quick look too, and Frankie is at the end of her leash, straining hard, and Nancy is braced, leaning back, leash wrapped around both hands.

Jerry points at Carrie. "You'll pay for that little trick. I'll see you at home, and you better be right behind me as soon as you drop that white trash off, you understand?"

He steps forward and starts to bend down and I put my foot on the pieces of paper.

"What's going on out here?"

Betty Franklin is standing in the doorway. Jerry straightens up and half-runs to his car. He jumps in and takes off, barely missing the post at the entryway to the parking lot.

She comes over to Carrie and takes her by the arm. "Carrie, you look awful! Are you all right? Do I need to call somebody?"

Carrie is shaking her head, looking at me and Nancy; she won't look at Betty. When she finally does she starts to say something and just starts crying instead. Betty wraps an arm around her and leads her into the building, and Nancy and I are left standing there with Frankie.

Neither one of us says anything for a minute or two, and finally I say, "Let's go see Gamaliel, Frankie."

She's ready to go, tugging at the leash, and Nancy hands it to me and we turn and head back toward the side yard.

Nancy slips her hand into mine, the one not holding the leash, and squeezes it hard. She clears her throat a couple of times.

"I'm scared for Carrie, Boone," she starts out, and then doesn't say anything for another four or five steps. "I mean, I don't think she ought to go to her house, do you? Jerry, he's, well, I'm just scared for her."

I don't tell her that I know what it's like to be in that kind of house, but I do. And I'm worried about Carrie, too.

I start to say something to her and don't, because Frankie's got her ears up, looking around. For a second I can't tell what she's listening to. Then, still pretty far off, we hear the sirens coming our way.

Chapter Twenty-One

When Carrie gets the call about Jerry she gathers us up and takes us home, and then turns right around and heads out, driving fast.

I put Frankie in the house and make sure she's got water and food, and then head for the truck. Nancy stops me.

"Let me take you there," she points to her car. "I want to know what happened too, and I can drive without worrying about getting pulled over."

I nod, thinking that I really need that damn license.

All the way over there I'm thinking about Momma and Daddy and how bad it was until she finally took off. Nancy keeps glancing over at me and eventually asks me what I'm thinking about. So I tell her a little about how it was before, when me and Frankie my brother and Hannah and Momma and Daddy were all in that little house, and how it changed when Frankie died, and how it kept just getting worse and worse and worse until everything went all to hell. I don't tell her about Daddy; I'll never tell anybody about that, but I tell her enough about how it was for her to get the idea.

Most of the time I'm looking at my hands, rubbing them back and forth on my knees, and when I finally look up at her she has this funny look on her face that I can't figure out, and her eyes are all teary.

When I ask her about it she won't say anything, just keeps looking at the road, and then says, "We're here."

So we're sitting in the waiting room and the door opens and Carrie comes in.

We both jump up and head over to her. She stops in the middle of the floor and looks at me, then at Nancy, and says, "You two didn't have to come all this way."

I don't say anything because I never know what to say when stuff like this happens, but Nancy says, "We were just worried about you, Carrie. So how is he?"

"Lucky more than anything," she says, and sort of laughs. "He took a curve too fast, probably because he was so mad, and the car is totaled, but he came out of it with just a broken leg and a couple of cracked ribs."

Good, I think, so she's probably safe, at least for a while. He'll have a hard time chasing her down if he's in a chair or on crutches.

And then she says, "You know this means I can't take you down to see Pop, Boone, not while Jerry needs me to take care of him."

At first I can't believe what I'm hearing and then I can, it all sounds so damn familiar; I start to say something, and then I look at Nancy and she's shaking her head no, so I don't say anything.

"It's okay, Carrie, I'll take care of it," Nancy says, giving me a look that I'm pretty sure means I'm supposed to let her handle this. "He's about to get his license, and until then, I can take him and Frankie to see your father."

Carrie just nods and turns around to head back to Jerry's room.

"Listen, Carrie," I say, ignoring Nancy's hand squeezing my arm. "I just want you to know I'll take care of the house. You don't need to worry about that."

She nods again, not turning around, and then she's gone.

I look at Nancy. "I guess we might as well go on back."

"I think so. Let her sort all this out."

On the way home we don't talk much, and don't talk about Jerry at all. Mostly it's just about school starting back up and my license and when we can go back to see Gamaliel.

"I think we should go back down to the home tomorrow," Nancy says.

188

"You got time for that?"

She smiles just a little. "Sure I do, Boone. I want to see you and Frankie with all those other old folks anyway, and meet your cousin. How about right after lunch?"

Frankie loves it, going from one old person to the next, starting with Gamaliel. He still doesn't talk, not a word, but it looks like there's a little more life in his eyes, and the nurse says he really looks forward to seeing Frankie. How he knows that I'll never figure out, but this time I'm pretty sure Gamaliel looks me right in the eyes for a full fifteen seconds, long enough to feel like a stare, before he drops his head and goes back to looking at his lap.

The rest of the people Frankie is making friends with are in better shape than Gamaliel; they can talk and sort of get around, and they're starting to talk to me after they've spent some time with Frankie. I don't see the woman who thinks she's related to me, but I can't ask about her because I don't know her name or anything about her.

Betty Franklin walks us to Nancy's car and tells us two or three times how good this is for everybody. She even gets Frankie's name right, and she tells us to come by anytime, not to worry about a schedule.

"There's always somebody who'd like to see Frankie," she says, looking down at her and smiling. "You have no idea how lonely some of our people are. This really is a Godsend."

I don't say anything to that, because I don't want to get into the whole church thing with her. I'm surprised that it hasn't come up already; it's usually the second thing you ask a person when you meet them for the first time. Right after how long you've been living here, it's what church do you go to, and if you don't go anywhere, people treat you like there's something wrong with you. Either that, or they try to have a little revival right there in the middle of the street or restaurant or wherever.

We say goodbye and I put Frankie in the back and get into the passenger seat. Nancy pulls out into the road and points us toward home.

Chapter Twenty-Two

The next few days go by quick. Nancy is trying to get me a license before school starts and she runs out of time, and that means she's spending a lot of time at my place. The subject of eating at her house comes up again at the end of one of our practice sessions. She's sipping a Thunderstorm with about three drops of shine in it, and I'm having an S&S.

"Mom wants you to come over tomorrow night and eat with us," Nancy says; she's watching a couple of wild turkeys in the field behind Gamaliel's house. They're taking their time, lowering their heads to peck the ground and then taking a few steps. Every once in a while one of them will stretch up to full height and scan the field. Probably heard something; it's amazing what hearing those birds have. Sure makes them hard to hunt.

I don't answer right away. I've got some decent clothes now, at least, so I'm not as worried about that. The thing is, the only thing I know about Nancy's parents is that they're rich. Well, rich compared to me. I don't know what to do around people that go around all the time bragging about how much they've got. They've probably got eight or ten rooms in their house and furniture in all of them that you're not allowed to sit on.

"Tomorrow night?"

"She's really looking forward to meeting you. I told her all about how good you were to Gamaliel and how you're taking care of his house. I haven't said anything about Jerry, so if you don't bring him up nobody else will either."

I still don't know. To tell the truth, I've never been invited anywhere for supper. I mean, I used to eat with Curt once in a while, but that wasn't really a meal. We'd get a sandwich or something and go outside, so that doesn't count at all.

"Look, Nancy, I don't know how to act around, you know . . ."

She's looking at me with a blank expression. "You act fine around me, Boone. Please come, I really want them to meet you. I've never had a boyfriend like you before."

"What does that mean?" I don't like how that sounds, like I'm some kind of freak she wants to show off. She must hear the anger in my voice; she hesitates and looks a little scared, and then puts her hand on my arm.

"I mean brave like you are, Boone. I did tell them about those guys last year on the four wheelers, how you protected your house and Gamaliel's. They don't know about you and Jerry, but they do know about that. I know Dad was really impressed. He wants to meet you."

When I say okay she leans over and gives me a kiss that goes on and on but not nearly long enough. She sits back and says, "Good. I'll come get you about five or five thirty, okay?"

She takes off and I spend the rest of the evening worrying about what I've just agreed to do.

Thursday morning I'm looking at my clothes thinking that they might as well be rags. What looked pretty good to me in the store looks like stuff nobody else wanted, which I think is what it is. I change my mind two or three times and I don't have that many clothes to pick from.

At four thirty I'm thinking that maybe I should just take Frankie and head out into the woods. I pour a little shine into a glass and fill it with Thunderstorm. It's really weak compared to the way I usually mix it, but I remember what Tiny said about his mom smelling it on him.

I finish it off quick and start to pour another one and stop. When I turn around Frankie's looking at me and I'm pretty sure she's saying, don't be an idiot, Boone.

"Okay, Frankie, you're right," I say, and she heads for the door like I just said "You want to go outside?"

I take her out for a quick run and Nancy pulls up while I'm feeding her. She comes inside without knocking and says, "Stand up and let me have a look at you."

I hate this kind of thing, but I stand up and she says, "Turn around slow."

When I come back around she's standing right in front of me and she pulls me in close to her and presses her whole body against mine. We stand there for a second and I'm thinking we should just stay here, and then she lets me go and steps back. "You look good, Boone. Ready to go?"

I nod.

"How much shine did you drink to get ready for this?" She's smiling, but it's kind of a nervous smile.

I think about lying to her and that's how I try to start out, but what I end up saying is, "I just had one, the way I usually mix yours. I was getting ready to have another and Frankie said that would be stupid."

She laughs and says, "Well, I'll need to check that out," and she gives me a quick kiss, and then a long one, and then steps back.

"Well, I don't think Mom's going to give you that kind of kiss, so I think we're okay."

I grin at her. "Damn, I sure hope she doesn't. I mean, I'm sure she's nice and all, but I wouldn't have any idea what to do if she did. Plus your dad might not like it."

She laughs. "You're a mess, Boone, you know that?"

We're getting ready to leave and she says, "Did I tell you my idiot brother is over at a friend's house? He won't be there until after we get done eating."

After I make sure Frankie's inside and all locked up and we get into the car, Nancy looks over at me and says, "Don't you be nervous, Boone, I'm plenty nervous enough for both of us."

I tell her I'm fine, but inside I'm scared to death. Nancy's great, she doesn't look down on me, but most people do, I can tell by the way they act around me. A new shirt and jeans won't make any difference to those people, and I don't know about Nancy's parents. I know if they start anything I'm liable to get mad, and I don't want to do that, and I don't have any way to get home if things start getting bad. So I'm scared.

There's no way I'm going to tell Nancy that, but I bet she knows anyway. When we pull into the driveway of her house she reaches over and squeezes my hand and says, "Well, I guess we're here. It's almost time to eat, we better get on inside."

Pretty soon I'm sitting there at the table with Nancy next to me and her dad across from me and I don't know what to do or say. I've seen that look before, that look her dad just gave her mom, and I've seen the expression on her face before, too. It only lasts a couple of seconds, but long enough for me to know.

I don't look at Nancy or at either one of them. The only safe place to look is my plate; there's a half-eaten chicken leg sitting there, and a little glob of mashed potatoes, and five peas. I know because I've counted them twice now.

Finally I say, "I hope Frankie isn't tearing up the house. I'm not usually gone after dark like this," and Nancy says, "Oh, I'm sure she'll be okay for a while longer," and her mom says, "There's pecan pie coming up in just a few minutes."

Her dad grins at me and says, "You've never eaten pie until you've had Mother's pecan pie. It's the best in the county, isn't that right, Sugar?"

Her mom kind of ducks her head and smiles at her plate; her face gets a little red, and Nancy says, "Want me to bring it in, Mom?"

I say, "You need some help?" and her dad frowns. "Let the women take care of that, Boone. I don't know about you, but I'm about ready for a good-sized piece and maybe a scoop of ice cream. That pie warm, Sugar?"

Nancy's mom nods and says, "Took it out of the oven about ten minutes ago. Boone, would you like some ice cream with your pie? It's vanilla; I think that goes best with pecan pie."

"Yes, ma'am," I say, and she smiles at me. "Such a polite young man," she says to Nancy. "Not like that last boy, what was his name?"

"Mom!" Nancy is red-faced, and it seems like she can't wait to get out of the room and into the kitchen.

Her dad laughs and says, "Don't tease her like that, Sugar, she's got a guest here tonight."

He's right, the pie is delicious, and I say so. Nancy's mom gets all embarrassed again, but I can tell she likes it, that I like her pecan pie.

"Do you want a cup of coffee, Boone?" she asks. She's on her way back to the kitchen and I say, "No thanks, I usually only drink coffee in the morning. I've still got a little Thunderstorm here anyway."

"Don't know how you can drink that stuff," her dad says. "As far as I'm concerned, it's only good for filling up the rest of your glass after you put a little whisky in first. You want some whisky to go with that soda, Boone?"

I almost spit the mouthful of pecan pie out onto the table, but I manage to keep it in my mouth and shake my head no while I'm chewing.

"You sure?" he says, and I try to swallow the food in my mouth and look up to see him grinning at me.

"You look like you almost choked on that pie, son," he says. "I promise I won't even try to sneak any in there. So tell me about these assholes on the four wheelers. Nancy says you're pretty handy with a shotgun."

"I don't know about all that," I say. I'm real glad to be able to talk about something else, anything else.

"I couldn't just let them walk in and take what they wanted, you know?"

He nods. "I know. You got balls, Boone, especially for such a little guy."

I don't say anything because I'm at Nancy's house, but what I want to say is, "Why don't you step over here and I'll show you what a little guy I am."

Instead, I say, "Well, there was only two of them."

He laughs out loud at that one, and when Nancy and her mom come back into the room he's smiling at me and I'm sitting there being really uncomfortable.

"You got a real winner here, kid," he says to Nancy, winking at me like we're buddies or something. "There was only two of them," he says to himself, shaking his head and grinning.

Nancy looks relieved, and comes over to stand beside me. "We better go check on Frankie, Boone."

Everybody stands up then, and we all sort of shuffle around for a second, and I figure out I'm supposed to say something.

"It was real nice to meet you both," I say and stretch my hand out to Nancy's dad.

I shake her mom's hand, too, and say, "Thanks for the supper. It was real good."

"You'll have to take some of that pie home with you," she says, and hurries off into the kitchen.

Nancy and I spend the whole trip back laughing at nothing and smiling at each other. I didn't know how glad I'd be for that to be over until we were on the road headed for home.

I try to get Nancy to stay a while and she says she can't, but then we're all over each other and she finally has to push me off of her and run out the door.

She's in her car when I catch up to her and I lean in for another kiss. She gives me a quick one and says, "If I don't leave now I won't be able to. I'll talk to you tomorrow, Boone. It was great, it went great."

I nod and step back from the car. "You drive careful, honey."

After she's gone I take Frankie out for a few minutes and then, when I get back inside, I mix a really strong S&S and sit in Gamaliel's chair and try to think.

I don't know what to do about it, but I know the look I saw pass between Nancy's parents. I've seen that same look pass between Momma and Daddy, and it scares me to think about Nancy being in that house. Then I think, it's Momma and Daddy, and it's Carrie and Jerry, and now it's Nancy's parents, and I wonder if this is just the way it is. Thinking about that makes me sick to my stomach.

I drain the rest of the S&S and throw the glass as hard as I can into the kitchen, and I don't even want to bother cleaning up the mess, but I don't want Frankie to get any glass in her paws. So I go clean it up, and get another glass, and don't bother with the Thunderstorm this time.

Chapter Twenty-Three

I'm almost as nervous as I was at Nancy's house last week. Nancy is with me, and that helps a lot, but it's still pretty damn scary.

The DMV office is almost empty; Nancy had picked Tuesday morning for me to get my license, because, she told me, she had called and asked the clerk what day had the fewest people coming in. We step up to the clerk.

"We need to speak to someone about a hardship license," Nancy says.

"You don't look like a hardship case," says the clerk. It's only 9:30 in the morning and she's already in a bad mood. Nancy is pretty smart to bring me in the morning, I think; this is going to be hard enough as it is. Later on in the day I bet this woman's a real bitch.

"It's not me," Nancy says, polite as you please. "My friend's parents left him alone, been gone for almost a year, and right now he has to depend on me and his other friends to get around."

"We'll see about that," says the clerk. "First he need to pass the written test. Unless you already took that and you're looking to cut down on the wait time," this last part was for me, I guess.

"No, ma'am, I haven't taken the written test. If you could get me started on that I'd appreciate it."

"Hmmph," is all she says, but she turns away and starts walking toward the back of the room. She turns around and says, "Well? You coming?"

Nancy pokes me with her elbow and says, "Better get on back there before she changes her mind."

I follow her on back to a set of tables with computers on them. She shows me how to get started and then just walks off, no "good luck" or anything. I start to get a little mad about how she's treating me, like I'm some kind of inconvenience instead of the reason she has this job, but when I look up Nancy catches my eye and shakes her head. She points to the screen.

The test is about what I expected; I hate taking tests, and there's nobody to help, let me have a quick look at their paper, give me any kind of sign, and some of it's easy and some of it I swear came from a different book than the one Nancy and I studied.

I'm allowed to miss five questions and still pass, and that's how many I miss.

The clerk hands me a form and tells me to get a family member to fill it out and Nancy reminds her that I don't have any family, that it's just me. For just a second it looks like she feels sorry for me, and I start to tell her I don't need her sympathy, but before I can she pulls out a different form and hands it to me.

"Driving test is through that door. There'll be an examiner waiting. You'll need to get that form filled out first."

I start to tell her that I don't have a family member and she stops me. "You don't want a hardship license. That's for people who are too young. You want to waive the waiting requirement, and a law enforcement officer, like a sheriff, has to sign off on that."

When I don't move, she points to the paper I'm holding in my hand. "You know Deputy Anderson? He has to fill that out before you can take your driving test." She turns back to her computer screen and I might as well have dropped off the face of the earth.

Nancy says, "If he's in town this morning, I bet he'll be over at the hardware store. I've seen his cruiser there enough times. Let's go see."

He's there, and I'm real glad I never got in any kind of trouble with him. He looks at me and kind of half grins. "Hello, Boone. Haven't seen you around for a while. Can I help you with something?"

When I tell him what I want he says, "You want me to help you get legal? Hand me that paper."

He's filling it out and looks up. "Hear anything from your mom or dad?"

I tell him about seeing Momma and her new man and the note that says they're in Memphis now, and that Daddy is still gone. He shakes his head.

"Real sorry to hear about your mom, Boone, bet that hurt. Here's the paper. You're going to get back in school now that you're going to be legal, right?"

I nod. "Thanks, Officer Anderson."

"See you around, Boone."

The driver's test is nothing special. I'd heard about it from friends of mine who are a little older. We're using Nancy's car, and I get in, the examiner gets in, and by that time it's close to lunch. She has me drive down the block, stop at the four-way, make a left turn, and go two more blocks. There's one traffic light on this route, and it's green, so I don't have to worry about that. A couple more turns and we're back at the DMV.

She hands me a signed piece of paper. "Here you are. Tell Shirley I'm going to lunch."

Five minutes later we are on the road headed back to the house. Nancy is driving since it's her car, and I'm looking at my temporary license. I stick it in my pocket and look over at Nancy and grin. "Thanks, honey, for getting me this."

She stiffens and says, "Could you not call me that? That's what Dad used to call me before, before, well, when I was little. I just got him to stop last year."

That makes me think of that look I saw in his eye when he was looking at Nancy's mom and I almost say something, but I don't.

"You got time to come in for a few minutes, Nancy?" I'll just stick with Nancy, I guess. "I've got stuff to make a sandwich, I think."

She's back to smiling now, relaxing in the driver's seat. "I'd like that."

It's no different driving with a license than without one, but it sure feels different. After Nancy heads back home I take the truck down to the grocery store and gas station and spend the rest of the afternoon with Frankie up in the woods above Gamaliel's house. We're into August now, and the woods are just what we need in the middle of the afternoon.

I hear the owl again, faint but clear, and that makes me think about Gamaliel. I'm not sure I even buy the whole superstition thing about death, and I know that it might not even be Gamaliel the owl is telling me about, but he's who I think of, and then I think that I can go down there anytime now.

Carrie needs to know that, I guess. She hasn't called since that whole thing at the nursing home and Jerry getting all busted up in the wreck, and I really don't want to call in case Jerry picks up the phone. I don't want to have anything to do with that piece of shit, even over the phone. She needs to know about my license, though, and I'm running out of money. The next set of bills is only a week away, and I spent most of what I had this morning on gas and groceries.

Frankie swings back around from behind the hill and I call her to me. "Time to go in, girl, I have to make a call." She and I head back to the house and inside, and I get the big fan going and open the windows. This time of year I need the breeze coming through the house.

Carrie picks up the phone, which I'm really glad about, and I make myself ask about Jerry.

"He's fine, Boone, just fine. He'll be back at work before long, I hope." I'm thinking that with a broken leg it'll be a while before he's going anywhere alone, but I don't say anything. I've already said as much about him as I want to, so I tell her about the license and the bills coming up.

"Good for you! So you can go see Pop anytime? I think that he'll really like that. Look in the mail in the next couple of days, I'll send you some money. Oh, that's Jerry calling me. Gotta go." She hangs up before I can say anything.

She's treating me a lot different now; I didn't hear anybody calling her. It's not my fault that the idiot flipped his car, and I was just protecting her when I stepped between them. I'm on my way to getting really mad at her when somebody starts pounding on the door. I don't get company here, except for Tiny and Nancy, so I hesitate before going down the hall.

The pounding gets harder and I can hear somebody shouting; it sounds like a kid. When I open the door it's Trevor from our old place.

"You got to come down right now!" he's shouting at me even though I'm only about three feet away from him. I just look at him, and he bangs on the door frame.

"You got to come down right now, I said! I already called the ambulance, but she's hurting real bad, come on now!" He's got me by the shirt front and trying to pull me out the door.

"What happened?" I'm letting him pull me out the door and then we're running down the hill to my old place. Never thought I'd go back there.

"She, she, she was heading toward the little field behind the house, you know, and she'd just about got to the gap in the fence and she stepped right on a yellowjacket nest and they swarmed her, swarmed her real bad!"

The little field is where I buried Daddy about a year ago. That gives me a really creepy feeling, thinking about that, but I try to stop thinking about him.

I'm trying to remember what Momma used to do for stings.

"You got any baking soda?"

Trevor looks at me. "What?"

"I said, you got any baking soda? You know, you use it in the kitchen for, well, I'm not sure what for. Supposed to be good for stings. You got any?"

"What's it look like?"

"I think a yellow box. How long til the doctors get here?"

"I don't know, I don't know. She's out there in the yard." He heads off toward the house.

"Bring a bowl of water, too," I call after him, and head out to where a woman is lying on the ground. She's making these little whimpering sounds, and she looks up at me when I bend over her. "Hurts."

I try not to run away, but I sure as hell want to, because I've never seen anybody swelled up like she is. I'd heard some people have bad allergies to stings, and even seen some, but nothing this bad.

Then she starts wheezing and grabbing her throat and it's like she can't breathe and about that time Trevor shows up with a box of baking soda and a glass of water.

"You go out to the road and wave the ambulance in here," I say. He doesn't move and I shout in his face, "I said go! They need to know where to turn in! Get your ass out there!"

He's crying, big loud sobs and tears running down his face, and he still doesn't move and I shove him backward. He finally takes off running toward the road and I turn back to the woman.

And I realize I'm watching somebody die, right in front of me. Her eyes are on mine, and she's trying to get a breath and she can't and her eyes are begging me for help and she's all swollen up all over and I don't know how many yellowjackets stung her but it must have been a whole lot. The ambulance pulls in and I wave at them and then look back at her and her eyes are open but she's not seeing anything.

I look down and I've still got the water and box of soda in my hands and I realize I just stood there and didn't do a damn thing. I just let her die.

Chapter Twenty-Four

The EMT's are doing their thing and Trevor's standing over on the side and I let the stupid baking soda and the glass of water drop from my hands and I turn around and walk back up to Gamaliel's house real slow. When I turn into the yard I look back toward the woods and I swear I think I see that damned owl, sitting on a branch. I get a little closer and see that it's nothing, just my eyes playing tricks.

Frankie's lying underneath one of the windows in the back room where the breeze from the fan is pretty strong. I mix an S&S and sit down, thinking about what just happened. I feel bad for Trevor and whoever else is in his family; it didn't look like that woman was coming back, even with the EMT's working their asses off. But I'm also feeling a little relief, because every time I heard that damn owl I thought of Gamaliel right away. This is how that kind of shit keeps going, I say to myself. Now part of me believes all that stuff about the owl.

The next day I get up middle of the morning because somebody's at the door. Damn, I think, what other kind of bad shit is going to happen now?

It's Tiny. I wave him on inside and head back to the back room. Frankie trots up to Tiny and nuzzles his hand and then goes back to her spot.

"How's your arm?" Tiny says, not sitting down when I point to Gamaliel's chair.

I nod. "Good. Haven't even thought about it in a week or so."

"Good. That offer of help still stand?"

That's why he didn't sit down. "Sure. When do you need it?"

"Right after lunch today. Mom's still on this cleaning out the buildings thing and I've got some good lumber in one of them but there's some other stuff that we haven't even looked at in years, old magazines, broken tools, you know, shit like that. It just needs to go to the dump, so if you've got some time in that busy schedule of yours, I could use another set of hands."

"Not a problem, Tiny, as long as I can just supervise and make sure you're working instead of sitting on your ass."

He laughs that short laugh of his. "Maybe you could pick something up every now and then, you know, throw it in the truck."

He waves at Frankie. "Got to go, girl. Grocery list in the truck." He turns back to me. "Say about one, give or take?"

I nod. "See you then."

When I pull up to the Thompson place a couple of minutes after one, Tiny is just heading out the back door. He motions for me to follow him and disappears around the side of the house.

When I turn the corner I'm on a part of their property I haven't seen before. There are half a dozen outbuildings of two or three different sizes. Tiny is standing in front of one of the smaller ones; his truck is backed up close to the door.

The building is not much bigger than the shed behind Gamaliel's house, but it's crammed full of all kinds of shit. The boards Tiny talked about are stacked against one wall and look like they're fine right where they are, but the rest of the place is a mess.

"You bring a pair of gloves?"

I pull them out of my back pocket. "So where do we start and what do we do? Are we sorting this or just tossing all of it except the lumber?"

"Everything but the lumber is going to the dump. Why don't you get about halfway back and start moving stuff toward the door, and I'll toss it in the truck."

"Okay, boss."

He grins at me. "Just make sure my back's not turned when you throw something toward me."

An hour later the shed is almost empty except for the lumber. Tiny is hard to keep up with, but I manage to move enough junk to keep him busy. I toss the last bundle of old magazines his way and look around. Place needs sweeping, but other than that, it's in good shape.

The truck bed is about two feet deep all over, and a few mounds getting a little higher than that. Tiny looks at it and then calls out, "Mom! What time is it?"

"It's 2:30. Why don't you do that dump run tomorrow? You've already worked poor Boone to death. I saw you stick him back in the back of that shed."

She comes out dusting her hands; they're covered in flour. "You want to stay for supper, Boone? Or maybe come back around 6:30? Give you a chance to rest and get cleaned up from all that trash Philip had you in."

"He'll be here, Mom," Tiny says, and looks at me. "Right?"

I nod. "That'd be nice, Mrs. Thompson. Thanks."

When I go back down to the house there's a car I don't recognize in the way; I can't get to my space. A man I've never seen before is standing on the porch.

"You live here?" he says.

"Who are you, exactly?" I'm tired and dirty and don't feel like messing with anybody.

"I'm Trevor's dad. I heard what happened from the ambulance crew. I just wanted to thank you."

I look at him and shake my head. "I didn't do anything, couldn't do anything. I've never seen stings that bad. I'm sorry, man, really sorry." I feel like I'm about to cry or something, and I didn't even know this woman.

I'm close to the guy now and I can see he is crying. "I don't think there's anything you could have done, son. They told me how bad it was. I was thanking you for sending Trevor up to wait for the ambulance. He didn't need to watch his mom die. You did the right thing there."

Now I am crying too, not much, but I can feel the tears. I shake my head, but I can't think of anything to say.

"You did the right thing there," he says again, and comes down off the porch. "I'll be going now."

Chapter Twenty-Five

Carrie's letter doesn't come until Friday, and when I open the letter it's not money, it's a check. I just stand there for a second staring at it. It says $300.00, more than I usually get from her, but I don't know what to do with it. I don't think the gas station is going to cash something like this.

It seems like when I run into something like this, something I don't know about or don't know how to get started, the first thing I think of is to call Nancy.

She picks up on the second ring.

"Hey, sweetie, what's going on?"

Nobody has ever treated me as nice as she does, and I don't know what to say or do with that.

"Uh, well, good. I'm good. I mean, nothing much. What's going on with you?"

"Dad keeps asking when you're going to come over. He really liked you, Boone, and he never likes the boys I bring around."

I'm trying to get my feet back on the ground here.

"So, listen, can you come over? I really need you, I mean, I need to talk to you."

"Is everything okay?"

"I just want to see my favorite girl, that's all. Anything wrong with that?"

I'm waiting to find out if I said the wrong thing there. Talking to girls has always been super hard for me. I usually just fumble around and then say something stupid and everybody laughs. Then I get mad, and they laugh even more. So I'm never sure.

There's a long silence and then, "You mean that, Boone? I mean about me being your favorite girl?"

It sounds like she's as scared as I am, and that doesn't make any sense. She's got brains and looks and money, so what does she have to worry about? Then I remember that look her dad gave her mom at the table, and I almost say something about it right then. I start to and then it just won't come out, not over the phone like this. So instead I say the things I'm already thinking right now.

"Well, yeah, sure I do. I mean, you're great, and pretty, and — "

"You need to stop that right now, Boone, I'm as red as a beet."

I kind of laugh, but I'm thinking that I'd really like to see that.

"You mean just your face?"

She's laughing now, kind of a nervous laugh, and it's like she can't answer me, like somebody's standing right there. I don't know what to say next, so I go back to the first thing I said.

"Listen, I really need to talk to you. Can you come over sometime today?"

She's getting her breath back now. "You sure nothing's wrong?"

I haven't told her about Trevor's mom, and there's this check, and then I remember what she told me once about a safety deposit box, and I think, I've got an I.D. now.

"I'll tell you when you get here, okay?"

When she pulls in, Frankie and I go to the car to meet her. She gets out and bends down and gives Frankie a good scratching behind the ears.

"I'm going to steal her from you, Boone, you know that? I'm just waiting for you to turn your back on her one time."

I'm just staring at Nancy. She is the most beautiful thing in the world, and for a few seconds all I can do is look at her.

She starts looking all over the place, everywhere except at me. "See, now I'm getting red again. You're embarrassing me."

"Can't help it. You do look a little red, though. Are you that color all over?'

She looks right at me now, and she's got a look in her eye like she's playing with me, like she's having fun. "Maybe someday you'll find out. Now what was so important you had me run over here?"

I don't really know where to start.

Nancy sees the look on my face and her voice turns serious. "What's wrong, Boone? Is it about Gamaliel? Is Jerry harassing you again? What's wrong?"

"Nothing like that," I say, shaking my head. "Actually, some of it is no big deal, I just wanted your help. There is one thing that kind of sucks, though."

She listens to what happened to Trevor's mom and by the end there are tears in her eyes. "Oh, that sounds terrible. But you couldn't have done anything for her, right? I mean, it was that bad, the reaction?"

I nod. "That's what it looked like, and that's what the guy said when he came up here."

"What guy?"

"When I came back from helping Tiny clean out a storage shed up at the Thompson place there was a guy on the porch. Said he was Trevor's dad, and he wanted to thank me."

She doesn't say anything, doesn't move. We're still standing out in the yard next to her car and Frankie is sitting next to her, watching me.

"He said it was good, sending Trevor to flag down the ambulance, so he didn't have to watch her, watch her . . . you know," I say, and I can feel the tears start up again.

Nancy doesn't say a word, just takes my hand and leads me into the house. She sits me down in

Gamaliel's chair and goes into the kitchen. In a minute she's back with a glass.

"Gamaliel said not to mix it with anything, not even ice, right?"

"Right."

She goes back in and comes out with her own glass; looks like it has about a teaspoon in it. I point to it and say, "Sure you can handle all that?" and try a smile.

"I'm going to try," she says, and takes a sip.

We sit for a while and don't talk, just listen to how quiet it is in the house.

After I finish my glass, I say, "There is something else, no big deal, but I could use your help with it."

"Okay," she says.

"You remember when I had that will, and you said something about a safety deposit box, and I didn't have any kind of I.D.?"

She nods.

"Well," I say, "I've got some I.D. now."

"But you don't have the will. You gave it to Carrie. What was in there, anyway?"

I shrug. "I don't know, she'll tell me eventually, I guess. Anyway, I've got this," I show her the check, "and I don't think the gas station's going to want to cash that. I thought I might get a checking account."

She looks at the time. "Well, it'd be close, trying to get there and do it today, but if you want to, we can run on down. Here," and she reaches in her pocket, "you better chew some gum, you know, just in case one of them wants to give you a kiss."

It takes me a second to realize she's teasing me.

"So, who's driving?" I've never been able to ask that question before.

She looks at me with a little smile. "Why don't I drive, since I just had a taste. Be sure you got your license with you, and bring that check.

The bank is pretty easy to deal with; I let Nancy do the first little bit of talking, and I just listen. The guy behind the desk asks for an I.D. and I give him the license and the check, and he gives it right back to me.

"You didn't endorse it yet."

I don't know exactly what he's talking about, but Nancy hands me a pen and says, "Did you forget to sign the back, sweetie?" She turns to the banker. "He'd forget his head if it wasn't screwed on tight."

He nods and says, "Right there, Mr. Hammond. Thank you. I'll be right back."

In about five minutes he's back with some checks and says, "You're all set. You know you won't have access to that money until Wednesday of next week, but everything looks good. Shouldn't be a problem."

"What do you mean, next Wednesday?"

This guy just took my money and now I can't get at it. I don't like the sound of that at all.

"Just standard policy, Mr. Hammond. We really never have a problem here, it's such a small town, but some banks have trouble with bad checks." He holds up his hand; I guess he can see I'm getting mad. "I can't just set the rules aside for you, you know, but, like I said, we really never have a problem here."

I look at Nancy and she says, "I had to do the same thing, Boone, when I opened mine. He's right, it's the rule, same for everybody."

There's not much else to do, so we stand up to leave. He sticks out his hand. "Pleasure to get your business, Mr. Hammond. Stop by anytime."

I'm thinking that the only other bank is down in Knoxville, so of course he gets my business, but I don't say anything.

As we're leaving, I say, "Well, I'd buy you a pizza or something but the bank's got all my money."

She laughs. "Don't worry about it, Boone, you can buy me a pizza on Wednesday next week."

When we get home I ask her to come in for a while, but she says, "I've been gone longer than I told them I would be. You going to see Gamaliel this weekend?"

I hadn't decided which day to go down there, but I had definitely planned to go, and I tell her that.

She says, "Call me when you decide which day. I'd like to go along; maybe it won't be quite as exciting as that other time."

We end up going on Saturday and it's a good trip, nothing like when we ran into Jerry and had that whole mess to deal with. So we've had two good ones in a row, and I think Gamaliel's starting to expect us to come by, maybe even look forward to it. He doesn't say so, still can't talk, but maybe I'm just getting better at reading the little stuff.

Frankie is loving this new thing in her life. She drags me from one person to another after we've finished visiting Gamaliel, and I can tell the old people are liking it too, having her come by.

We're on the way home and Nancy, in the passenger side of the truck on the other side of Frankie, reaches past her and lays her hand on my leg.

"You know it's a really good thing you're doing there, Boone. Those people love seeing you and Frankie come around the corner of the building."

I'm working as hard as I can to keep to my side of the road, and I can barely hear what she's saying. All I can think about is her hand on my leg, and I'm wishing Frankie was on the outside and she was in the middle right up next to me.

She must have figured out what was going on, because she laughs a little, pats my leg one more time, and says, "I better let you drive, sweetie."

She pulls her hand back and I say, "Would've been worth putting it in the ditch to have you leave your hand there."

"You're a mess, Boone, you know that?"

She leaves almost as soon as we get back, something about a family thing she can't miss, but she says she'll try to see me a bunch next week. "School's starting up soon, you know. I'm guessing you won't be going, but I will be, so I'll be busy studying and stuff."

Monday morning I'm back at the bank. I go up to the same desk I sat at the last time, and the same guy is there. Mr. Wakefield, his nameplate says.

"Hello, Mr. Hammond. Didn't expect to see you quite so soon."

"How are you, Mr. Wakefield?" I stick my hand out first this time, and he takes it and then asks me to have a seat.

When I tell him I want to get a safety deposit box, he looks surprised, but then says, "Well, we have three different sizes. If you'll step over here, I'll show you your choices."

The only one the box would fit in is the biggest one, but it's way too big, and I figure I can put the rolls in a bag and get by with the small one that way.

We go through the paperwork and he shows me how the whole thing works. When he asks me if I want to put something in the box while I'm in the vault, I say no, I just wanted to get it set up.

I get up the next morning and put all that money in a paper bag. It's small enough, I'm pretty sure, to fit in the box I'm renting; I don't realize how hard that trip is going to be until I'm out on the road. I am more nervous than I've ever been in my life, and I bet I spend the entire trip going ten miles under the speed limit. When I pull into the bank parking lot I have to sit for a minute to get my breathing back under control.

The trip back is easy.

When I was cleaning up the shed a while back I had found a chain, like what they used to put on ceiling lights so they'd be easier to turn on, so the key is hanging around my neck under my shirt. I start to take it off when I get home and decide not to, that it's safest where it is right now.

Chapter Twenty-Six

The next time I see Nancy is a week later. School's real important to her, and as soon as the year starts, she's waist-deep in clubs and projects and shit like that. Not too many classes; she's ahead of a lot of her class as far as getting all the requirements out of the way. She's got English and a civics kind of class and the rest are things just to fill up the day. Gives her more time for the clubs and stuff, I guess.

Tuesday afternoons are not full of stuff, at least not yet, so she comes over straight from school and is talking a mile a minute about all the stuff going on, how the team's supposed to do, and so on and so on. When she finally takes a breath I say, "I need to talk to you about something kind of important."

She immediately thinks it's Gamaliel, and I tell her no, it's not him, it's not any kind of bad news. We're sitting in the back room and I say, "I'll be right back."

When I come back I hand her the spare safety deposit box key and say, "They told me at the bank I needed to keep this safe, and I don't have anywhere like that. I mean, this isn't my house or anything. So I was hoping you could keep it for me. I probably won't ever need it," and I show her the key on the chain around my neck, "but just in case, you know. I trust you, Nancy."

I start to say something else and she's up and got her arms around me, squeezing me tight, and we stand there that way for a minute. Then she backs off and says, "You know you're the only person that thinks I'm, I mean, that thinks I'm enough of an adult to keep something like this. I could just kiss you," and she does, and then sits back down quick before I can get something started.

"So what's in the box?"

"It'd be better if I took you down there sometime and showed you. You wouldn't believe it if I just told you about it." What I'm thinking is if she knew about it she'd try to make me give it back, and I don't think I'm going to do that. The old man said it was for me, for when he was gone. I'm just keeping an eye on it, haven't spent a dime, I just needed it to be safe.

I look over at Nancy and she's kind of pouting, but then says, "Okay, Boone. You let me know when you're ready, and I'll keep this safe for you. You know you need a better chain than that if you're going to hang that thing around your neck and carry it with you all the time."

She takes the extra key and puts it in her pocket. "I'll find a place in my bedroom to put it; it'll be safe with me, Boone. I promise."

"Thanks. So how's school? Is Hargrave still the principal?"

She tells me about stuff at school, which I'm not interested in at all, I just want to keep her here as long as I can. She looks at her cell, though, and says, "Oh my God, it's already six! I need to get home right now. I'll take care of this, Boone, and I'll see you real soon."

And just like that she's gone.

The thing about having somebody like Nancy is how I feel when she's not around. I used to be fine by myself, well, by myself except for Frankie. It didn't bother me a bit to go without seeing folks for days at a time. Now when I'm alone for more than a while I start not liking it much, and that bothers me. I can't see Nancy whenever I want to, Gamaliel's a drive away and doesn't do much besides sit, and Tiny's busy about half the time and running with his friends the rest of the time.

Wonder what else there is to do around here.

I pour myself an S&S and while I'm sipping I start thinking about last year when Gamaliel and I were finishing off that run he had started with Daddy.

I get out the recipe for shine that Gamaliel left me and study it for a while. Some of it's going to be hard to follow, that whole "a good handful" of this, and "mix until it looks right" stuff, but I think there's enough information there for me to give it a try. It'd be a lot easier if I had a partner, like Gamaliel used to be.

Nancy, well, that wouldn't work; she's got school, and probably wouldn't be much interested in doing something illegal, even though it's just a little shine. Tiny, he might be up for it, but I'm just getting to know him. He'd be the best, I know that. He could find a place on the Thompson farm where nobody goes, where it'd stay hid.

I drift off thinking about how to do this and whether or not to try to get Tiny in on it. Last thing I remember thinking is how hard it is to find somebody you can trust these days.

The old place that Nancy and I saw when she was driving me around a while back must've come back to me while I was sleeping, because I get up with that place on my mind. I think I remember her saying there was a lot of state land there, and it looked like nobody had been messing around there for quite a while.

"Frankie!" I say, and she's right there, next to the chair, wagging her tail, ready to go out. "You want to go for a ride?"

I'm hoping I can remember how to get to that part of the county. Maybe it'll come to me when I'm on the road. I hope so.

I load Frankie into the front seat and climb in. In a few seconds we're rolling past Trevor's house; it looks abandoned. For a second I think about putting the still back where it was last year, and then decide to go check out this other place since I've already started. There'll be time after I get back home to have a look around Trevor's place.

Funny, I haven't thought about it as my old place in a long time.

Turns out to be pretty easy to find that piece of property. I remembered the left turn on the way into town, where I usually go straight, and pretty soon I'm driving right by it. I pull into the next driveway, which is quite a ways up the road and long enough that I can't even see the house, and back out into the road, head back to the pair of ruts going up to the old house, and park around behind it.

It's been a long time since anybody's lived here, I can tell that right off. Frankie is out, practically knocking me out of her way, and has her nose first up in the air and then on the ground, back and forth, staying pretty close for now. I go up to the door, which is still in place but just barely. The hinge screws are coming out and the door looks like it's about ready to fall out of the frame and land in the grass. I grab the knob and rest my other hand against the door to steady it and ease it out of the frame and lean it against the outside wall.

Inside it's dark and almost completely bare. The room is small, about the size of the front room at Gamaliel's house, and the only piece of furniture is an old ladderback chair set against the wall.

I stand for a minute to let my eyes adjust to the darkness. When I can halfway see I step on into the room and turn around slow, just looking. The place has been stripped bare, all right. Nothing on the walls, the floor is bare, and, aside from that old chair, there's no furniture. There's a fireplace at the end of the room opposite the door I came through with a rough pine board for a mantel. On the mantel is a box, looks like the kind of thing you get at Christmas with candy inside. I walk over to it and pick it up, give it a shake. Something rattles inside.

The light in here is so bad I decide to take it outside to have a look. When I get it outside into the light I notice that it doesn't have any dust on it at all.

When I open the box, the only thing inside is a kind of a glass tube with a bulb on the end and a box of matches. I've never seen a meth pipe before, but I bet that's what this is. So maybe it's true that nobody lives here, but somebody is sure using this house.

I'm disappointed. I was hoping for a place I could go if I needed to get out of Gamaliel's house, but I'm not ready to fight a meth head for this place.

"Frankie!" I call and hear her coming back through the undergrowth. She's carrying something and drops it at my feet. It's an old boot, looks like it's been out in the weather for a while. I look at the boot, then at the box in my hands, and I think they're probably connected somehow.

I'm starting to feel like death is following me around. Of course I don't know for sure that there is a dead meth user on the other side of that little hill, but that's the first thing I think of, and I don't like thinking about this kind of shit. I stand there for another minute, and then I take the box back into the house and put it back on the mantel where I found it.

"C'mon, Frankie, let's get out of here," I say, and she picks up the boot.

"No, girl, that stays right here." I reach down and take the boot from her; she doesn't want to give it up, but I eventually get it out of her mouth and toss it into the brush.

"In the truck, girl, let's go."

She takes one more look where I tossed the boot and jumps up into the truck.

On the way home I'm trying to decide whether or not to tell Anderson about the pipe and the boot. I wasn't doing anything wrong, there was no "Keep Out" sign anywhere, I was just looking for a place to run my dog. I was really looking for a place to maybe set up to make shine, but that's definitely out if there's other people around.

I finally decide it's none of my business, and I'm going to leave it that way. When I get to the intersection, I turn back toward home and pull into the yard.

So the place out there on state land is off the list. I'm still thinking I might try to make a little shine, but I lost all my energy when I found out I couldn't use that old place.

Maybe there's another place like that. Tomorrow I'll go out and just drive for a while.

When I realize what I just said to myself I can't help but grin. Having that license really does change things.

About three hours later I forget all about that drive. It's full dark outside, and I'm out in the back yard with Frankie, giving her one more run before we settle in, and I don't really notice the headlights coming up the road until they swing into my yard.

Chapter Twenty-Seven

It's Nancy's car, and I didn't have any idea she was coming over. I just have time to brace myself when I see her get out of the car and start toward me at a dead run. I catch her and she grabs hold of me and she's breathing hard and I can feel her heart beating, or maybe that's mine. I don't know. She's in bad shape, I can tell that, and I've got a feeling I know what it's about, and I'm already getting mad as hell.

She's looking at me now, and her eyes are red and swollen, and her face is wet, and she's trying to say something and nothing's coming out, and she shakes her head and puts her face back into my shoulder and we just stand there.

I don't know what to do except to hold her, so I hold on as tight as I can, and in a minute or two her breathing starts to slow down some. Then she says something and I can't make it out because her head's still buried in my shoulder. I say, "Do you want to go inside?" and she nods against me and we sort of move in that direction. Frankie is circling around; she knows something is bad wrong.

"Frankie," I say. "Let's go to the house, girl."

We get inside and I try to get her to sit down and she won't, she won't let go of me. So we stand there, holding so tight it's starting to get uncomfortable, and Frankie just sits there staring at us.

All kinds of stuff is going through my head right now. Did that asshole Randy or whatever his name was show back up at school? Did some other guy go after her in the hallway or outside the gym? There's a place there that, as soon as you turn that corner, nobody can see you unless they are following right behind you. Did she have a wreck? I didn't see anything wrong with her car. Maybe she ran over an animal or something.

Then I remember that look on her Dad's face at the dinner table that night, and the anger flares up hotter inside me. If that son of a bitch laid a hand on her . . . .

I'm so mad I can barely think, but I'm guessing I might be wrong about that. It wasn't Nancy he was looking at, it was her mom. The more I think about it the more I think I'm right about that part, and I don't know what to do about it.

Nancy's starting to ease up on her grip, and pretty soon she pushes away from me and says, "I have to get cleaned up. Back in a minute."

She heads into the bathroom and Frankie and I are left just staring at each other.

In a few minutes she's back and this time she sits down and looks up at me. "Could you make me an S&S, sweetie?"

"Sure," I say and go into the kitchen. When I come back with one for each of us and hand hers to her, she reaches past it and takes mine and says, "You can have that one."

"I made mine a little strong," I say.

"Figured you would," she says, and takes a sip, then another. "Do you need to fix that one up for yourself?"

I nod and go back to the kitchen. While I'm adding shine to my drink I'm wondering what in the hell is going on here. This must be really bad, I think, for her to do this. She's all the time on my case about how strong I make mine, and here she is, taking it right out of my hand. I start back and then turn around and pour just a little more into mine.

Nancy's already made a pretty good dent in her drink by the time I sit down. She looks at me for a long minute before she says anything.

"You know, don't you?"

I nod. "I think so, but I really want to be wrong. You'd better tell me."

She shakes her head. "I don't know whether I can or not, Boone." She takes a deep breath, and lets it out all in a big whoosh. "I've never told anybody. Ever."

The only thing I can think to do is wait, so I just sit there.

She stretches out her hand. "Come over here, Frankie. That's a good girl."

Frankie acts like she's trying to climb into her lap and she starts laughing. "You're way too big for that, girl, you know that. You can sit right here next to me."

She takes another drink and shakes her head. "Honestly, Boone, I don't know how you can drink this."

"You get used to it."

"Well, if I ask you for another one, you tell me no, okay?" She sips one more time before she sets it down. She looks over at me. "Okay?"

"Sure. You want a sandwich or I got a pizza in the freezer, it'll take a few minutes, but, you want something to eat?"

She shakes her head. "No, I was at the table eating just before I left. I got no appetite now, none at all." And then her face changes and she starts to cry again. Not sobbing like last time, just tears rolling down her cheeks.

I'm useless here. I know this, and it makes me mad, mad at myself. Anybody else would know what to do here, I'm sure of it. Tiny would know what to do, hell, even Curt would know, and he's a damn idiot. But I don't know, I'm useless here. Nancy is talking.

"I'm sorry to just bust in on you like this, but I had to come here, Boone. I couldn't go to anybody else, I can't tell my friends this, they'd tell their friends, at least Rhonda would, and it'd be all over school in about a minute and then Dad would find out and I can't let that happen."

She didn't have to say that. I know I don't have any friends to tell, except maybe Tiny, and he doesn't run with the high school crowd, hasn't for years. I could tell Gamaliel, that'd be safe, but really I got no friends to tell. So I'm safe, I guess.

I mean, if I had friends, I wouldn't tell. I can keep a secret, I've proved that already. Of course Nancy doesn't know that, I've never told her about Daddy. But I could keep a secret, even if I had any friends. It just pisses me off to be reminded that I don't.

I don't say any of this to her.

I look over at Nancy, and she's looking down at Frankie, rubbing her behind the ears.

There's nothing for me to do, since I don't know what to say or when to say it. I take another drink and sit there, holding the glass in both hands, with my elbows on my knees.

"I guess you're just waiting for me to say something."

When I look up Nancy is looking at me instead of Frankie. I shrug.

"I figure you'll tell me when you're ready to."

She smiles, just a little one. "You know that's what I love about you, Boone. Sometimes you know exactly the right thing to say."

I'm trying to think of the last time I said the right thing to anybody, but I'm all of a sudden so nervous I'm trembling. Nobody, not even Momma, used my name and the word love in the same breath. At least, not that I can remember. I sit as still as I can so Nancy can't tell how worked up I am.

When I glance back up she's looking off through the window, so I let out a big breath, quiet as I can, and say, "I'm going to make a sandwich. You sure you don't want one?"

She nods. "I'm sure, but you go right ahead." She holds out her glass when I stand up. "Just Thunderstorm this time, okay? I might have drunk that a little fast."

I manage a grin. "Sure thing. I'll bring it right back."

After I get her a Thunderstorm, I throw together a sandwich. It uses up the last of the mayonnaise and I have some trouble unwrapping the slice of cheese and I almost cut my finger off slicing the tomato, but finally I get it done and bring it back in along with a new S&S for myself. As soon as I sit down she says, "Mind if I have a bite of that?"

She takes it from me and takes a bite, nods her head, and takes another one, then hands it back. I

237

look at what's left and say, "You sure you're not hungry?"

Nancy covers her mouth with her hand and says, her mouth still pretty full, "Okay, maybe a little. I'm good now, though."

"I get it," I say, taking a bite myself. "Nothing much tastes better than tomatoes in August."

She nods, swallowing. She gets up and heads into the kitchen. When I see her reach for the jar of shine, I say, "You told me to tell you no if you asked for a refill, remember?"

"I'm not asking you, sweetie, so it's okay."

She doesn't put more than a tablespoon in her glass, as far as I can tell, so I let it go. She stops on the way back to her chair and kisses me on top of my head.

"So, I probably owe you an explanation, don't I?"

I really don't know whether I want to hear this or not, but what I say is, "If you want to tell me what's going on, I'll sure listen to you." And I take another bite of the sandwich because I don't know what else to say.

This is scary and uncomfortable and kind of exciting all at the same time. I like Nancy a lot, more than anybody ever, and I want to do what I can here, but I don't know what that is. But mostly I can't stop thinking, she came to me. She could have gone to anybody, anybody at all, and she came here.

Nancy's looking at me like she can tell what I'm thinking and I get all embarrassed, even though I know she can't do that.

The silence gets longer and longer, and I'm about to say something else even though I can't think of anything new to say, when she stands up and walks over to one of the windows. She's got her back to me when she starts talking.

"I don't know, Boone, I mean, I don't know what to do. Or maybe nothing I can think of seems like a good idea. I can't leave, I'm almost done with school, and besides, there's Cyrus, and I think he's fine, I mean will be fine, but it's different for boys, you know? And I can't get in the middle of it, I know that's a terrible idea, but it's so hard to be in that house while it's going on, you know what I mean?"

She's still got her back to me. "He's never laid a hand on her, at least as far as I know, and he's never touched me or Cyrus, I mean, I know about me, but I don't think he's done anything about Cyrus, it's just how he talks to her, I mean Mom, you know, and the things he calls her, and what he says about her right to her face, and she just stands there and takes it.

"And she's so good and she's trying so hard, and it's never enough, never, and sometimes it doesn't bother me so much but tonight I was in the dining room, you know, where we ate that time you came over, and Mom and Dad both want you to come back, they both really like you, and I was in the dining

239

room and Mom was in the kitchen and I guess she dropped something because there was this crash like a plate breaking and Dad was out of his seat and into the kitchen and he started in on her and I just couldn't sit there and listen any more and that's why I came over here."

The first thing I think is, so is that it? He hasn't even hit any of you? I don't say anything, though, because I'm thinking, I mean, for her, this is a big deal, and then it makes sense to me, when I figure that out. She grew up nice and easy.

The next thing I think is, what the hell is wrong with her dad? They've got money, nice house, cars, plenty to eat, they got nothing to worry about. I'm thinking, if I had all that, I'd never be mad again, ever.

I try to make that part of it make sense and I just can't. Nancy's family, they live like people on TV do. She's still standing there at the window, looking out into the dark, and I look at her and I can't understand why she has to be afraid, why she has to run away from her house.

"I know you think this is silly," she says, still with her back to me. "I mean, your parents aren't even around, and here I am complaining to you, and you're probably thinking, boy, I wish I had what she's got."

That's pretty much exactly what I'm thinking, but for once in my life I know enough to keep my mouth shut.

"I know it's not the same, not like not having them around at all, but he doesn't have to yell at her like that, she's trying as hard as she can, and it's just a damn plate!"

Even I know it's not just the plate, but before I can say that, she turns around to face me.

"It just hurts to have to see that, and I think, what's it going to be like for her when I'm not there? I think he kind of holds back because I'm still around, and I'm afraid that when I move out he'll get worse."

"I get that," I say, because that's the first thing she's said that I do get. She starts to talk again but I keep going.

"I mean, when Momma and Daddy were around he treated her like shit, especially when things didn't go right for him, and I'm kind of glad they're not together anymore, because I think it'd just have kept getting worse and worse.

"I'd like to tell you that I'll come over and fix it, but I can't, darlin', I don't know how, and I didn't even know how to fix my own family."

And I stop because I'm thinking back on what I just said and the only word I can remember saying is darlin' and I think I've blown it again, like when I called her honey and she didn't like that, said it reminded her of her dad calling her that.

Before she can say anything I start talking again. "I can't fix it, but I can tell you that anytime you need to get away from it, you can come over here. I do know what it's like to have to get out, get away from it. That's why I used to go up to that pool in the woods, remember? You and me went up there and you almost fell in."

Nancy laughs. "Oh my God, I'd forgotten all about that. That was when you first told me about making moonshine."

I grin at her. "That's right."

She comes away from the window and plops down in the chair. "I need to call home, tell them I'm okay. I hope Mom picks up."

She calls and I can only hear one side of the conversation.

"Hey, Mom, it's me. Just wanted to let you know I'm okay, and I'll be back in a little bit."

"No, Mom, I'm not up in my room. When you and Dad — "

"I'm fine, really, I just had to get out of there for a while. Listen, you don't have to tell Dad I was even gone. I'll be real quiet coming in."

"Are you sure?"

"All right, I'm on my way. Don't say anything."

She turns to me when she's done. "I got to go, sweetie. They didn't even know I was gone, can you believe that? Sounds like Dad's already asleep down in his study. When he's really mad he goes down there and drinks, and if I'm quiet coming in, he'll never know I was gone."

"You can stay here if you want to, you know," I say. "As long as you want to."

She gives me a big smile. "Careful what you offer, Boone. I might be over here so much you'd be tired of me."

"No chance of that."

"Walk me to my car?"

I go to the door and hold it open for her. "You're sure you don't want to stick around?"

She comes up to me and gives me a long, long kiss. "I'm sure I do want to stick around, but Mom's there by herself with Dad, and I need to go."

We walk out to the car. "Call me when you get there, okay?"

"I will."

"Be careful, darlin'." I really don't want her to go back over there, but I can't figure out how to keep her here.

She gets in the car and drives away.

Frankie's waiting by the door when I come back. I go to the kitchen and fix another S&S and sit down in Gamaliel's chair.

"Frankie, I don't exactly know what to do here. Nancy's making a mistake, sneaking around on her daddy like that. I know, I did the same thing with mine. We all did — Momma, Hannah, me — the only one who didn't so much was Frankie."

Frankie jumps up, her tail wagging, and heads toward the back door.

"No, girl, we've already been outside tonight. Anyway, I did all that and worse, that's how I know it's a bad idea. It just made Daddy madder when he found out, and he always found out.

"I'm thinking I need to say something to her. She said her dad hasn't done anything to her, but if she keeps doing this and he catches her, who knows what he'll do. I sure know what my Daddy would do. He'd beat the hell out of me. Probably different for a girl, though."

As soon as I say that I think about something Momma said, in one of those letters she wrote back when she was still doing that, about getting Hannah out of there while she was still young enough. I never was sure exactly what she meant, but I think I know now, or maybe I always knew and just didn't want it to be true, not even for a bastard like Daddy, and if I'm right, I'm glad Daddy blew his head off or else I'd have done it for him.

I'm not real steady on my feet when I get up to answer the phone. It's Nancy, telling me she got there okay. She says she can't talk, which is fine with me, the way my head is right now.

After I hang up I mix up one more, real strong, and I make it almost halfway through before I fall asleep.

Chapter Twenty-Eight

I spend the next two days worrying about Nancy. She calls once on Friday, but it's a really fast call, and it doesn't make me any less worried. Saturday I decide the hell with it and I call Betty Franklin to tell her I'm on my way down to see Gamaliel and the rest of the old people.

There's a long silence at the other end of the phone.

"Mrs. Franklin? Is it okay if I come by later on today?"

For a few more seconds there's still nothing, and then she says, "You mean for the memorial service?"

After I hang up I try to remember what just happened. I know I was shouting into the phone part of the time, and I think she didn't shout back, just stayed on the line, and I know that I blamed her for a lot of stuff that wasn't her fault.

I know I should have been yelling at Carrie.

Why didn't Carrie call me and tell me about Gamaliel?

I start to call Betty back and apologize, but I can't make myself do it. I start to call Carrie, ask her why I wasn't even invited to the memorial service, but I don't do that either. I think I know what's going on, and I think I know what's about to happen to me real soon.

That son of a bitch.

Jerry is behind this, I know he is, sure as I'm standing in Gamaliel's house.

I try to remember what Betty said, about what time the thing at the home is, because I'm going to be there. Won't Jerry be surprised.

Three o'clock. I'm pretty sure she said three, so I'm going to be there at a quarter til. I check the time; it's ten-thirty, so I've got plenty of time.

I think about calling Nancy and decide not to, and then, just as quick, I know I really need to talk to her. I don't need her to go, probably be best if she didn't, but I need her right now.

There's no answer at her house, so I try her cell. It goes to voicemail.

"Nancy, it's me. I really need you right now, it's Gamaliel. Give me a call."

After that I can't think of anything to do. I take Frankie out for a run, but I cut it short because Nancy might be calling. When I get back inside I sit down in Gamaliel's chair and Frankie comes up right beside me and lays her head on my leg.

I'm still sitting there a half hour later when Nancy finds me.

"You didn't answer your phone, Boone, worried me sick. I got your message. Is is bad? Is Gamaliel okay?"

I just look up at her.

Her hands go to each side of her face. "Oh God, he's gone, isn't he? Oh, Boone, I'm so, so sorry. I know you loved that old guy, and I know he loved you, too."

She runs out of things to say and just stands there, looking at me with a sadness in her eyes I've never seen there before.

I don't say anything, I don't know what to say that would make any difference. I want it to be Friday so I can decide to go see him then, see him one more time. Or maybe that's when he died. I don't think I'd want to be there for that.

Nancy's looking around the place and I know she's thinking about how mad I get sometimes, and she's looking for broken stuff.

"I haven't thrown anything, darlin', not yet anyway."

She looks back quick, kind of embarrassed, and says, "I know, Boone, I can tell you're just real sad. Tell me what I can do."

I shrug.

"So what did Carrie say when she called? How did she — "

"She didn't call me."

Nancy's mouth hangs open for just a second, and then she grabs a chair and pulls it over next to me. She lays her hand on my leg and I twitch a little.

"What do you mean, she didn't call? How did you find out?"

I tell her about deciding to go down and see the old man and calling Betty Franklin, and her being confused, and me yelling at her, how the memorial service is at three today.

"What are you going to do?"

"I'm going to go apologize to Betty and then go to the service."

She nods and pats my leg. "I'm going with you."

"You know you don't have to do that," I say, but I'm really glad she's offering.

"Of course I'm going with you. I'm your favorite girl, aren't I?"

"It's not a date, Nancy."

There's a little flash of something on her face, I don't quite catch it, and then she says, real low, "I know that, Boone, I just thought — "

"Sorry," I say, not letting her finish, and it's true. I really am sorry. "It's a bad day, is all."

She looks hurt, and I don't get that. I said I was sorry, but I guess I need to say something else.

"Truth is, I think I need you there with me. You can keep me from killing Jerry as soon as I lay eyes on him."

She tries a grin. "I can do that."

"And you need to go with me to see Betty so you can step on my foot or kick me under the table if I start getting real stupid."

"Okay, Boone. Do you think I'll need a leash?"

I can't help but laugh. "No, I don't think you'll need that."

We both stand up and she puts her arms around me and I stand there for a second and then start crying. Nancy hangs on tight and I'm bawling like a little kid and I can't stop. I knew this was coming, and I didn't want him to live a long time just sitting in that chair, but I can't stop crying.

It takes me a while to get back under control and Nancy's right there, she doesn't talk or tell me it's going to be all right, she just stands there, patient, waiting for me to get it back together.

Finally I put my arms around her for a second and then take a step back, and I put my hands on her shoulders and give her a kiss, and then say, "What would I do without you?"

She turns a little red and takes hold of my wrists, pulling my hands away. "I'm going to go home and get cleaned up, you do the same, and I'll be back here in plenty of time to go over there."

Chapter Twenty-Nine

One of the smaller buildings on the grounds of the home is a chapel. I never paid much attention to it before, but, sure enough, as soon as you pull into the parking lot, there's a sign, and right under the words, "Main Building/Administration" there's an arrow pointing off to the right and the word, "Chapel".

Nancy's driving. She says that way if things get ugly she can haul my ass out of there and get me back home.

Home. I don't want to think about it, but I can't help myself. Now that the old man is gone, I'm wondering how long Carrie will be able to keep Jerry from kicking my ass out of there. Or if she'll even try.

I know it seemed like the worse things got for Daddy, the more Momma protected him, and I never understood that, not after the way he treated her. It's like when he was really down, she needed to be the one taking care of him. I guess it's the only way she knew how to be necessary.

I shake my head; there's time enough to think about that. Right now I need to talk to Betty, make things right with her.

Nancy and I go in together, through the front double doors and down the main hallway. Betty's office is about halfway to the first intersection, on the right, and the door is open.

When I stop at the doorway she's sitting at her desk, frowning at a computer screen and tapping her finger on the desk. She looks up and sees me and says, "Hello, Boone. I'm very sorry that you lost Gamaliel, and that I had to be the one to tell you about it."

"Is it okay if I come in?"

She points to a chair. "Of course."

I pull Nancy into the office with me and say, "Mrs. Franklin, I don't know whether you remember my girl, Nancy," and I feel her squeeze my hand, "she came down with me for the memorial service."

"I do remember you, you were here one other time with Boone," Betty says, and puts out her hand. Nancy lets go of mine and shakes hands with her. "Hello, Nancy. I wish the circumstances were better."

"Yes, ma'am."

We all just stand there for a minute and then Nancy pokes me in the side with her elbow.

"Oh. I'm sorry to bother you, I just wanted to apologize for earlier today. I said some stuff to you I shouldn't have, used some language I shouldn't have, and I wanted you to know I'm sorry."

Betty smiles for just a second. "Oh, Boone, you don't need to apologize to me. I saw how you were with Mr. Everett. I know it was a shock. Besides, I've had much worse said to me right here in this office. I appreciate you taking the time to come by, but, really, it's okay. How are you holding up?"

I don't answer right away and Nancy says, "He was pretty torn up earlier; he's better now."

Betty nods. "Are you here for the service? We have a chaplain that does a wonderful job." She looks at the computer screen. "He should be in his office right now, and it's still about twenty minutes until the service. I know he'd like to hear something about Mr. Everett, something personal. Come with me, I'll introduce you."

"Oh no, I don't know about that," I start to say, and Nancy elbows me again and says to Betty, "That would be just fine."

Betty leads the way down the hall and I turn to Nancy. "What was that all about?"

"This guy probably doesn't know Gamaliel from Adam," she says. "Just tell him a couple of stories and he'll be happy."

I don't like it, not at all. But I follow Betty down the hall and we make a right turn into another hall. This one's short, only a few doors before the door to the outside. I can see a building out there with a cross on the front, up above its door.

Betty stops and knocks on a door, the last one on the right before we'd be outside, and a voice says, "Come in."

She opens the door and says, "Mark, this young man is a friend of Mr. Everett, the person you're doing the service for at three."

Nancy and I step into the small room and Betty says, "I should really get back to my office, I'm expecting a call. I'll be at the service, though."

"Okay, see you then," Mark says. He stands up and holds out his hand. "Good of you to stop by, Mr., uh,?"

"My name's Boone," I say and take his hand, thinking, if my Daddy was the one going into the ground today and he knew a black man was going to be running the service, he might just get up out of his coffin and walk out of the chapel. The only people Daddy had less use for than Mexicans were black people.

"Won't you sit down?" Mark points to a couple of chairs, and Nancy and I sit down.

"So, Boone, you can really help me out here," Mark says. He looks from me to Nancy and back again. "And your name, Miss?"

"Nancy."

I glance over at Nancy and I can tell she's uncomfortable. Didn't know that about her, and it may not be him being black. Might be something else.

"Pleased to meet you, Nancy. Now, Boone, tell me something about Mr. Everett."

"Well." I know there's some stuff I can't say anything about, so I'm trying to be careful. "Well, Gamaliel is, or I guess was, a good guy. Helped me out a lot when he didn't have to, and he was always good to me. Except for that time he shot me, that is."

Mark's face doesn't change, not much, but he sits up a little straighter in his chair.

"The time he shot you?"

So I tell him about the assholes on the four-wheelers, and how Gamaliel was just trying to defend his house and didn't know I was in the woods, and about us trying to patch each other up, and about his fiddle, and how he used to do woodwork, and how he kind of tried to look after me once he found out I was left by myself, and he holds up his hand.

"He sounds like a fine man and I wish I could hear more, Boone, truly I do, but it's almost time for the service. You've been a big help, and I thank you for that. Will I see you and Nancy in the chapel?"

We nod and he says, "I need a few minutes to get ready. See you over there."

Chapter Thirty

Nancy and I are two rows back from the pulpit, which puts us about a third of the way down the room. It's a small chapel. In front of us are three empty chairs and Betty. Across the aisle on the front row are Carrie, on the aisle seat, and Jerry beside her, his cast sticking out in front of him. When Nancy and I came in a few minutes earlier Carrie looked at me and turned away quick; Jerry didn't even turn around when she leaned over to say something to him.

I twist around in the seat to look at the rest of the place. It's about half full, fifteen or sixteen people altogether. Some of the folks I recognize from my visits with Frankie, and one old guy gives me a quick smile when our eyes meet.

Mark comes in from the back and walks down the aisle to the front, not looking either way. He passes a little table that sits even with the pulpit. The pulpit is over on the left, in front of Jerry, and the table is in the center, lined up with the aisle. There's a couple of

255

vases on the table with flowers in them, and a silver vase between them that has a lid on it. I tap Betty on the shoulder and when she turns her head I whisper, "What's in the silver vase?"

"He wanted to be cremated, Boone," she whispers back.

It takes me a second. I lean over to Nancy and point to the table. "That's all that's left of Gamaliel, in that vase?"

She nods and leans over, her lips touching my ear. "It's called an urn. I've seen a few of them before. It's a nice one."

I start to ask her what is going to happen to it after the service and Mark stands up and steps to the pulpit. There's a little noise while everybody shifts around and gets comfortable.

"Thank you all for coming," Mark starts out, and he's using his preacher's voice. He sounds real different than he did in his office a half an hour ago.

"We are here to celebrate and remember the life of Gamaliel Taylor Everett. He spent his entire life in these Tennessee hills, almost all of them in the same house, the one just on the other side of the highway, to the east of here.

"He married once, to Elizabeth, his 'Lizzie'. She went to be with the Lord twelve years ago, and now Gamaliel is joining her."

I lean over to Nancy. "Gamaliel wouldn't like all this heaven talk."

256

"Shhh."

Mark hasn't missed a beat. "Only one of his two children could be here today. Tragically, his son was lost in an accident in Europe two years ago. Carrie is here, along with her husband Jerry, to join us in this celebration and remembrance.

"We never know the hour we will be called to leave this life and go on to our reward. Gamaliel lived a good and full life, on his own until just a year ago, in the house where he and Lizzie raised their children and built a life together."

"This isn't about Gamaliel," I whisper to Nancy. "You could put anybody's name in there and it would sound just the same. It's like he's in a play, you know, memorizing all his lines."

"Shhhhh!"

This time it's Betty that's shushing me. I look at her for a second and then back up at Mark. I know what I'm talking about here. She never knew Gamaliel, not like I did. Mark's not talking about Gamaliel, he's talking about an old man, and it's starting to piss me off.

Mark clears his throat. "Gamaliel Everett worked for the aluminum company down in Alcoa for most of his working life, making the drive back and forth, until he retired. He, uh," Mark looks down at his notes, "had friends, friends all through his life, and there are many stories about Gamaliel that bear telling. For instance, there was the time he — "

Mark stops talking and looks down at his notes again, but this time he doesn't start right back up. After a second he clears his throat and says, "I started to tell a story about Gamaliel from late in his life, a story with humor and compassion and drama all rolled into one. But as I stand here, I realize that I can't do justice to that story. There is someone here, however, who can not only tell it, but who lived it right alongside our departed friend Gamaliel."

Oh, no, I say to myself, don't you do that, Mark, you bastard. I feel Nancy's hand on my shoulder; I look over at her and she's smiling, but her eyes are teary, and when she catches me looking at her she nods at Mark.

Mark is still talking. "As I said, the person who should be telling this story is in the room with us this afternoon, and I think not only is it right, it's what Gamaliel would want, for his story to be told the right way, the honest way."

You just need to shut up right now, I'm thinking, but there's also a part of me that wants to get up there and really talk about Gamaliel, instead of listening to all this bullshit that could be about anybody.

"I'd like to have him come up and tell us about the man whose life we're here to celebrate," Mark says, and he's got his rhythm back now, the preacher is back in the pulpit. "It is surely what Gamaliel would have wanted, and I know it's what we need to hear.

Mr. Boone Hammond is here, in the second row, and I'd like to ask him to come up and say a few words about his friend."

He points to me and Nancy is giving me a little push and I look around. The old guy who smiled at me earlier is nodding at me and I catch Carrie looking at me and she looks away again, but I think I see a smile on her face for just a second.

One more push from Nancy and I'm on my feet and heading toward the pulpit.

When I get up there Mark shakes my hand and says, "It's all yours, Boone. Be sure and tell them about the time he shot you. That's a great story."

Then he sits down and I'm up there all by myself.

I look out at the people in the room. Most of them I recognize from my visits with Frankie, a few I've never seen before. I realize that they don't know any stories about Gamaliel at all, since he didn't come here until after he couldn't talk.

"Gamaliel was a good guy," I start out, and immediately think, how stupid does that sound. I don't belong up here, it should be Carrie talking about her daddy or somebody that knew him when he was younger.

"Go ahead, sweetie, tell them about how you two met," I hear Nancy's voice from the second row and I look out at her. She's got a big smile on her face, and she's nodding at me.

"Right. How we met. Well, I needed a pump for my bicycle tire, and his house was the closest one. He damn near ran me off his property that first time." Maybe I shouldn't say damn but I don't care much, I didn't want to be up here in the first place. Mark and I are going to have a talk after this.

"But he told me where to find it, and pretty soon after that there was the lottery ticket that he cashed for me and wouldn't take any money for doing it," and once I start talking about the old guy the stories start piling up and when I get the nerve to look at the people I see some of them are nodding and smiling.

So I tell them about spending more and more time with him, since my family had left me there by myself, and about when he told me to start calling him Gamaliel and how I didn't know where the name came from until Carrie told me.

"We had a few good times together, didn't we?" I look at Carrie and her eyes are brimming and she's staring at me and not moving a muscle.

I tell them about getting a dog, "You all know Frankie, she's named after my brother, the one that died," and I almost start crying myself when I say that, but I stop for a second and then I'm all right. I tell them how Frankie took to Gamaliel from the first and how he threatened to take her away from me or get an even bigger dog to kick Frankie's ass.

I don't say anything about the moonshine.

When I tell them about him shooting me because he thought I was one of the guys that were there to rob him and about us trying to patch each other up pretty much the whole room is laughing, and somebody says, "Tell it again!" so I do and they like it just as much the second time around.

I roll up my sleeve and show them the scar from the bullet and say, "He didn't mean to hurt me, he was just trying to defend his home, and I was coming in from the same direction as the thieves were.

"He was maybe the best guy I've ever known," and now I am crying and I don't even care, "and I'm going to miss him a lot. He was a man I could trust, and I knew that, and he knew he could trust me. We were really good together, me and Gamaliel. So I've got this scar and it reminds me that there are good people out there, people I can count on, people I can trust."

I stop for a second and then I roll up my other sleeve. "And I've got this other scar, haven't had it very long at all, and it reminds me that there are people out there who don't care about anybody but themselves, who I can't count on, people I can't trust and who I know that I better not ever turn my back on, ever."

I'm looking right at Jerry when I say this, and he looks like if he had a gun he'd shoot me down right there in the chapel. I lock eyes with him for what seems like a full minute and then look back out at everybody else.

"Gamaliel was one of the good guys, and I'm proud to say I knew him. I — I — " and I drop my head and start bawling like a little kid and Nancy is right there in a second and she and Mark lead me off the stage and back to my seat.

I don't really remember much about the rest of the service. I don't think it lasted too long, and by the time Mark is wrapping things up I've stopped blubbering and stuff. Nancy still has her arm tight around me and I remember I didn't ask her to come with me but I'm sure glad she did.

"What time is it?" I ask her as Mark comes up to us.

"A little after four. You talked for almost half an hour, sweetie, and it was great."

"It certainly was," Mark joins in. "Gamaliel would have liked what you said, Boone, I'm sure of it. And what the people were saying about it, well, you brought us a part of Gamaliel that we'd never seen and would never have known about."

"I ought to kick your ass for getting me up on that stage," I say, but my heart's not in it, and I realize I'm smiling while I say it. "I might still do it, too."

He grins back at me. "I know, but I guess I'll have to take it, then, because I would definitely do it again."

Betty joins our little group. "Boone, we need to talk sometime soon. Whenever you've got some time, I mean. That was lovely, by the way. Perfect."

I'm getting embarrassed by all this attention, and I think Nancy notices, because she says, "I really need to get back home and study, and you should check on Frankie, don't you think?"

"Yeah, I do," I say, and turn to Mark and Betty. "We need to get going, nice service. What's going to happen to that silver vase? Is Carrie taking that?"

Chapter Thirty-One

"Usually it goes with the closest relative, so, yes, Carrie will be taking it with her."

"What's she going to do with it?"

I don't know anything about this stuff. When people die you put them in the ground, you don't burn them up and put the ashes in a vase.

"I don't know, Boone, you'll have to ask her about that."

I don't want to have anything to do with Carrie for a while. I'm still pissed that she didn't invite me to the service; I figure that's Jerry's doing, but it still makes me mad every time I think about it.

What has happened, or is happening, to Carrie feels like what happened to Momma, especially after Frankie died. I mean, it was pretty bad before, but after that, after she lost her favorite son, she just gave up on everything. The only thing that got her going, finally, was worrying about Hannah. She sure as hell wasn't worried about me. Maybe she was looking to me to protect her from Daddy and then when I couldn't do it she gave up on me too.

It feels like Carrie's giving up, that she's not fighting Jerry anymore. Maybe with him home all the time he's really been working on her, maybe she feels sorry for him and needs to take care of him, maybe he's beat the fight out of her. I don't know.

I'm tired of thinking about it. I've been thinking about this most of the way home, and Nancy hasn't pushed me to talk to her.

We pull in and I get out and look at the place, wondering how much longer I'll be able to stay here. It's not a great house, not like Nancy's house, but it's a lot better than where I was living, and a hell of a lot better than living out of the truck would be. Or is going to be.

Nancy gets out and we walk up to the back door together. We can hear Frankie inside jumping up and down on her front feet the way she does. It's been a while since she's been outside, and I open the door and call her out.

While Frankie is checking the yard for new smells Nancy and I stand together next to the truck.

"You want to come inside for a while?"

"I can't, sweetie, Dad's cousin is in from Nashville and we're having a big family meal. You want to come eat with us?"

I'm actually kind of glad she can't stay, even though I'm the one who asked. I think I'd like to be alone, hang out with Frankie, and remember Gamaliel.

When I tell Nancy that she nods. "I get that, Boone, I know you two were close."

"I wish I'd had him for a father instead of the one I got." I have to turn away so she won't see me all blubbery. Again.

She touches me on the arm. "You had him for a while. That was good, right?"

I nod.

"Listen, I'm going to get out of here. You be careful tonight, okay? Don't get out on the roads or anything."

She's not my Momma, I think, and I switch from sad to mad in a heartbeat. I open my mouth to tell her to mind her own damn business and then close it again. That's what Daddy would do, and I see him in Jerry, and Nancy's Dad, and sometimes in me, and I hate that. I don't want to be him. I look at Nancy and think, I'd kill anybody that treated her the way Daddy treated Momma.

I bet Gamaliel wasn't like that. How Carrie got mixed up with an asshole like Jerry I'll never figure out.

Surely he wasn't like that.

I watch Nancy's car disappear over the hill and whistle for Frankie and we go inside.

No Thunderstorm tonight. No ice. Just shine, the good stuff, the triple-filtered stuff. I pour one, a good strong one, and sit in his chair and think about the old man and all the stuff I left out of the stories I told at the service. There were more than a few, mostly about shine and how we got to be partners.

I nod off before I can finish the second glass and sleep until way up into the night.

After that it's off and on sleeping until middle of the morning. I'm dozing off and on and the phone wakes me up.

"What?"

"Boone, is that you? It's Mrs. Thompson, Philip's mother. I was just calling to check on Mr. Everett. I hadn't heard any—"

"He's dead. Service was yesterday."

She's quiet for a minute. "Oh, Boone, I'm so sorry. I didn't hear a thing about it."

"Me neither."

"Really?" She's quiet again, then, "I guess I don't understand."

"I don't either. I wouldn't have known if I hadn't called the home to see if Frankie and I could come by and see him and the others."

"Well, I'm so sorry about all of it, Boone. I'll tell Philip, and if you need anything you be sure and let us know, you hear?"

I nod, and then say, "I will, ma'am. Thanks for calling."

We just sit there with nothing to say for a minute and then I say, "I got to go now, Mrs. Thompson."

"Of course, Boone. I'll let you go." And she hangs up.

I'm sitting there with the phone still in my hand when it rings again.

"Hello?"

"Boone, it's Betty Franklin."

"Okay." I'm not sure why she's calling me. Gamaliel's dead, and I got no reason to go back there.

"Some of the residents here, well, they're sad about losing Gamaliel, but you know he didn't interact with anybody."

I know this. I could barely get him to make eye contact.

"They're sad about losing him, like I said, but they're also sad because they're afraid that they'll never see you and Frankie again."

I don't say anything, and after a second she goes on.

"I told them I would call you and tell you that you're welcome to keep coming here and bringing Frankie."

Her voice gets quieter. "Actually, they didn't say this, but they really need the two of you. They don't have much to look forward to, you know."

"What are you talking about, Betty?"

If she's telling me I need to keep going down there, she's crazy. Nothing there but a bunch of old people waiting to die.

Turns out that's exactly what she's talking about.

"You know how much good you've done down here, Boone? People talk about the last time you and Frankie were here and when you're coming again, and I've already had three people ask me if this, I mean losing Gamaliel, means that they won't get to play with Frankie anymore."

"What makes you think I'd come back down there, down there where Gamaliel died, and I don't even know how he died and I wasn't invited to the service and then I had to get up there and do the damn preacher's job for him because he didn't know Gamaliel at all? I mean, what the hell?"

It hasn't been that long since I was apologizing to Betty for going off on her and here I am doing it again.

"I'm sorry, Betty, I'm doing it again," I say before she can say anything. "I don't mean to yell at you, it's just soon, you know?"

"I know, and I should have given it a few days, Boone, I know that, but I have to tell you that people here really like you and Frankie. They really do."

I need to get off the phone; I can't think about this kind of stuff, not right now.

"Betty, listen, I got to go. Let me call you back about all this."

"Okay, Boone, you take your time, I just wanted you to know what good the two of you do here."

After I get off the phone with Betty I just stand there in the kitchen, staring at the sink. Finally I shake my head, hard, which is a mistake, but it gives me something else to think about.

"C'mon, Frankie, let's go outside before anybody else calls us."

We spend a few minutes in the yard and then I decide to go back into the woods and have a look at Trevor's place from the back. Last time I checked it looked abandoned, and I'm curious. I'd like to know if they're gone.

When we come around through the woods and get to the edge, I can get a good look at the place and it sure looks like nobody lives there anymore. The way it's starting to fall apart, I'm not sure anybody is ever going to live there again, which I think is a good thing. That place has seen its share of death, more than its share, just in the time I've known it. Frankie, then Daddy, then Trevor's mom. Maybe the place is cursed or something.

Thinking about that makes me want to get the hell away from there, so Frankie and I head back to Gamaliel's place. Tiny's truck is in the side yard when we get back.

"Mom said the old guy died," he says as soon as I come up to the back door. He's sitting there, rolling a pair of dice around in his hand. Click, click, click.

"Yeah."

He stands up and sticks the dice in his pocket. "That's rough, man. I know you two were pretty tight."

I nod. "Tight as anybody ever in my life."

He looks down at the ground. "Yeah, I got that feeling."

"Tight as that nut we had to take a hammer to on the old truck," I say.

Tiny looks up and grins a little. "Tight as a tick?"

"Tight as a banjo head." I don't have any idea what that even means, but I remember hearing it somewhere.

"Tight as Mr. Timmons' ass right about now?"

It takes me a second until I remember he's due back in court next week for more stuff from the lake house. I nod, think for a second, and and then say, "Tight as old man Stevens with a dollar."

Tiny laughs. "You got that right." He thinks for a minute. "Tight as the Rayburn boys when they get to playing, what was it, 'Blackberry Blossom'?"

"Tight as the knot in that oak I was trying to split the other day."

He grins. "Tight as a virgin?"

I laugh. "I can't top that one, Tiny."

I'm hoping he doesn't ask me anything about that, because I've never found out how tight a virgin is, or anybody else, far as that goes. I wonder if Nancy's a virgin. I bet she is.

I step over to the door. "You want to come inside for a minute, have an S&S for the old man?"

"Thought you'd never ask," he says, and follows me inside. Frankie is right behind us.

I mix a couple of drinks and we sit, Tiny in Gamaliel's chair and me in the other one, and I tell him about not knowing about the service until the day of, and how the preacher got me up there to talk about Gamaliel, and Tiny says, "Damn preachers."

I nod and say, "I told Mark, that's the preacher's name, I was going to kick his ass for doing that to me and he said, 'Well I guess I'd take it cause I'd do it again', but I didn't do it. Seemed like a waste of time, plus, he's bigger than me."

Tiny laughs again, and says, "I've never known that to stop you before, man."

We sip for another few minutes, and then Tiny says, "Where'd you say you got this stuff?"

I don't know what to do, so I don't say anything.

He keeps going. "I always wondered how hard it would be to make some myself, but I never did anything about it." He looks over at me. "What about you, Boone? You ever wonder what it would be like to make your own?"

He knows. I can tell he knows that Gamaliel used to make this stuff, and he's wondering if I know it too. He's got to know I've got more shine than I let on at the beginning. I'm trying to decide what to do and then I think, what the hell, Jerry's probably about to kick me out of here anyway, I'll be living in the truck and won't have a place to make shine when he does that. Might as well take a chance. I don't think he'll turn me in. I just hope he can keep a secret.

"Actually, Tiny, it's not all that hard. You just got to be careful."

I'm looking into my glass when I say this and don't look up for a few seconds. When I do Tiny is staring at me with a little grin on his face.

"Not all that hard, huh? Care to tell me how you know that?"

Well, you've done it now, I tell myself. At least the old man won't get in any trouble. He's probably laughing at me right now.

"Maybe I wasn't completely straight with you about where this came from."

Chapter Thirty-Two

He's staring at me. "You son of a bitch! You and Gamaliel?"

I nod.

"Where?"

I point up the hill, into the woods.

"You are shitting me." He's still got that little grin on his face.

"I shit you not, Tiny."

He shakes his head. "Right under Mom and Dad's noses. I'll be damned."

I shrug. "Not sure how long it was up there before I knew about it. It was on our land, I mean on the land we used to live on, before."

"Is it still up there? The still, I mean?"

I shake my head. "I took it down when I, I mean when we, when we weren't living there anymore. Gamaliel had a deal going with Daddy and I just stepped in when he took off, and then when Gamaliel went into the hospital I figured I'd better do something about it. I didn't want anybody to find it, you know?"

"So where is it?"

"Here and there. Mostly it's just buckets and stuff like that, made up to hold in the steam. The coil is out in the shed, that's the thing that looks most like a still, like the old pictures in the history books."

Tiny sits back in his chair. "I will be dipped in shit."

I can't think of anything else to say, and I'm afraid I've said too much already, so I shut up and get out of the chair, take his glass and mine into the kitchen, and mix a couple with the good stuff, just to show him what I've got. I figure if he tells anybody it's all gone anyway, so I might as well enjoy it.

He takes a sip, then a long drink. "Man, that is smooth!"

"Triple filtered. Gamaliel says, I mean said, it makes all the difference."

Saying that makes me sad, having to talk about him being not here, never here again. I need to find out what happened to Gamaliel. I mean, how he died. Usually I don't care about that kind of stuff but I'm thinking I'd like to know if it was quick, or if it hurt, or anything like that.

I miss the first part of what Tiny says. When I start listening, he's saying, "So how long does it take? Is there a recipe or do you, like, make it up kind of as you go? Where are you going to set it back up?"

"I don't know about that, Tiny."

"Of course you're going to set it back up! You're part of a, you know, tradition. You can't just let that kind of thing go, man. I mean, I've got lots of friends who — "

"You can't tell anybody about this, Tiny. I mean, nobody."

He's been leaning forward, all excited, and now he leans back in the chair and goes quiet for a minute and then says, "You're right, Boone. You're right."

"You know if I thought you were going to tell anybody I'd have to kill you," I say, trying for a really low, scary voice. Tiny looks over at me and then starts laughing.

"Yeah, I guess you would at that. Okay, Boone, just you and me."

I take a deep breath and blow it out. "Good. Good."

"So I want in."

That surprises me a little. "You want to make shine with me?"

"Sure I do. Long as we're smart nobody'll find out, and you and me'll have plenty to drink and maybe a little to share."

"Well, hell, yes!" I say, and raise my glass to him.

He raises his, and we both take a big drink.

I set mine down first. Tiny does the same, and we sit and grin at each other for a while.

"So," Tiny finally says, "how much of this do you know how to do?"

"Hold on a second," I say, and go into the kitchen. Under the basket Gamaliel had all his bread and crackers and stuff piled up in is the recipe. I pull it out and take it back to the sunroom, hand it to Tiny, and say, "I've got this, and I've done the last four or five steps with Gamaliel. The beginning's going to take a little work."

He takes the paper from me, looks at it, and then reads it through slow. He looks up at me and says, "What the hell's 'a good handful'?"

I shrug. "Like I said, it's going to take a little work."

We go through the recipe together and most of it makes good sense. The first couple of tries might not be the best, but both of us think it's worth a try.

"I've got a spot I'm thinking about," Tiny says.

"On your farm?"

He nods. "Out on the edge of it, really. Our land backs up against some state-owned property that nobody wants; it's too steep and it's all rocks and clay. Last year the state said something about a natural area or park or something but they haven't done a thing, and I don't think they're going to."

"Has it got water?"

He frowns. "Not real close, but I think there's a stream over on the state land about a hundred yards from where I'm thinking about. We'll have to look at it. How much water are we gonna need?"

"A lot, I think. I don't think it's anything we can't carry if we have to."

"How about all the rest of this stuff?"

I show him the list of businesses. "This was with the recipe."

"Did Gamaliel give you all this?"

"You mean the recipe? He told me where to look for it. It just took me a while to find it."

Chapter Thirty-Three

The next couple of days I'm back and forth about a bunch of stuff.

I'm pretty sure I can trust Tiny, but I don't have a whole lot of experience of being able to trust people, so sometimes I think it was a good idea to tell him about the shine and sometimes I think it's the stupidest thing I've done in a long while.

The whole thing with Betty has me all mixed up, too. I don't want to go back there and walk around where I used to hang out with Gamaliel. I don't owe them anything; they didn't even tell me about him dying. But a couple of the old guys were okay, and there's that old woman that I just saw that one time, who said she was related to Momma, and Frankie sure seems to like it there, all those people telling her how great she is. She just eats that up.

Jerry, now that son of a bitch I'm not mixed up about at all. It wouldn't surprise me at all to find out he's the one who didn't want me to know about the memorial. He's probably got Carrie so scared she'll do whatever he says. I know what that's like. I've seen it. So I'm expecting any day now to get a phone call from one of them telling me to get out, and I've got nowhere to go. Nowhere.

The biggest thing, though, is Nancy. I'm all torn up about her.

I like her more than anybody else, ever. Hell, I think I might love her, but I can't tell her that. I mean, look at her, smart, rich, probably going off to college, and me, poor, not even a high school education, maybe out on the street before September's over.

Then I think about her dad and how he looked at her mom and how her mom acted around him. I don't know a lot, but I know what's going on there. Seen it too many times to think it's anything else. And she's right in the middle of it. I don't know what I'd do if she got hurt. Probably something really stupid.

Tiny calls me middle of the week.

"You doing anything right now?"

"I was going to meet my banker, but I can put it off."

"Banker, my ass. Well, if you can put off that meeting, I thought we might take a run up into the woods. You know, just to look around."

He says he'll meet me in their big field out behind Gamaliel's house.

"Bring your shotgun and Frankie if you want to," he says.

I know Frankie would love a long run in the woods, so I grab the gun and a pocket full of shells, call Frankie, and we head out across the back yard and up into Thompson land.

Tiny's got his gun, too, but we end up not firing a single shot. It's still summer, and the trees are full and the underbrush is thick. We'd be shooting blind if we were aiming more than twenty yards out, and, anyway, we're not here for game.

The spot Tiny had told me about was just about perfect. Not too big a clearing, but enough to set something up.

Tiny points to a big rock, looks kind of like an anvil but twice as big. "That's the property line. We could set up just on the other side, in case any of my family should wander up here. That way it'd be on state land, not ours."

"Makes sense to me."

We scout around a little more. Just like he said, there's water not quite a hundred yards away, and enough laurel for cover from anybody that didn't just happen to walk right into the clearing.

I'm starting to get excited about this; I wanted to do it with Gamaliel, but the old man's gone, and I think Tiny's going to be somebody I can trust.

We head back to Gamaliel's house after spending a little time just wandering around. Frankie is in dog heaven; she's never been to this area before, and she's wearing herself out following one scent after another.

Tiny points to her. "She's going to sleep for about fourteen hours when you get her back home."

I say, "It'll be good for her. She hasn't had a run like this in a long time."

When we get back in early afternoon, she goes straight to her spot in the sunroom and collapses. I can tell she's dreaming a little, the way her legs keep jerking like she's running, but other than that she's gone.

Tiny says we should start taking stuff up there a little at a time, which is a good idea.

"Don't go the same way twice in a row," I say. "We don't want a path."

We agree to start on Friday, two days away, and Tiny heads back home.

After he leaves I turn to Frankie.

"Well, girl, what do you want to do about the nursing home? Do you want to go see Betty, and Mr. Sanderson, and Kelsey? We could go there tomorrow if Betty says it's okay."

As soon as I start naming people down at the nursing home Frankie is on her feet, at the door, ready to go. She looks back at me and then at the door. When I don't move she trots back over to me and nudges her nose up under my hand. Then she just stands there like, "Okay, you know what to do. Get going."

I give up and move my hand until it's behind her ears and start scratching. Frankie's eyes close and she stands perfectly still, loving every minute of it.

"Damn, dog, sometimes I'm jealous of you," I say. "It sure don't take much to make you happy, does it?"

Frankie doesn't answer. She's too busy being happy.

Thursday I decide to call Betty and see about paying a visit.

"You come on down here anytime you want, Boone," she says as soon as I bring it up. "You know the folks would love to see you and Frankie."

"I was thinking about noon or so today if that's all right," I say, looking at the clock. It's about ten, a few minutes past, and I've only been up for about a half an hour.

"Noon is great," she says.

Frankie and I don't get there until about half past, and most of the residents there have finished their lunch. A lot of them are outside, just sitting around. Most of them don't notice when we come around the corner until Frankie starts going from one person to another, and then everybody wants to pet her.

Thing is, she won't stay with anybody for more than a few seconds, and I finally realize she's looking for Gamaliel.

"C'mere, girl," I say, and give the leash a tug. Frankie pulls for just a second and then trots over to me.

"He's gone, Frankie," I say quietly. "Gamaliel's not here, not anymore."

She doesn't understand, of course. There's no way she would, unless she had been here when he died. That reminds me, and I start off toward the main building, Frankie trotting behind me.

Betty has somebody in her office, so we stand around in the hallway for about five minutes, until she's done and the visitor leaves. She catches my eye and says, "Come right on in, Boone. You too, Frankie."

I stop just inside the door. "I won't take up much of your time, Betty. I was just wondering about how Gamaliel died. You know, was it quick, did he suffer, that kind of thing."

Betty doesn't say anything for a long minute.

"Betty? What's going on?"

She still doesn't say anything and I'm about to ask again a lot louder when she says, "You know, Boone, some people just, well, they just decide. I didn't believe it before I started working here, and I don't have any proof, nothing scientific, nothing at all, but I think your friend decided he was done with life."

"What the hell are you talking about?"

The question is out of my mouth before I think about it, but already I know I didn't need to ask it.

Gamaliel would have hated what his life had turned into, I know that for sure. He was too old by the time I met him to do much besides stay around his house, but he was on his own and took care of himself and was his own boss and I know he hated being wheeled around, fed mush and who knows what kind of shit, having somebody get him up, get him dressed, wipe his ass, put him to bed. I'm sure he was completely miserable. If he could've talked, I bet he would have been begging somebody to put him out of his misery.

Betty's just watching me, like she knows what I'm thinking.

Eventually I look at her and say, "Yeah, I could see Gamaliel doing that. Why do you think that's what happened?"

"I don't know, exactly," she says, looking at me and then down at the desk. "He was stable and doing well, I mean, considering everything." She drums her fingers on the desktop. "He didn't fall, or suffocate, or have internal bleeding, at least as far as we know, it was just that one minute he was here and the next he was gone."

"What do you mean, as far as we know? Were you in there, in his room, when it happened? You said one minute he was there and the next he was gone. Did you see it happen?"

She doesn't answer me, just picks up the phone. After a second she says, "Would you ask Maryanne to come in, please?" She puts the phone down and says, "You'll need to ask Maryanne about that. I wasn't there, but she was."

While we're waiting on this Maryanne person, I say, "So what did you mean when you said as far as we know?"

"What?"

"You said he didn't have internal bleeding as far as you knew. What did that mean?"

"I just meant that it's pretty rare to do an autopsy on someone in a home, Boone. That's all. We didn't have any reason to suspect anything other than a natural death."

There's a knock on the door and I turn around.

Maryanne is maybe a year or two older than me. She looks like she has some Mexican in her. She's a little shorter than I am, and really good looking. She stands there like she thinks she's in trouble about something, and I wonder if she's one of those illegal Mexicans Daddy used to cuss about and accuse of taking all the good jobs.

"Come in, Maryanne," says Betty. "Don't worry, you're not in trouble." She turns to me. "One of the things about being a supervisor is that everybody that gets called to come here thinks they're in trouble of some kind."

Maryanne steps in and still looks scared. Then I realize she's looking at Frankie. I never think of Frankie as being scary, but she is kind of a big dog, and I've never seen Maryanne around here when Frankie has been visiting.

"It's okay," I say, "she won't hurt you unless she thinks you're trying to hurt me." I smile at her, but she doesn't smile back. She comes in the rest of the way and kind of slides sideways so she's on the other side of Betty's little office. That doesn't put her very far away from Frankie, so I step around the dog so I'm between Maryanne and Frankie. "Is that better?" I say, partly to her and partly to Betty, who's been watching all this.

"I think so," Betty says. "Maryanne doesn't know what a great dog Frankie is. Maryanne, you should see how the patients love her, and Boone, too."

Maryanne looks at me. "You're Boone?"

I nod.

"Mr. Everett's son Jerry told me that you were not supposed to have anything to do with his father."

Chapter Thirty-Four

"What did you say?" I'm so mad I can barely ask the question. I look over at Betty. "You need to tell me what's going on here!"

Betty looks like she's never heard this before, and I want to believe that, but I'm so pissed that I'm not sure I believe anything anybody around here says.

"Boone? Would you and Frankie excuse us for just a minute?"

I'm still looking at Betty, but she's not looking at me. She's looking at Maryanne, and I think maybe Maryanne really is in trouble now.

"I want to hear this," I say, but I know what I should do is step outside.

"Please, Boone, let me try to get this sorted out, okay?"

"Okay," I say, staring at Maryanne. I tighten up on Frankie's leash and we go out. What I want to do is leave Frankie in there; maybe she'll help Maryanne remember whatever it is Betty's going to be asking her about.

After a couple of minutes I decide to go back outside and see if anybody's still hanging out after lunch, but the little courtyard is empty. Frankie and I walk around the back of the main building and have a look. We've never been here before.

I can see the chapel off to the right, just the back end, but I figure that's what I'm looking at. There's an open space, kind of like the space with the fountain, but bigger, no pond or fountain, and a couple of gravel paths winding back and forth. On the opposite side of the open space are a few more buildings. One of them looks like a big toolshed; the front door is open, and I can see shelves and a lawn mower. The other two look like houses, smaller than Gamaliel's house, and I can't tell any more than that.

"Boone?"

I turn toward the main building and Betty is standing there.

"Can you come back in my office, please? I think I know what's going on now."

I'm curious about those other houses, but Frankie and I head back in and follow Betty to her office. Maryanne is still there, looking a little red-eyed.

Betty sits down behind her desk. "Boone, would you close the door?"

I push the door shut and turn back to her. "Okay. Now what?"

"Maryanne made a mistake earlier, but we don't think it was her fault," Betty says. "Maryanne, why don't you tell Boone what you told me?"

Maryanne won't even look at me at first, but eventually says, "Jerry, I mean Mr. Phillips, he never said son-in-law to me. He made me think he was Mr. Everett's son. That's why I said that to you."

"With two different last names?" I'm not buying this, not yet.

She spreads her hands, looking helpless. "I didn't think about that, I guess. He was here so often, and his wife seemed so nice, I didn't ask any questions."

I can see Jerry letting her believe something like that, so I'm thinking I should just let this go. I already knew he was a lying piece of shit, and this just backs that up.

"What I really want to know is how he died. Betty said you were there."

She nods. "I was there, it was the middle of the morning. I was cleaning up, like I usually do, and Mr. Everett was just lying there, you know, just lying there. When I looked over at him he would be looking at me, and then I went into the bathroom to check on, you know, tissues and soap and things like that, and when I came back in, he still had his eyes open, but he had stopped breathing. I ran to get the nurse, and she called the doctor, but everybody knew he was gone. I'm very sorry. Mrs. Franklin told me how close you two were."

I nod. "We were, we were very close, Maryanne. Do you think, I mean, was he hurting? I hope he wasn't hurting."

She shakes her head. "I don't think so. I think he just went away."

"Thank you, Maryanne," Betty says. "You can go now."

She is out the door like a flash, and I turn to Betty. "Thanks for that, Betty. I don't know what I'd do if I thought he suffered."

Betty gives me kind of a sad smile. "You're a good person, Boone."

"Well, I don't know about all that," I'm looking down at the floor and thinking about all the shitty stuff I've done, just in the last year or so. And that doesn't even count the stuff I've thought about doing.

"I do," she says. "I can tell. I'm pretty good at reading people, and you're one of the good ones. I still smile thinking about those stories you told at the service. Most of them I didn't know, and neither did the rest of the staff, or the people here. It was good to hear about that side of him."

I just stand there, mainly because I don't know what to say when people tell me shit like this.

"The other thing is, I'm really glad you decided to give it another try," she says. "The people here, some of them, nobody gives a damn about them. Excuse my language," she says, seeing me look at her like, what did you just say?

"I see the way they are around you and Frankie, and it's a good thing. I just hope you don't take that away from them, now that they've had a taste."

I don't like this kind of talk at all. It feels like she's trying to make me feel guilty if I decide not to come back or don't come back as often as she thinks I should. I can't stay in here and listen to this any more. There is one thing I'm curious about that she can help me with, though.

"Do you still have an old lady, taller than me, I only talked to her once. She was standing off by herself."

"That sounds like Mrs. Alder. Her family moved her to another facility closer to where they live. Why do you ask?"

"Nothing," I say. "Nothing. I think I'll go out and say goodbye to whoever's out there."

"Okay," she says. "I do hope you keep coming, Boone. The people here — "

"I know, they need me," I say. I can't hear any more of this, I really can't. "I get it. I'll call you before I come back down, okay?"

I'm out the office door and down the hallway as fast as I can go, thinking, Mrs. Alder might be closer to her family now, but she's farther away from me, and maybe I'm family, too.

Chapter Thirty-Five

Tiny shows up on Friday, just like he said he would.

"So what's the first step, Boone?"

I look at him; he's like a little kid, like he can't wait to open presents. At least I guess that's what it's like, having presents to open.

Daddy never would let Momma get any gifts from those places that made up packages for poor people. He sure was a proud man, considering he didn't have all that much to be proud about. Anyway, Momma would always try on Christmas and birthdays to make something special for supper. Maybe a dessert, maybe real homemade cheeseburgers. A few times we got presents wrapped in newspaper. It was always something she had made, some piece of clothes or something like that. I hear all those people on TV and places talk about how the homemade presents are the best, and I guess if you get a lot of stuff from the store that might be true, to get something homemade every now and then. If that's all you ever get, though, it's just one more thing for the other kids to make fun of you about, and one more reason not to talk to any of them about birthdays or holidays or anything like that.

"Hey, Boone. Man, you're a million miles off. You thinking about Nancy?"

Tiny's got a grin on his face and I can't help but smile back.

"Maybe."

"Well, stop it and let's figure this out. I want to get started."

We're sitting at the table and I lean back, thinking for a second.

"I think we divide up what needs to be carried up there and decide when to go. We don't want to go at the same time or by the same way. Gamaliel said always be more careful than you think you need to be. Better to do too much than not enough."

Tiny nods. "Makes sense to me. So what goes up there?"

We make a list and divide it up. "We'll stack it all in the shed for now," I say. "I'm almost always here, so when you come by to get some of your stuff, we can decide then when I'm going to make my run, and keep swapping back and forth. Should just take a few trips."

"Starting to feel like we're doing something against the law," Tiny says.

"We are," I remind him. "Just because those big companies are making what they call moonshine nowadays doesn't mean that a couple of guys can do the same thing."

"Well, that's not fair."

"Right. It's not."

We stare at each other for a few seconds, then Tiny gets up and stretches.

"I think I'd like to walk the property line later on today, Boone, so if I'm going to help you get that shed organized, we need to go ahead and knock it out now."

"Sound's good," I say. "I'll probably hang out here today and maybe take Frankie for a run tomorrow afternoon."

By Sunday we've got everything up there and Tiny drops by in the middle of the afternoon. We go over the recipe and make plans to start our first trial run.

"Got plenty of dry wood up there already," Tiny says. "I think we're going to have to be up there together at least a few times."

"Right," I say. "Now we start paying attention to the weather. Rain or too much wind, and we can't do anything."

"What does the wind have to — okay, never mind."

"Right again," I say. "What do you have going on Tuesday morning?"

And that's how we start our partnership. We divide up the jobs; I order some cracked corn from one of the stores on Gamaliel's list and yeast from another one. He had the phone numbers listed, and when I call to make the order, the person at the first store says, "Mr. Everett, good to hear from you, but you don't sound like yourself. Everything okay with you?" I tell them he's not here, which is true, and he wanted me to make some phone calls for him.

I have to wait for an hour on Tuesday for Tiny to show up. Frankie has been sitting under the big rock and is up on her feet, looking down the hill, a good forty-five seconds before Tiny sticks his head out of the brush. When he sees me looking right at him he looks disappointed.

"Thought I was being real quiet there."

"You were," I say. "I didn't hear a thing. Frankie heard you a full minute ago."

He looks over at Frankie and shakes his head. "Figures."

He takes off the backpack; it hits the ground with a thud.

"What's first?"

I point to an old washtub and a couple of buckets. "Every time either one of us comes up here, we should go get a couple of buckets of water from the spring we found and pour them into that tub."

"Okay."

"We can cover it up with this," and I pull an old tarp out from behind the rock. "Weight down the corners and it should keep leaves and shit from blowing into it."

"Wouldn't mind much if it rained into it, though, right?"

"Right. So when we get a little water in there we can take a look at that recipe.

"It says we need sugar, cracked corn, yeast, and rye. I got the corn ordered, should be here in a couple of days. I bought a bag of sugar, and you should do that too so they won't wonder why I'm buying so much. I ordered some yeast, too, so when we get that, we just need some rye grain and we're good to start."

"I know a guy who grows rye in one of his fields," Tiny says. "How much do we need?"

"Couple of pounds, is all. We get all that and put it in that keg I brought up from the old still and let it set for a week and a half or so, until it stops bubbling."

"You ever figure out how much a good handful of yeast is?"

I look at Tiny's hands. "Gamaliel's hands were bigger than mine, so I think we use your hand and just grab some and throw it in there."

"Okay. Sounds good to me. After that, we cook, right?"

"Well, we got to pour it through a pillowcase to get all the solid stuff out, but then, yeah, then we cook."

Tiny's been leaning forward and now he leans back on his hands and says, "Sounds good, Boone. Sounds real good."

Tiny agrees to go up a few times with a bow saw to get some wood ready for when we need it. A chainsaw would attract attention, and we don't want that. When I mention the bow saw, Tiny says, "Man, there's a whole way you have to think to do this stuff, isn't there? I mean, I would've just grabbed one of our chainsaws and headed up there, but you're right. Keep it quiet. I get it."

He heads off and I watch him going, thinking, so you would have grabbed one of your chainsaws. How many chainsaws do you guys have?

Man, you have no idea how good you've got it.

Chapter Thirty-Six

Nancy calls me on Labor Day morning.

"You okay?"

I have to think about why she's asking me that.

"Yeah, I just been hanging out with Tiny and stuff. Oh, and I went back to the home the other day."

"Without me?"

She sounds disappointed, and I start to say I don't need her holding my hand all the time, but then I think maybe I do need that, so I just say, "I wanted to try it on my own, see if I could do it. I know you're in school and all, and if I'm going to keep doing this, I can't always have you along."

"Oh. So, how was it?"

I tell her about Maryanne, except the part about her being young and good looking, and about how Gamaliel died, and about talking with Betty.

"You really believe that, don't you, Boone? That he just decided to die?"

"Yeah, I think I do, darlin'. It kind of sounds like him, like it's how he would want to go out."

She's quiet for a few seconds and then says, "I bet you're right. Anyway, the reason I called is that we're grilling burgers for Labor Day and I thought you might want to come over and have one."

"Or two?" I haven't figured out how to fry a really good burger, and a grilled one sounds awfully good to me.

She laughs. "Or two. What do you think?"

"I think I'd like that. What time?"

"About four or four-thirty, I guess. You want to bring Frankie?"

I hadn't thought about that. They don't have a dog, but I know the neighbor does, a German Shepard kind of dog, pretty big.

"You sure that would be okay? Will that work with the dog next door?"

"Oh. I'm not sure, to tell you the truth. Hold on a second." She's gone for half a minute and comes back and says, "Dad says that dog's kind of mean. Maybe you'd better leave her at home."

"Sounds good. So, about four?"

"See you then, sweetie."

At about fifteen til four I give Frankie a little extra food and a pat on the back. "Be back soon, girl."

I drive the the truck over to Nancy's house, wondering if this meal is going to be like the last one.

First thing that happens, Nancy's dad offers me a beer almost as soon as my feet hit the driveway.

"Hello, Boone, good to see you again! Glad you could come over. Have a cold one."

Nancy is behind him shaking her head, hard.

I say, "I better not, got to drive home later, but thanks anyway."

He looks at me. "What are you, a little girl? Come on, have a beer with me."

Nancy comes up about then and says, "Dad, you know Boone's not legal yet."

Her dad snorts. "Not legal, my left foot! He's enough of a man to defend his property, isn't he? Nancy told me that story about you going up to try to help your neighbor and getting shot in the process. Damn brave of you, son. How is Mr., what was his name again?"

"Dad, I told you, Mr. Everett passed away just a week or so ago," Nancy grabs me by the arm and whispers, "I'm sorry," into my ear and leads me around to the back.

Cyrus is in one of the chairs next to the grill and waves. "You must be Boone. Nice to meet you. Nancy talks about you a lot, you know. She thinks you like her." He grins at Nancy and she gives him a dirty look.

Nancy's mom comes out of the house with a tray of hamburgers and a stack of cheese slices. "Hello, Boone, good to see you again. I'm so glad you could join us."

"Afternoon, ma'am."

She beams at Nancy. "He is so polite."

Yeah," Cyrus says, "not like that — "

He doesn't get to finish because Nancy's dad comes around from the front and says, "Boy, is that grill ready for me to start?"

Cyrus loses his grin and he pretty much completely changes. He gets out of the chair real quick and steps over to the grill. His head is down, his whole body is slumped, and he looks like a whipped dog. I recognize that look right away and it just confirms what I thought last time about Nancy's dad.

"I — I — I think so, Dad," his voice is different, too, and I catch Nancy looking at me to see if I've noticed it.

What I'm thinking is how soon can I get out of here. This looks like a really nice house, nice family, all that stuff, but underneath it feels a lot like the one I grew up in, the one that blew up a little over a year ago. I hate to think about Nancy growing up in this kind of place.

She's the oldest, but she's not catching any of her dad's shit, and I wonder if it's because she's a girl. It sure looks like Cyrus is catching all of it, at least right now.

"The damn grill should have been hot already, boy," her dad isn't shouting, but his voice has an edge to it that's kind of scary. I look around to see what everybody else is doing about that.

Nancy is looking at the ground, and then at me, and then back at the ground, so she knows that I'm picking up on it. Her mom is so cheerful that it feels faked and it probably is; I bet she's just hoping that I'm not noticing it. Maybe she thinks other families aren't like this and so people won't catch the little stuff that gives it away, and if she's happy and shiny and busy enough, they'll get through one more evening.

The thing is, I don't know what to do. I don't know whether Nancy wants me to help her mom pretend that nothing's going on or not. I don't know whether I'm supposed to let her know that I get it, that I know what's happening, or not. I don't know whether to stand up for Cyrus or not.

Damn, I wish Gamaliel was still around.

By the end of the evening I'm so tense that I'm sure somebody has noticed it. But it looks like everybody's pretending to be normal and happy and all that shit. I can feel it, though, just underneath, and a couple of times it feels like it's so close to exploding that one word from me would touch it off.

"You're a quiet kind of guy," Nancy's dad is saying to me. "I like that. Shows strength. You hang onto this one, little girl," he shouts across the patio to Nancy, who's sitting with her mom. They're getting the ice cream out of the electric ice cream maker. I've seen a couple of them on TV but never up close, and I've never had ice cream from one before.

"Daddy!" Nancy acts like she's embarrassed, but gives me a big smile before she's back to working on the ice cream.

"Those were sure good burgers, Mr. — "

"None of that 'Mr.' stuff from you, Boone, you hear me? You call me Stan." Her dad is on his fourth beer since I got here.

"My family taught me to be respectful, but since you asked me to, I'll try. Those were awful good burgers, Stan."

He turns to Cyrus. "See that, boy? The kid's got respect. He'll go a long way with that. You could learn a lot from Boone."

Oh, shit, I say to myself. What's Cyrus going to do with that?

He might be used to it by now, or it might really piss him off. I wait a second before I look over at him, but he's looking across the yard to where the German Shepard is penned up.

I get up and head that way and Cyrus follows me. When I get close to the pen the dog starts raising hell and Cyrus says, "Our neighbor says he'll take your arm right off." He's not looking at me. "Course you already knew that, didn't you? I mean, I hear I can learn a lot from you, so you must know everything, pretty much."

"Man, that just ain't true," I say. "Just because your dad thinks I know a lot doesn't mean I do. He barely knows me."

"Knows you enough to rub my face in it," Cyrus mutters.

"Don't lay that on me, man," I say, starting to get a little mad. "I just came over here to eat a cheeseburger."

"Yeah, right. You came over to kiss Dad's ass because of my sister."

I give him a look. "You know better than that."

He doesn't say anything, just mumbles something too low for me to hear. I know I should just let it go, but I can't do it.

"Nancy tell you anything about me?"

"Just that she felt sorry for you being so poor and all."

"Is that right?"

"Yeah, that's about it. Same thing my mom says."

"Look, I know you already lied to me, first time we talked, that whole Randy thing. I got no reason to believe you now."

I look over at him and it looks like he's getting ready to jump me.

"That'd be a real big mistake, Cyrus," I say, real low and even.

"What would be? You think I can't take you?"

"I think after I finished kicking your ass your dad would start in where I left off. You'd best walk away, pretend this never happened, and I'll do the same."

He starts to step toward me and then turns and heads back to the house. He says something again too

305

low for me to hear, and I'm thinking that if I was anywhere besides Nancy's house I'd mash him right into the dirt.

"Ice cream's ready!" Nancy's mom is calling us back in, and I'm looking forward to trying this stuff.

It may be the best thing I've ever put in my mouth, and I tell Nancy's mom so. She gets all embarrassed and pleased at the same time and makes me have another bowl. It's not hard to, and I probably wouldn't have fought her too much on a third bowl, but she doesn't offer.

I make it through the rest of the evening without any trouble; Cyrus is all mad and feeling sorry for himself, which I understand, because I've been in that same place. Only difference is that I was the oldest and I had a brother that was everybody's favorite. Stan is on his second six-pack and is pretty much leaving Cyrus and Nancy's mom alone; actually looks like he's about to fall asleep in his chair. Nancy's mom doesn't have to put on so much of an act with Stan dozing in the chair, so she starts acting like a real person.

Nancy is behaving herself, but just barely. She's sitting right up next to me and keeps putting her hand on my thigh and rubbing it. She'll lean over and rest against me and once when I say something about what a great meal it was she says, "Why, thank you, sweetie," and gives me a kiss on the cheek. Cyrus makes choking noises, but Nancy's mom just smiles. Her smile's kind of sad, though.

When I get up to leave Nancy's mom looks around and can't find anything to send home with me, since we ate all the burgers and most of the ice cream. She tries to send what they have left with me and I say, "I can't do that, I had two bowls already, and I'm afraid it might melt on the way home anyway."

I can tell she feels bad, like she's not a good hostess if she doesn't send something with me, but it really doesn't bother me and I try to let her know that.

Eventually I get away from her; Cyrus doesn't even look up when I say goodbye and I'm thinking, if Stan was awake you'd be in trouble for that, Cyrus, don't you know that?

Nancy says, "I'm going to walk Boone out to his truck," and her mom smiles and says, "Don't stay out there too long in the dark, dear."

Nancy laughs. "I won't, Mom," she says, and we head around the corner of the house to where the truck is sitting.

Chapter Thirty-Seven

Tuesday I get up around ten and spend a little time with Frankie out in the yard, since she was kept up so much last night. She's thinking of this place as her home, it's easy to see that. There's a route she takes every day, checking her territory for intruders or just something interesting.

I figure it's only a matter of time before Jerry makes some kind of move on this place, and when I think about that, I don't know whether or not to fight him about it. I believe what Carrie told me Gamaliel said about me staying here as long as I want to, but I didn't hear it, and he's gone, and if it comes down to it, it'll be her word against Jerry's if she'd even be willing to stand against him.

During the service she looked like she was, well, enjoying is not the right word, appreciating hearing the stories I told. Since then I haven't heard a single word from her, and it's coming up time to pay bills, and she's supposed to take care of those.

What if she thinks that now that Gamaliel's gone, paying those bills is not her problem anymore? The more I think about that the more I'm afraid that's exactly what she might be thinking. If that's true then she needs to tell me so, to my face, instead of just not talking to me at all. I think about calling her, but I don't do it. For one thing, I don't want to take a chance on Jerry picking up. He's the last person in this world I want to talk to. For another, I've got this feeling that when I do talk to her it's not going to be good.

I'm thinking it's Tiny's turn to go check on the mash. We got all the ingredients end of last week and just guessed on how much yeast to throw in there to get it going. I've only been up once and it was starting to do something, but I wasn't in on this part of it with Gamaliel, so I'm not sure what it was doing. I know that batch we finished had sat for so long that there wasn't anything happening, like bubbles or whatever, and I think we need to wait until it calms down. I give Tiny a call.

"Hey, it's Boone. What are you up to today?"

"I don't know, probably head into town later, maybe go for a walk if I have time."

So it is his turn.

"Sounds good; if you do end up going to town, stop by here, I might want to ride along or ask you to pick up something for me."

"Yes, sir, Massa Boone, I'll be right sure to do that."

We both laugh and I say, "Well, as long as you've got a plan. Maybe I'll see you later."

After I hang up I think, okay, I'll need to go check day after tomorrow.

So I've got the day free, and what I really want to do is see Nancy. I can't, because she's back in school, but I think Tuesday is one of her free nights. If she doesn't have too much work to do maybe we can spend a little time together.

I still haven't talked to her about Labor Day, and I think she knows that I saw stuff at her house that reminded me of how I came up, especially how Cyrus got treated by Stan.

I'd like to tell Cyrus that I know what he's going through, but I figure he's too mad at me to hear anything I've got to say. Can't say I blame him, his dad treating him like that in front of company. We weren't much for company when I was his age, Daddy already had a reputation as a mean drunk and nobody would have wanted to come over. Well, Curt came a few times, but we'd just head right out into the woods and never really saw my folks.

All this family stuff makes me think about Hannah. I don't even know if she's still with Aunt Claire, and they don't know I'm living in this house. They couldn't call me if something happened to

Hannah, and now that I think about it I'm ashamed of myself. Poor kid got dumped just the way I did.

I'm going to call her real soon, I promise myself. I'm sure she's still with Aunt Claire; I can't see Momma's new man, whatever his name is, letting her add a little kid to their group.

She just left the both of us, first me, then Hannah. That makes me mad when I think about it, about how she picked Jake, I think his name was Jake, over her own blood. From what I saw of him, he wasn't much better than Daddy.

Pretty soon I've forgotten all about calling Hannah and I'm feeling like I need to talk to Nancy. I feel that a lot these days, like she's some kind of solid ground for me. She's seen me mad, and scared, and a little crazy, and still stands right with me. I've never had anybody like that before, not even Momma. She wasn't strong enough, not by herself, and I don't think she had anybody to stand with her besides us kids. Then when she lost Frankie, she just collapsed. No, Momma never stood with me the way Nancy does. I really need that.

I'm still thinking about calling Nancy when she calls me.

"Boone? Are you busy right now?"

"I'm almost never busy. Only thing I was doing was thinking about calling you."

Usually she'll laugh at something like that, but not this time.

"Well, I guess it's okay that I called you, then?"

"What's wrong, darlin'?"

"Well, nothing really, I guess."

I'm starting to get worried here. "Nancy, I can tell something's wrong. Why don't you just tell me?"

"Is it okay if I come over? I mean now?"

"It's always okay if you come over. I'll be right here."

I look at the clock after I'm off the phone. She's cutting a class to come over here. I don't like how this is going. Nancy never cuts class.

When she gets here she jumps out of the car and ignores Frankie, which isn't like her at all. She runs up to me and grabs me and holds me so tight I can barely breathe. I don't think she's crying, but she's not letting go enough for me to get a look at her. So I do the only thing I know to do. I squeeze back.

After a long time she eases up and says, "Got time to fix me an S&S?"

"Sure," I say. "I was just getting ready to have one."

I fix a couple, weak for her and strong for me, and she says, "I need to talk to you, Boone, and it's serious."

Immediately I think she's getting ready to dump me, and the anger flares up strong. I'm wondering who the guy is, and I'm about to ask when she says, "It's about last night."

Okay. Wrong again, as usual.

"Okay, what about last night?"

Nancy drinks half her S&S before she puts the glass down. She looks at me and then down at the floor and then back at me, looking me right in the eyes.

"You remember how after that first time you came over, I came by here and told you all about how Dad treated us, and you said you understood?"

I nod.

"And how you said that your daddy treated you the same or worse?"

I nod again.

"So you know, don't you?"

"Know about what?"

She looks upset. "Don't do this, sweetie, not right now. Like I said, this is serious."

"You mean about your mom?"

She waits.

"And your dad?"

She's still waiting.

"And about him and Cyrus?"

Her eyes get real wide when I say that, but she doesn't move.

"What I don't know about is you."

She looks down at the floor and keeps her head down this time. "How do you know all this?"

"Well, I don't know all this, I mean, I don't know details. You want me to tell you what I do know?

Then you tell me whatever I don't know that you think I should. Okay?"

She nods.

"Okay, well, here goes." I stop for a second, wondering how much I need to tell her about me to kind of balance this out.

"You remember what you told me before, right? About how your dad talked to your mom and how she just stood there and took it?"

She's back to looking me right in the eyes.

"You didn't say much about Cyrus, and nothing about you, but I know what's going on between your dad and Cyrus. I know he puts your brother down and makes fun of him and generally tells him he's worthless, and I know it cut your brother like a knife to have your dad tell me how great I am, and please call me Stan, and all that stuff. When we were out at the dog pen, you know, your neighbor's dog, I thought he was going to jump me, and if things were reversed, I know I would have done it. So I know Cyrus has more self-control than I do.

"So you're the big question for me. If your dad's done anything to you, I swear I'll go over there right now and kick his ass all the way across the county line."

Nancy smiles a little at that. "I believe you would, sweetie."

"So has he?"

She doesn't say anything.

314

"Nancy, has he done anything to you?"

Slowly she shakes her head. "No, not really. There was one time, about a year ago, he was really drunk, and I turned to look at him and he looked away real quick, but the way he was looking, before he looked away, was pretty creepy. And I'm not even sure about that, Boone, honest I'm not, so no, he's never done anything to me."

"If he ever does — "

"I know, I know. But he won't. I'm not worried about me. I'm worried about Cyrus, Boone, I really am. I'm afraid Dad'll say or do something to Mom or to him and he'll just lose it. Can you talk to him for me?"

So that's why she's here. She's worried about her little brother. I get that, and I know that right now he wouldn't hear a thing I have to say, not after last night. I tell Nancy that, and I can see she knows it's right, but she doesn't like it.

"I'll talk to him anytime you say, you know I will, and I'll tell it to him straight, you know that, too, but right now I'm not the guy."

She sighs and leans back in the chair. "I know, I just got started thinking about it at school and I had to come over and see you. Kind of silly, right?"

"No, you call me anytime. I mean anytime, you hear me?"

"I will."

"You want to stay and eat something? I was going to make some spaghetti."

"You can cook spaghetti?"

"Well, not the sauce. That comes in jars., but I can boil water."

She gets up. "I'd better not, Boone. I cut a class to come over here and I'm due home pretty soon, so I'm going to get out of here."

"If you change your mind later, I usually make too much."

She smiles. "Thanks. Maybe later on this week."

After she's gone I think about what just happened. Things are starting to look pretty good overall. Nancy really trusts me, comes to me when she's scared or hurting, and I've never had anybody depend on me like that. The thing with Tiny is off to a good start, and even if this first batch doesn't work out, I've got a partner that I think I can trust. If I decide I want to keep going to the home, Betty says I can come anytime, and sometimes those old folks are okay to hang around with. They've got some great stories.

The only thing still up in the air is Carrie and Jerry, and I can't help but think that sooner or later Jerry's going to get me booted out of here.

That means I'd have to have a place to go, and I don't have any idea about how to even start thinking about that. I've never looked for a place to live in my life. Before Daddy died and Momma ran off, they decided and us kids just went along. After that it was Gamaliel that handed me this place, and I'm still here. Where to go next I have no idea.

I'm not going to worry about that just yet. Tomorrow I'll go up to the still, maybe try to find a different route, and see how things are going. All that really means is looking in the keg and seeing if it's still bubbling. If it is, we leave it alone. If it's slowed way down or stopped altogether, I'll get hold of Tiny and we'll come up with a schedule for the next step. I need to remember to pour out the first little bit that comes through the coil. Don't want to poison myself or Tiny on our first try as partners.

The next day I go up there and it's still bubbling away, doesn't even look like it's slowing down yet. I wonder if we put too much yeast in; we wrote down everything we did, but didn't pour the yeast from Tiny's hand into a cup or something to get a real measurement, in case we need to change it for the second try. I get the recipe out and look over the list, to see if I missed anything. Looks good, and we ordered the extra stuff from the companies Gamaliel had listed, so maybe I'm just getting anxious. It really hasn't been long enough to be worried that we did it wrong.

ChapterThirty-Eight

I'm back at the home; it's been a week, almost, since I was here, and I'm figuring out that I miss these people. Maybe I needed Gamaliel more than I thought I did. Frankie's pretty much given up looking for Gamaliel and she's got a few folks she makes sure she says hello to. One of them is Mr. Booth, who has to use a walker but still gets around, and says hello to Frankie and immediately starts talking to me about weather, what it was yesterday, what it is right now, what he thinks it will be tomorrow. "I'm an excellent predictor of weather," he says every time we talk. "You know why? Because I never try to predict more than twenty-four hours into the future. Those seven-day forecasts don't mean shit."

Angela is another one. She won't tell me her last name and looks around like she's worried if I ask, so I've stopped asking. She tells Frankie she can trust her, and then points to me and says, "What about that one, Frankie? Can we trust him?"

There's half a dozen more that are regulars and, even though they're a little strange, they're okay, and it seems like they think I'm okay. Nobody here cares what I wear or how new my truck is or who my daddy was.

I'm getting ready to take off when I hear my name and look up. Mark, the preacher from the service, is coming toward me.

"We need to talk," Mark says.

I've pretty much forgiven him for dragging me up to the pulpit at Gamaliel's service. We haven't done much more than say hello when we see each other, but Frankie seems to like him, and that counts for a lot with me. She's never been wrong, not yet, and I count on her to tell me if somebody's not one I can trust.

"Okay," I say.

"So when's good for you? I'm here two days a week all day, Tuesdays and Fridays, just the morning on Wednesdays, and Sunday morning of course, but I'm kind of busy on Sundays."

"How about day after tomorrow?"

He nods. "Friday's good. What time?"

"I don't get up too early, so how about eleven?"

"That works. See you then."

A little before eleven Friday morning Frankie and I walk down to Mark's office and there's a piece of paper taped to the door. "We're outside next to the chapel."

We go out the door, me wondering who "we" is, and head over to the chapel. There's a big hickory tree on the far side of the chapel that has an outdoor table and some chairs. Mark is sitting in one of the chairs, and Betty is in one of the others.

Okay. Betty's okay. I was afraid he was going to have somebody I don't know in on this conversation about something, and I'm still not sure why he wants to talk to me.

"Hi, Betty."

"Good to see you, Boone."

I turn to Mark. "I'm here. What'd you want to talk about?"

Mark points to one of the empty chairs. "Have a seat, Boone. Don't worry, this isn't anything bad. Just the opposite, in fact."

I don't ever trust anybody who tells me ahead of time what kind of news they're bringing me, especially when it's coming out of nowhere. But I sit down, mainly because Betty's there, and she's always been straight with me.

"Okay, so what's this all about?" Frankie curls up right next to my chair, and Betty smiles at that.

"She's such a good dog, Boone," she says.

"She is that," I say.

We all sit there looking around, until finally Mark clears his throat and turns to Betty. "Should I start, or do you want to?"

Betty nods. "You go ahead."

Mark kind of scoots back and forth in his seat, getting comfortable, and I'm thinking, if he starts preaching at me I'm out of here right now. But it's not his preacher's voice; he's just talking, like a regular person.

"I've been thinking about you, Boone, ever since the service for Mr. Everett. I know I put you in a kind of scary situation, and you said something about kicking my ass if I ever tried that again.

"I hope you've noticed that I haven't tried that again, although I have to say I've been tempted. You're good at that, Boone, you really are."

Betty jumps in. "Some of the residents here still mention it when they're sitting around after a meal, and they always talk about how much they didn't know about Mr. Everett. Some of them didn't even know his name was Gamaliel."

"Listen," I say, "I'm still trying to figure out why it is you wanted to talk to me, and I'm not getting it. So what's going on here, really?"

"Just let me talk for a second," Mark says, not in a mean way, more like he's asking permission. "I'm still working my way through this.

"I've been working with old people for years now." He looks at Betty and says, "I know you don't like me to call them old people, but that's what they are. That's what they call themselves and each other. They know what and who they are.

"And I like that about them, that they know. They've lived, Boone, they know things, they have stories to tell, lessons they've learned, this really is a place of great riches if you look at it in the right way.

"Do you understand what I'm talking about, Boone? You were close to Mr. Everett, you must understand what he was carrying around, all the things he saw and heard and learned in his ninety plus years."

I catch myself nodding. I get what Mark is saying. There was so much more about Gamaliel than anybody knew, more than I knew, or Carrie, or anybody here.

"But that's only half of it. They have this treasure to offer us, all of us, but there's a need there, too, a real need, a strong need. They need somebody to tell their stories to, somebody who knows how to really listen to them."

I'm thinking about all those times Gamaliel and I sat around, sipping and talking, and what Mark's saying feels right to me. Looking back, I think he was glad to have somebody to tell his stuff to.

"Gamaliel had lots of stories that weren't right for church, Mark," I say.

He grins. "I'm sure that's true, and I'm not sure I would have tried to stop you if you had told them. But that's in the past. Maybe one of these days we could sit down and you could tell me some of them."

Not a chance, Mark, I say to myself. I'm not telling you about our little moonshine operation, and a lot of the stories have that right in the middle.

He goes on. "But that's not what we wanted to talk to you about, not really. The whole thing with Mr. Everett was so good for all of us here, staff and residents alike, that it started us thinking."

Betty says, "That's right, Boone, especially about the staff, I mean. They had been taking care of Mr. Everett every day and had no idea what his life had been like, and that has helped them look at who is here now in a completely different way. Plus, they talk about how much easier and more interesting their jobs are when the residents talk about their lives the way you talked about Mr. Everett's life."

Mark says, "What we're thinking about, Boone, is to try to help rescue some of these stories that are all around us and will be lost if we allow them to be.

"We've seen you and Frankie with the folks here. I think it started out with Frankie more than you, but these people recognize when somebody's just putting up with them and they also recognize when somebody sees that they're a real person. These people like you a lot, Boone, they know you're a good person."

I'm getting tired of hearing people go on and on about how good I am. They don't know about Daddy, or the shine, or about me fighting with Jerry, or pretty much abandoning my little sister, or anything else. I know I'm not a good person, and it pisses me off to hear people go on about it.

"I'm maybe not as good as you think I am," is all I say to the two of them.

Mark waves me off. "I know what I know, Boone. For instance, that guy at the service, the one in the cast, I think Jerry was his name? I saw the way he was looking at you when you were talking, especially about your scars. The difference between the two of you, well, he's carrying a lot of anger around with him. Some of it's aimed at you, but there's more there. I half expected him to disrupt the service, he was so angry. I know you saw it too, but you didn't let it stop you from doing right by your friend.

"That's what I'm talking about. When I say I know you're a good person, I don't mean perfect. I don't know you well at all, but I can tell you you're not perfect, not even close.

"But that's not what I want to talk to you about. All this stuff about who's good and who isn't is pretty much a waste of time, in my opinion. All of us have a little of both.

"What I think you need is something worth doing, and what I know these people need is somebody to remind them that they're genuine, that their life still means something. They need to tell their stories, Boone, and not just to themselves. They need to tell them to another human being. And maybe they need somebody to pass their stories along after they're gone."

I don't like the sound of that at all. It sounds like he wants me to do his job for him when one of these people dies, get up there in the pulpit like a damn preacher. I think about what Daddy would say if he saw me in a pulpit and I laugh out loud.

"What's so funny?" Mark asks, and Betty looks puzzled, too.

"It sounds like you're trying to give away your job, Mark, and I got to tell you I'm not interested. If you're looking for me to get up in that pulpit every time somebody dies and tell stories about them, you're crazy."

Mark is shaking his head. "Nothing like that, Boone, although I would like to get a working relationship started with you. What I need is somebody to help me fill out these peoples' lives, make them a whole person. There may even be a book in there somewhere, one of these days.

"The thing you can do to help with that is not to take over my job. I mean, you did an excellent job talking about Mr. Everett, but you two had history that none of us have with the rest of the residents here. No, what you can do, you and Frankie, is be the person who they tell their stories to, the one who listens to them. Then, once in a while, you and I could sit down and you could tell me their stories, good and bad, clean and dirty. I'll take care of the preachy stuff." He winks at me. "I could tell there were some stories you wanted to tell at the service but couldn't."

I have to agree with that part. I look down at Frankie.

"Listen, can we take a little break here? I'd like to get Frankie up and moving, and I could use a walk, too."

"Excellent idea," Betty says. "I feel like walking myself. Mark, care to join us?"

"No, I'll pass," he says, and I swear he gives Betty a thumbs up about something. "You two go ahead. Let's get back together in, say, half an hour?"

"Good," Betty says. "Boone, why don't we walk around back?"

"Okay," I say. I've been kind of curious about those other buildings, and maybe Betty will tell me what they are. "Frankie, girl, let's go for a walk."

Frankie's almost always up for a walk, and we start out down one of the gravel paths.

Chapter Thirty-Nine

"So what did you think about what Mark had to say?" Betty says after a minute or two. We're behind the main building now, and I can see the rest of the property, looks like about ten or twelve acres altogether, and the Smokies past the trees at the fence row, not too far off.

"I don't know, Betty, it sounds like he wants me to pretty much keep doing what I'm doing, except I sit down and talk to him every now and then. I mean, it's not like I have to force these old guys to talk to me, although Mr. Abernathy still just talks to Frankie. He tells her all kinds of stories, though, and since I'm right there, well, it's like he's talking to me."

"I'm sure he is," Betty agrees.

"I just don't know why you two felt like you needed to have this big meeting, that's the part I still don't understand."

Betty stops and so do I. Frankie is out as far as the leash will let her go, moving back and forth across the lawn.

"Have you seen these before?" Betty is pointing to the small buildings between us and the fence that I'm guessing is the property line.

"I noticed the maintenance shed," I say. I'm seeing now that there are four buildings in all, the shed and three others that look like little houses.

"Let me show you inside one of them," she says and pulls a ring of keys out of her jacket pocket.

We go to the one farthest away from the main building and she unlocks the door. She opens it, steps through, and says, "Come on in."

I look around for something to tie Frankie's leash to and Betty says, "She can come in, too, Boone. It's okay."

"Okay," I say, and we step inside.

It's a little house, all right, and we're standing in the living room. There's a couch and a chair, and a little TV, and a bookcase. I can see a kitchen right next to the living room, and a really short hallway that I'm guessing goes to a bedroom and a bathroom.

"What do you think?" Betty says.

I'm not sure what she means by that.

"It's okay," I say. "I didn't know you had houses back here."

The place is smaller than Gamaliel's house, but not much.

"It's okay," I say again, because I don't know what else to say. This is starting to feel a little weird; I don't know what's going on here. I'm about to ask her when she says, "How long has it been since you talked with Carrie?"

"It's been a little while," I say. Funny that Betty brings up Carrie. I've been getting kind of worried about that, that she hasn't called. One of the bills is due day after tomorrow, and I'm running a little low on money, not counting what's in the safety deposit box at the bank.

She nods. "I talked to her yesterday. Actually, she called me, Boone."

I'm starting to get mad now.

"Betty, are you going to tell me what the hell's going on here?"

"That's exactly what I'm about to do, Boone, it's just hard to find the right way to do it," she says, and when I look at her I can tell she's kind of nervous about something.

She clears her throat. "Carrie called me to talk about you, Boone. She's worried about you."

"I'm fine, Betty. She could call me herself and ask me that."

"That's not what I meant. See what I mean about this being hard? What I meant was, she's worried about what's going to happen to you."

I don't say anything, because I think I know what's coming.

"I don't know any other way to say this, Boone. You're about to lose that house you're living in."

I just nod. I figured that was what she was going to say.

"Jerry's been pushing her to sell the place. She says that he's telling her they need the money, and I think she's going to put it on the market soon, maybe next week."

"Next week! Next week? What the hell, Betty? Why in the goddamn hell am I hearing this from you?" I'm shouting and Frankie is freaking out and Betty is backing up, almost out of the house, and I'm standing in the middle of this little room and everything is going to shit around me.

Betty just lets me run on for a minute or two; a staff member comes out of the maintenance building to check on the noise and she waves her off. After I stop for breath, she says, "I talked to her for a long time, Boone. I think she's scared. I don't know what all that's about, but I think that's part of what is going on with her."

"She was just going to let Jerry or the law or whoever come marching up there and throw me out on the street!" I'm still shouting, but I'm not out of control.

That makes me stop and think. Damn, there's still quite a bit of shine up there. I need to get it out of there, and my clothes, and Daddy's shotgun, and, well, there's not much more.

"I got to go, Betty. Sounds like I'm going to need a place to stay, unless I live in the truck," I say, and start toward the door.

"Nothing's going to happen for another week, Boone, she told me that. More likely it'll be the end of the month before anything real happens."

"I'm still going to need a place, Betty. You don't understand."

"Well, what about here?"

I'd been looking at the floor and now I raise my head to look at Betty. "Don't screw with me, Betty, it's a real bad time to do that."

"I'm not screwing with you, Boone," she says and doesn't even hesitate to use the word screw. For a second I think, you're not supposed to talk that way to a kid, and then I think, you're not a kid anymore, Boone, you'd better remember that.

"I mean it, Betty."

"So do I. This whole thing today with you, me and Mark, we'd been talking about it already, but after I got Carrie's phone call, well . . . ."

Now that was the wrong thing to say to me.

"So this is some kind of charity? I don't need your damn charity."

"Sorry, Boone, I shouldn't have said it that way. Everything Mark said was the truth. These people that we're taking care of here, they need you. And Frankie, too, of course, but mainly they need you.

"The worst thing that can happen to somebody is to lose their voice, to have nobody listen to them. I don't know if you have any idea what that's like, Boone, but it's awful."

She has no idea about me, but she's wrong about one big thing. I know exactly what that feels like. I've been that way pretty much my whole life.

She goes on, "You can be their voice, Boone, don't you see that? It's not charity, not charity at all. You would be doing them a great service.

"Anyway, I don't know what kind of plans you have for the next year or two, but you could spend it doing something really important. Plus we'll pay you."

I just stare at her.

"Almost nothing, as far as money goes, but a little, and a place to stay and a meal in the cafeteria any time you wanted it. I would expect you to do something with our residents at least three days a week, you understand. You couldn't just move in here and sit and watch TV. That would be charity, and I'm not any more interested in giving charity than you are in getting it."

I hold up my hand. "Stop a minute. You're saying I could live here, in this house, and Frankie could, too?"

Betty smiles. "Oh, it's a package deal. You and Frankie together are much better for our folks here than either one of you separately."

"And all I have to do is hang out with them three times a week?"

"Well, there's more to it than that. I'll also expect you to sit down with Mark at least once a week and share their stories with him. This is no good if it stops with you. You understand that, right?

"A long time ago, this was the only way people knew who they were, or where they came from. Passing it along is part of the deal. You can't get all these great stories and keep them for yourself."

"I'll do it."

She looks surprised. "Just like that?"

I shrug. "Who do I need to talk it over with?"

"I guess that's right," she says. "Let's go find Mark." She seems pleased as she can be, and when she tells Mark, he gives me a big hug, which makes me feel a little weird, since the only person who has hugged me in, well, a year or more, is Nancy. It's not a long hug, though, and it doesn't seem to bother him that I'm not hugging him back. He's got a look in his eyes I haven't seen before, and he keeps saying, "This is good. This is really good for everybody. This is going to be great."

It takes a couple of days to get everything set up and about fifteen minutes for me to get my stuff together and out of Gamaliel's house. Tiny agrees to keep an eye on the still; we should be running the first batch through the coil any day now. Nancy is overjoyed, glad to have me away from Jerry more than anything else. So I make the move, and don't even call Carrie. I leave a note on the kitchen counter, drive away, and don't look back.

I look around at my new home. It's been a while since I've had a TV, but I bet I'll get used to it pretty quick. I get everything put away, including a few jars of the triple filtered stuff and most of what's left of the regular shine; Tiny said he knew just the place he could put a few jars where his folks wouldn't find them, so he's got the rest. There's a hall closet, and that's where I put Daddy's shotgun and that old rifle I found in the shed. I figure Gamaliel would rather me have it than that shithead Jerry. I'm hoping I won't have any use for either one of them here, but you never know. I pick a spot for Frankie's blanket, and she goes over to it, turns around a few times, and settles in. Once all that's done, there's one thing I need to do that I've been putting off for a while now. I go into the living room, pick up the phone, and punch in the number. It rings three times, and somebody picks up.

"Hello? Aunt Claire? It's Boone. Can I talk to Hannah?"

End of Book Two

Boone's story continues in "Keeping Secrets," Book Three in the series. Available in both print and ebook format.

www.ingramcontent.com/pod-product-compliance
Lightning Source LLC
Chambersburg PA
CBHW031617100726
47898CB00006B/1825